BEFORE

It was the perfect day for a party. The summer afternoon was a temperate seventy-nine degrees, the sky was cloudless, and the Atlantic crashed hypnotically down the bluffs. He got ready, dressing in linen pants, a fitted white polo, and broken-in leather flip-flops. As he splashed water onto his cheeks, he saw a refined, debonair face in the bathroom mirror. He looked like the strong but silent type. Teddy Roosevelt, maybe. He smiled, delighted at the reference. Wasn't Roosevelt the one who said *Speak softly and carry a big stick?* Maybe he'd think of himself as Teddy tonight. As a little inside joke.

By 7:30 p.m., streaks of pink and orange made an ombré effect across the horizon. The beach was empty; a flock of seagulls perched on the wooden lifeguard stand. Partygoers glided toward the luxury beach club and condo complex, bottles tucked under their arms, phones in their hands. Past the gates, twinkling votive candles spanned the long seating areas by the pool, and brightly colored rafts bobbed atop the placid clear water. As the guests swarmed the space, beer bottles were popped open. Everyone began to talk and laugh. Swells of Bob Marley, the Beach Boys, and Dave Matthews drifted through the air.

Teddy sat on a chaise, beer in hand, and watched as Jeff Cohen, a staple on the beach scene, carefully made his way across a slack rope that had been set up between two trees. When Jeff reached the end without falling, he grinned at Cole, whose indie film about surfing nuns had won first prize at a couple of festivals last year. "Wanna give it a try?"

Cole chuckled. "That's not exactly my thing." He raised his Nikon camera and took a snap of Jeff as he jumped to the ground.

Chelsea Dawson, Jeff's ex-girlfriend, gave Cole a flirty grin. "Cole, you're so going to be a famous paparazzo someday."

Cole snorted. "Uh, I have bigger career goals than loitering in a parking lot, waiting for celebs. Unless it's *you*."

"Nah, I'm my *own* photographer." Chelsea pulled something from her purse. An iPhone in a sparkly pink case was attached to a motorized selfie stick; when she hit a button, the device extended, lights illuminated, and a miniature fan began to whir. Her blond hair whipped prettily in the artificial wind. Her skin glowed under the golden bulb. The cobalt shade of her dress brought out the steel-blue flecks in her eyes. As she grinned into the lens, a hush fell over the crowd. Everyone turned and looked at the perfection that was Chelsea Dawson.

She examined the results and then tapped the screen. Moments later, Teddy's phone buzzed, but he didn't bother to check the alert. He knew what it said: *New post from ChelseaDFab.*

Another Bob Marley classic blared from the speakers. Someone did a perfect jackknife off the diving board. Teddy decided to check out the bonfire. Down at the beach, the

THE AMATEURS:
FOLLOW ME

SARA SHEPARD

HOT
KEY
BOOKS

First published in Great Britain in 2017 by
HOT KEY BOOKS
80–81 Wimpole St, London W1G 9RE
www.hotkeybooks.com

Copyright © Alloy Entertainment and Sara Shepard, 2017

The right of Sara Shepard to be identified as Author of this work
has been asserted by them in accordance with the
Copyright, Designs and Patents Act, 1988

A CIP catalogue record for this book is available from the British Library.

ISBN: 9781471406324
also available as an ebook

2

This book is typeset using Atomik ePublisher
Printed and bound by Clays Ltd, St Ives Plc

Hot Key Books is an imprint of Bonnier Zaffre Ltd,
a Bonnier Publishing company
www.bonnierpublishing.com

stoners were arguing about whose fudge was better – Cindy's, a local store, or Lulu's, from one town away. "Dude, all the fudge is made by the same company, probably in a big vat," a glazed-eyed guy said. "It's a *conspiracy*."

Teddy chuckled along with them, but then he was distracted by a sharp, familiar voice. "When did you turn into such a hater?"

He whirled toward the sound. Chelsea stomped across the sand, high heels in her hand, her face a knot of pain. Jeff trailed behind her, his long hair in a messy man bun, the tails of his button-down flapping. A couple of the stoners glanced at Chelsea and Jeff, too, then went back to their fudge argument.

Jeff waved a cell phone in her face. On the screen was Chelsea's latest Instagram post. "Look, I just don't understand why you feel you have to post photos that show your boobs to ten thousand strangers," he was saying, loud enough for Teddy to hear. "There are a million prettier pictures of you than this one."

"Fifty-one thousand, eight hundred seventy-*three* strangers," Chelsea shot back.

"Okay, so almost fifty-two thousand skeevy dudes know what your boobs look like. As a woman, I'd think you –"

Chelsea groaned. "Don't do the feminist thing with me. Your opinion doesn't matter so much anymore. Besides, it's important for me to build my brand."

Jeff laughed incredulously. "It's not like you're a Kardashian."

Chelsea's expression hardened. Spinning around, she headed for the beaten-down path that led through the dunes, behind the apartment complex, and all the way to the public parking lot. "Hey!" Jeff cried. "What did I say?"

"Forget it."

"You're more than a pretty face, Chel. You should have more self-respect."

"I *do* have self-respect." Chelsea's eyes blazed. "It's you who doesn't respect *me*."

"What are you talking about? I'm –"

Chelsea's expression snapped closed. "Just leave me alone."

Jeff looked like he'd been slapped. Chelsea slipped into the reeds. After a few moments, Jeff swiveled and settled down on a lawn chair at the bonfire next to one of the stoners. He stared into the flames, looking like he might burst into tears. The stoners suddenly seemed to notice him. "You okay, man?" one asked, but Jeff didn't answer.

Taking a deep breath, Teddy grabbed his phone from his pocket and composed a message.

You all right?

He could picture Chelsea stopping on the overgrown beach path. Rooting through her bag, pulling out the phone he'd given her. On cue, his phone quietly pinged.

I'm fine. Thanks.

His fingers flew. *Wanna talk about it? I can meet.*

Up popped an emoji of a face blowing a kiss. *Nah. I'm really tired. We'll talk tomorrow.*

He squeezed his phone hard. That had been her one last chance, and she'd blown it. Well then. Now to put the plan he'd crafted into motion.

Teddy stood as unceremoniously as he could. No one saw him as he walked away from the bonfire, though he chose to follow Chelsea by a different route than she'd taken. A quarter

4

mile later, a streetlamp made a gauzy golden circle across the pavement, the beach tag hut, and the concrete structure that held the men's and women's bathrooms and showers. A lithe shape streaked through the light near the beach path. Teddy breathed out, sweaty and anxious.

A car passed, its xenon headlights blinding. Teddy crouched behind the changing rooms, his thighs trembling, his heart contracting in his chest. He'd been so desperate to get close to Chelsea. For her to know him. If she'd bothered to give a shit, if she'd reciprocated the kindness he'd shown her, he would have let her in, told her who he really was, where he really came from, how he'd become this way, who was responsible for turning him into this. Instead, she had blown him off time and time again, so she only knew the basics, the lies. She knew him by the name everyone called him, a name he'd ditch when he moved to his next location – Washington, maybe, or Texas. It wasn't even as good a name as Brett Grady, which he'd used in Connecticut. He'd been quite fond of Brett Grady, actually. He sometimes still called himself that when he was alone, or bored, or right when he woke up, when he didn't yet remember who he was pretending to be.

The man formerly known as Brett Grady pulled the mask out of his pocket. The slippery piece of fabric felt energized and electrified, like a living thing. He fit it over his face and walked quietly across the pavement. Next to the path, Chelsea stood by the bike rack, her hand curled over a random bike's handlebars. It was such a pretty hand. Milky white. Long-fingered. Elegant.

It was a shame he'd probably have to break every bone.

THE NEXT MORNING

CHAPTER 1

On a sticky, sweltering Saturday morning in July, Seneca Frazier stood on a brick-paved side street in downtown Annapolis, Maryland, wearing the long-sleeved uniform of the Annapolis Parking Authority. The getup was 100 percent wool and didn't breathe. Unless she got into air-conditioning in the next three minutes, she was going to pass out from heat stroke.

Brian Komisky, the officer she was shadowing, inspected a parking meter next to an off-white Range Rover. His hazel eyes lit up. "Bingo! One minute left, and this baby's expired." He offered Seneca the gray handheld computer that electronically processed parking tickets. "Wanna do the honors?"

Go, me, Seneca thought as she held out her palm for the device. It was demoralizing that making a prehistoric iPad knockoff spit out a thirty-dollar parking ticket was the highlight of her day. It wasn't like she'd set out to score a summer internship with the APA. She'd wanted to intern with law enforcement, and her dad even begrudgingly helped her get the interview, calling upon a friend on the Annapolis PD. But somehow she'd gotten stuck on parking duty instead of actually solving crimes.

9

She and Brian inspected more cars on the block, but everyone was paid up on their meters, so they headed to Brian's van. Sweat dripped down Seneca's back as she walked. They passed a little boutique called Astrid, and Seneca noticed a gaggle of girls in flirty sundresses squealing over something on their phones. She felt a pang. According to her overprotective, worrywart of a dad, that frothy, bubblegummy life was the one she *should* be living.

In another universe, maybe.

Brian started the van, and Seneca cranked the AC on high and pressed her face directly against the vent. Brian peered at her before pulling out of the spot. "You okay?"

Seneca tried to tell herself that the sudden chill she felt was from the subzero air. "Right now, I'm just trying not to melt into a puddle," she said.

"C'mon, Seneca. You've been vacant all day. What's on your mind?"

Seneca sighed. Was she that transparent?

"Is it . . . a boy?" Brian asked gently, turning down the AC a touch.

Seneca felt herself blush. *"No!"* Though it was kind of true. She was thinking about a boy. Just not *that* way.

A wrinkle formed between Brian's eyes. At twenty-four, he was already married to his high school sweetheart, and Seneca understood what his wife saw in him. His penny-colored hair was thick and wavy, his hazel eyes were kind, and his impressive physical size always made Seneca feel safe. No one would mess with her with Brian around. And by no one, she meant Brett Grady.

Or whatever the hell his name really was.

10

It started three months ago, when she and Maddox Wright, a friend she'd made on a website dedicated to cold murder cases called Case Not Closed, looked into what happened to Helena Kelly, a murdered girl from Dexby, Connecticut. They teamed up with Aerin Kelly, Helena's younger sister; Madison, Maddox's stepsister; and another site regular, BMoney60 – Brett Grady. Together they discovered that Helena had been having an affair with Skip Ingram, a much-older man, and that Marissa Ingram, Skip's wife, had most likely killed Helena. Case Not Closed team *out*.

Or . . . not.

Only after Brett Grady skipped town did Seneca figure out that their so-called friend wasn't who he said he was. Once she put together that his name wasn't even Brett Grady, Seneca realized that Brett had fed them every clue that led them to Marissa Ingram. He'd been so subtly cunning that Seneca believed she'd come to each conclusion on her own, and she'd felt like a brilliant crime solver. Which was an improvement over feeling like the girl who'd flunked out of her freshman year at the University of Maryland – aka the truth.

But Brett knew everything because *he'd* killed Helena. And she wasn't his only victim. He'd also killed Seneca's mom, Collette, a murder Seneca had spent years trying to solve. And Seneca had discovered a slew of other cases involving blonde-haired, blue-eyed women with Brett's name written all over them.

Seneca didn't dare share her theory with anyone besides Maddox, Madison, and Aerin – and she only discussed it in clinical terms, verifiable facts. Not the emotion of it. Not the

11

crushing terror that they'd all been duped by someone they'd considered a friend. That they'd been working side by side with the very person who had destroyed their lives. She was desperate to tell the cops, but she didn't have any hard evidence Brett had done anything. She didn't even know his real name or age or where he was from. If only Seneca could find Brett, follow him, get something on him . . . but he'd disconnected his phone. Stayed away from CNC message boards. Shut down his social media accounts. Seneca wondered whether Brett went AWOL because he knew she was onto him, but if that were the case, wouldn't she be dead by now?

At the next stop sign, Brian swung the van to the left. "Let's take a break and get some ice cream for lunch. My treat. Sprinkles? A waffle cone?"

"Whatever." Seneca slumped, embarrassed that Brian thought she'd actually get this bent out of shape over a *boy*.

Brian pulled into the ice cream stand, a glorified shack with a small service window and a large grassy area that abutted a swampy back creek of the Chesapeake. Seneca peered nervously around the gravel parking lot, looking for Brett, as she'd done ever since he'd vanished into that crisp April evening in Dexby. She thought of the map she'd constructed on the inside wall of her closet. Each pin on the map corresponded with the locations of the cases Brett had commented on through Case Not Closed under the handle BMoney60 – crimes he *also* might have committed. His trademark was weighing in with one simple but salient clue that broke the case wide open, like he'd done with the Ingrams. There were pins in Arizona, DC, Florida, Georgia, Utah, Maryland, Connecticut, and Vermont.

Where would Brett show up next? All she knew about Brett was what he'd done in the past, not what he planned to do in the future.

A long reed jerked. Seneca tensed. A mouse shot out and disappeared into the grass. She exhaled, suddenly drained.

She and Brian ordered vanilla cones and took a seat under a filmy umbrella that provided little shelter from the punishing heat. "Well, you know what they say," Brian said, "there are plenty of fish in the sea."

Seneca licked the cone furiously to keep the ice cream from melting onto her hand, letting out a grunt.

"Maybe you need to go on a date," Brian continued. "I might know someone."

Seneca felt her cheeks blaze. "Brian, will you please drop it?" Love was the furthest thing from her mind.

Her phone beeped. As she rummaged in her messenger bag, Brian squinted at a Honda Civic in front of an antique shop across the street. "That bastard's in a loading zone." He reached for the ticket machine as though it was a semiautomatic weapon. "Not on my watch."

"I'll catch up with you in a sec." Seneca found her phone and squinted at it, but the glare was so bright she had to curl her hands around the screen. When her vision adjusted, she saw the alert she'd set up months ago. Her breath caught.

BMoney60 has just posted on Case Not Closed!

Hands shaking, she clicked on the link. A Case Not Closed thread appeared, something about a girl named Chelsea

Dawson disappearing from a party in Lafayette, New Jersey, last night. BMoney60's comment was four names down the list: *Easy one. It's gotta be her ex, right? I was at that party – saw them fighting. It was VICIOUS.*

Whoa, read the responses from the eager amateur sleuths. *Let's dig in. The cops need to question him.* But Seneca had gleaned something very different from the post. It was as though a tiny pinprick of sunlight had emerged in the sky after months of rain.

Brett Grady was back.

CHAPTER 2

Aerin Kelly lay on a chaise on the top deck of a sixty-six-foot yacht named *That's Amore* in the middle of Newport Bay. She was pretending to sleep, but the guy she was hanging out with, Pierce, kept fiddling with the strings of her plaid bikini bottom, and it was distracting.

"Babe." Even though it wasn't yet noon, Pierce's breath smelled like beer. "Babe. I *need* you. Now."

"Mmm." Aerin opened one eye. Pierce was shirtless, showing off the rock-hard abs he'd perfected working out with his personal trainer, Jules. His hair stood up in peaks, and he wore aviator sunglasses with green-tinted lenses he'd special-ordered. Pierce was always getting things custom made. He thought buying anything off the rack was pedestrian.

"Good, you're awake." Pierce passed her a bottle of sunscreen. "Can you put more lotion on my back?"

"Can't your friends do it?" Aerin groaned.

Pierce grinned at her. "I like it better when *you* rub me down."

Aerin begrudgingly squirted SPF onto her palm and kneaded the spot between his shoulder blades. "Thanks," Pierce said. He gave her a kiss, then traipsed off to find his friends.

15

Aerin flopped back onto the chair and tried to find her zen again. It really was a perfect day – the Newport air was warm but not too hot, the mansions that peppered the coast gleamed like diamonds, and she was aboard the largest yacht on the harbor.

Helena would approve.

She flinched. It was like her sister was a commercial jingle playing on auto loop in her brain. Aerin didn't *want* to think about Helena. She certainly didn't want to imagine her *here*. She was still so angry with her. Helena had lied to her, had chosen to run away with an older man and leave her family behind without a word. Aerin still loved her sister, but sometimes she wondered if she ever knew her at all.

And did Aerin even know what actually happened to Helena? The world accepted that Marissa Ingram killed her sister, but Seneca Frazier's theory about Brett Grady gave Aerin pause. Aerin didn't want to believe it. Marissa's motive was neat, tidy, and logical, while the idea that Brett – whom she had *almost kissed* – had done it was nonsensical, irrational, and terrifying. How could her sister have even *met* Brett Grady?

Aerin jumped to her feet. A change of scenery always helped when her thoughts tumbled down this particular rabbit hole. On the lower deck, Pierce and his buddies, Weston and James, were opening beers. She walked down to them, plucked the open Anchor Steam from Pierce's hand, chugged it, and handed it back with a wink. "Sorry," she said, wiping her mouth. "I needed that."

Pierce's grin was delightfully scandalized. "Babe, you can steal my beer *anytime*." He loved that Aerin was a little crazy. He'd told her so when they'd met at a party in Paris, where Aerin's parents had sent her on a pity trip after Marissa Ingram's arrest instead of actually talking through things. Her parents might have made a lot of promises after it all went down, including spending more time together and going to family therapy. It had taken them only a few weeks to slip back to their old ways.

Instead of working through her grief in Paris, Aerin maxed out her credit card at Chanel, buying treats for kids she barely knew. She went to seedy dance clubs, drank champagne straight from the bottle, and staggered home alone through dodgy neighborhoods in the middle of the night.

And on that trip, instead of facing the possibility that Brett Grady might *actually* be Helena's killer, Aerin agreed to travel to Nice with a guy she'd just met. On Pierce's private plane, she sloppily made out with him, then did some body shots of Patrón, then rinse and repeat. The first thing she did at Pierce's family's villa was drunkenly strip, sprint to the swimming pool, and slip on the slick stones, practically cracking her head open.

Was she acting out? Sure. Laden with baggage? She'd break an airport scale. Absolutely aware of it? Of course. But what was she supposed to do? Go to therapy? Rebond with her estranged parents? Write a college essay about how she was a survivor? Cue burst of sarcastic laughter.

The alcohol zooming through her bloodstream began to soothe her frenetic brain, but she could still hear the jackhammer inside her, thudding and splintering. *Move. Do something.* She marched to the cockpit and plopped down on the plush leather seat. "Mind if I take us for a cruise?" she called to the boys.

"Go for it," West yelled back.

Aerin pressed the lever that powered the engine. The boat jolted to life, skimming past water-skiers, a pleasure cruiser with *Newport Ferry Tours* emblazoned on its side, and a medium-sized yacht with a half-naked couple entwined on the prow. Her hair flapped in the wind, and she relished the rushing air on her face. She pushed the lever forward. The boat zoomed faster. White caps lapped against the hull. She felt so powerful. She pressed the lever forward again and let out a wild yell that matched the roar of the motor.

"Yeah!" West called out, pumping his fist.

Aerin clipped a buoy and sent it skittering across the surface of the water. The lighthouse was ahead, and she focused on it. What would it feel like to crash the boat into its rocky shoreline? Would the boat be ruined? Would they catapult overboard? Would they die?

Would she see Helena if she did?

"This is awesome!" Pierce screamed.

But something began to shift inside her. Aerin noticed how hard she was gripping the steering wheel. Her heart was pounding, and she was out of breath. The adrenaline high had vanished, and now she just felt . . . drained. Messed-up.

She steered away from the lighthouse, slowed down, and slid off the captain's chair. "Why'd you stop?" Pierce called from his perch.

"Because we almost crashed," Aerin said shakily. She stared at her hands, suddenly not quite recognizing them as hers. "*I* almost crashed."

The boys just laughed, like she'd made a joke. She hurried down the stairs into the cabin. It was dark and cool, and she sank into the leather booth in the elegantly appointed dining room and took a few deep breaths, trying not to cry.

"Babe?"

Pierce stood on the stairs, a concerned look on his face. Aerin felt a lump in her throat. Maybe he was more perceptive than she thought. And maybe, just maybe, she was finally ready to talk about what was going on. But as her eyes adjusted, she noticed he was holding something. It was the bottle of Banana Boat. He turned around and pointed to his lower back. "You missed a spot. I'm getting burned."

Aerin wanted to hurl the bottle at him, but she found herself squirting lotion into her palm. What did she expect? She and Pierce didn't have that kind of relationship. They didn't have *any* kind of relationship, really. As she rubbed it into his muscles, she felt a pang for Thomas Grove, the cop she'd met while investigating Helena's death. Thomas would have noticed she was slowly going crazy. Thomas would have wanted to know why she'd almost smashed a million-dollar boat to pieces.

Wrong, Aerin thought. She wasn't even speaking to Thomas anymore. He'd quit the police force and gone to college in New York City shortly after Marissa Ingram's arrest, when Aerin needed him most. He was probably having a great time right now. Aerin probably never entered his thoughts.

Something buzzed. Aerin's gaze flicked to the granite bar, where she'd deposited the large cream-colored leather Chanel satchel Pierce had bought for her in France. Something was buzzing inside it. She dug her phone out of the smooth silk pocket. Seneca had sent her a text. *You need to look at this.*

19

She opened the accompanying link. The headline caught her eye. *Chelsea Dawson, 21, Disappears in Lafayette, New Jersey*. Next to the story was an image of a girl in a see-through blue dress. Aerin stared at the girl's blue eyes, her white-blonde hair, the dimple next on her left cheek. Aerin's blood turned ice-cold.

She looked exactly like Helena.

CHAPTER 3

Maddox Wright finished his treadmill run with three minutes on the 11.0 mph setting, his pounding feet echoing through the LA Fitness in Dexby, Connecticut. Normally, he preferred to run outside, but it was way too hot and humid even for an elite athlete like him.

Breathing hard, he hit the END button, wiped down the handgrips, and guzzled a water bottle he'd filled with chocolate milk. He found it disgusting to drink chocolate milk post-run, but John Quigley, his soon-to-be coach at the University of Oregon said in his bestselling self-help book, *The Path to Gold*, that chocolate milk had the optimal mix of proteins, carbs, and fats to refuel after a workout. Maddox made a point to be Coach Quigley's model athlete-in-training.

"Hey."

A tall, fit girl with green eyes and glossy, kissable lips smiled at him from the water fountain. As she moved closer to Maddox, he realized she smelled like sugar cookies.

"You were really booking it." She lowered her long eyelashes. "Are you some sort of pro?"

Maddox shrugged modestly. "I'm headed to the Olympic trials next summer, if all goes well."

The girl widened her eyes, then thrust out a hand. "I'm Laila. Wanna grab a smoothie? You can tell me more about it."

An instructor's voice boomed out from a nearby exercise room: *Pick up the pace! I want to see higher kicks!* Maddox's tongue felt coated with chocolate ooze. He cleared his throat and blurted, "Actually, I've got to get home."

Laila blinked. "Oh. Okay."

Maddox gave her a polite smile and hurried toward the front door. A scoff stopped him, and he noticed his stepsister, Madison, perched in the little nook that sold athletic gear. She was giving him such an indignant glare you would have thought Maddox had just walked across the gym floor naked.

"What?" he snapped. It made no sense that Madison was here. Whenever Maddox asked his sister if she wanted to go to the gym with him, her typical response was something like, *Well, I power-walked the Dexby Diamond Shoppes in my dream for hours last night searching for the perfect Gucci purse charm, so I'm pretty exhausted.*

Madison tucked a piece of straight, shiny black hair behind her ear. "Did you seriously just blow off Laila Gregory?"

Maddox stiffened. "Did you seriously just spy on me?"

He headed for the front door, and his sister jumped up after him. "Victoria's Secret just signed Laila as a runway model," she hissed in his ear.

He snorted. "As if a Victoria's Secret model would be hanging out in this dump."

"Her family lives in Dexby." Madison pointed back to the row of machines. "Go back in there and apologize. Explain that you're a reformed dork. This could be huge for you, Maddox."

Maddox rolled his eyes. "Even if I did believe you, I need to focus on running right now. Not random girls."

"Only you would blow off a Victoria's Secret model for *running*."

Maddox unlocked his Jeep, opened the door, and tossed his gym bag onto the seat. The bag tumbled into the foot well, and the contents spilled out. His phone bumped against the frame of the car, and the screen lit up, displaying the wallpaper Maddox had chosen this morning: a picture of Seneca Frazier the night of the Ritz-Carlton party in New York, her dark, curly hair in her face, her glowing, light brown skin, the corners of her mouth stretched into a lazy, tipsy smile.

Maddox lunged to hide the screen, but it was too late. Madison breathed in sharply. "Oooooh!"

He stiffened. "There's nothing to *ooh* about." He cursed himself for choosing that wallpaper. Of *course* Madison was going to ask questions.

There was a knowing look on Madison's face. "At least this explains Laila Gregory."

"It doesn't!" Maddox was keenly aware that his voice had shot up an octave. Why was it, though, that Madison had a particular knack for sussing out Maddox's private, most mortifying secrets?

Because, okay, he thought a lot about Seneca. He had no chance with her, romantically, but ever since she left Dexby three months ago, no girl had measured up. He couldn't stop

23

thinking about the bouncing, boyish way Seneca walked, or her raucous laugh, or the crinkle that appeared between her eyes when she was puzzling something out. He'd relived the moment they'd kissed at least two thousand times. Whenever she emailed him these days – which was becoming less frequent – he pounced on the message, stopping whatever he was doing, even running, to read it. But her emails were so chilly, so spare, just briefings about cases Brett Grady had been interested in on Case Not Closed. They weren't peppered with details of books she'd read or new music she'd listened to. There were no updates about whether she'd had dinner at her favorite greasy Asian noodle place in downtown Annapolis. It was like she was pretending what had gone down between them – how close they'd been to becoming something – had never happened.

A few times, Maddox composed an email to Seneca that cut through the bullshit, laying out how he was still crazy about her and that he worried she might be becoming a mild agoraphobic – she was spending a lot of time in her room, on Brett Watch. That he couldn't begin to imagine how devastated she was right now. The betrayal he felt was nothing compared to what she must be going through. *I'm here*, he wrote. *We're in this together.* But when he reread his words, they seemed cheesy. Seneca was the last person who wanted unsolicited help; maybe he should just leave her alone. And so he always wrote an equally toneless email in reply, burying the truth deep.

But *Madison* didn't need to know that. He glared at her now. She looked so smug, like she'd solved some major mystery.

She was wearing a heart-print dress and bootie sandals with stacked pink heels. Her hair was pulled into a high ponytail, and she smelled like she'd just smoked a pound of weed.

"What are you doing at the gym, anyway?" he asked grumpily.

"I came to find you. You got mail." She presented a slender envelope. *Maddox Wright*, it read, and then his address. In the upper-right corner, there was only a name. *Brett Grady*.

Maddox felt the blood drain from his cheeks.

The letter had a generic American-flag stamp and a postmark from Cleveland, Ohio. It had been addressed on an old-fashioned typewriter, but there was something wrong with the lateral alignment, and the letters jumped up and down across the page. It gave Maddox a spinning sense, like he was looking at an optical illusion.

He peeked at his sister. She was watching him carefully, the playful look on her face gone.

"Oh." He moved to stuff the letter into his bag, but Madison grabbed his wrist.

"Don't play dumb. Anything Brett says, I want to know, too," she said.

Maddox could feel his heart pounding through the thick canvas. When he'd first heard Seneca's theory about Brett, he'd thought she was crazy. Brett was a cool guy – they'd hit it off a year before at a CNC meetup. But the more he thought about it, a lot of Brett's behavior during the investigation *was* sketchy. *Could* Seneca be onto something? Could Brett have used a fake name and lied about who he was? Was it such a leap to think that Helena's killer had steered their investigation all along, pointing them to the wrong suspect? That beneath Brett's seemingly harmless exterior lurked a monster? That possibility terrified him. He'd let him in. They'd partied together. He'd never once guessed that he'd been lied to.

The sun crept behind a cloud, turning the sky a purplish gray. Locusts began to screech, the sound discordant and ugly. Maddox felt a rushing sensation in his ears and peered nervously over his shoulder, half sure Brett would be lurking nearby. The gym's rusty Dumpster lid banged shut in a gust of wind. A large graffiti eye was spray-painted on its side, watching him. Goose bumps rose on his arms.

Suddenly, Madison shot forward, ripped open the envelope, and extracted two sheets of folded paper. "Hey!" Maddox tried to yank it back, but his sister had hurried across the parking lot. "We're both reading it," Madison snapped.

"Madison . . ." Maddox rushed over to her, blood sloshing in his ears. Single-spaced typewritten words marched jaggedly across the page. He caught sight of the words *Dear Maddox* on the first line and felt the same way he did when he stepped onto a boat slip: groundless, shaky, suddenly unsure of the rules of the world.

The air around him went still. As he read each sentence, his stomach began to twist with disbelief. He read the letter one more time, trying to process what Brett was saying.

What up, Maddox –
Hope all is well with you. I bet you're wondering where I am, huh? I know you've been looking. I know

26

all of you still talk. So really, this is a letter for everyone. I miss you guys. But look, I might have withheld a few important details when we last hung out. I thought I'd share a few of them now, in case you want to know.

Seneca – I know how eager you are for information, so here's a nugget: Remember when you'd go to Target to buy books? Did you know Mama flirted with someone at the Starbucks while you were thumbing through paperbacks? Even kissed someone?

And, Aerin – Did you know that when a certain pretty blonde took Metro-North into the city, she always chose a seat farthest from the bathroom? And did you know her favorite bar in Grand Central was the Campbell Apartment, and that old dude she was hooking up with wasn't the only guy she met there? I bet you didn't.

I know you know what I did. And I know you want to find me. I'm not done with you, either. Game on, everyone. You've gotten my first clue, so come and get me. But if you think about going to the cops with this, someone's dead.

Stay real,
Brett

"What. The. *Hell?*" Madison whispered, stepping away from the letter as though it was seeping radiation.

When Maddox tried to fold the letter, his hands shook. "W-we have to call the police."

27

"Are you insane?" Madison cried. "He told us someone will *die* if we do!"

From inside the car, his phone started ringing. Dazed, Maddox wrenched the Jeep door open and found it on the floor. He wondered if Brett was now *calling* . . . but it was Seneca's name that flashed on the screen. His heart dropped.

"Maddox?" Seneca barked when Maddox answered. "Are you there? I have Aerin on the phone, too. We need to talk to you."

Maddox couldn't feel his legs. Spots formed in front of his eyes. His vocal cords seemed to have knotted together. "Wh-what's going on?" he heard himself say.

"Brett just posted on Case Not Closed. Something about a girl who went missing in New Jersey. The police weren't too concerned about it at first, but then they found blood in the parking lot near the party. It matches her blood type. BMoney60 posted that he thinks her ex-boyfriend did it. He said he was *at* the party."

"Chelsea Dawson looks exactly like Helena," Aerin chimed in.

Maddox's chest tightened. "Maybe *that's* what he's talking about in his letter. That post is his first clue."

"Letter?" Seneca asked sharply. "What letter?"

Maddox shut his eyes. "Brett sent me a letter. Just now." His voice trembled. "Madison found it in the mailbox. We were just about to call *you*."

"Hey, guys," Madison added reluctantly.

"Brett sent you a *letter*?" Seneca sounded appalled. "Read it!"

Maddox thought of what the letter said and shut his eyes. The last thing he wanted to do was read it aloud to Seneca. "Um . . ."

Madison ripped the letter from his hand. "*I'll* read it," she said, as if sensing why he was so hesitant. Maddox gave her a small, grateful nod. Madison unfolded the pages again and, with a grim look, began.

CHAPTER 4

Seneca had moved to the tiny bathroom inside the ice cream stand, where she could speak in private. She stood in the cramped space, which had drawings of anthropomorphic ice cream cones on the walls, and listened to Madison read the letter. As the words washed over her, she felt a bright, almost-surreal mix of anger, shock, disgust, and devastation. Then, to her astonishment, she felt the urge to burst out laughing. It had happened only one time before – at her mother's funeral, at the very moment they were closing the casket. It was like the wires in her head were crossed.

But on the heels of the desire to laugh came the desire to throw something. Shatter the mirror over the minuscule bathroom sink. Kick the door so hard she broke the bones in her foot. She wilted against the wall, her emotions suddenly doing a 180 again. Now it felt like a big hole was spreading inside her, turning everything to ash. Could this be real? Could this be how Brett and her mother met? Oh God, she *knew* that Starbucks Brett mentioned, tucked into the front of the Target outside Annapolis. For all she knew, she'd seen Brett behind the counter, serving her mom a latte.

But *kissed*? Brett and her mom had *kissed*?

Seneca leaned over the sink, feeling sick. The idea was now seared into her brain.

When Aerin's voice came through the phone, Seneca jumped. "Why would Brett write all of that?" Aerin asked in a small, thin voice.

"Because he's insane?" Madison cried.

"I know, but why would he confess?"

"He didn't confess anything," Maddox argued. "It's all so vague. There's nothing we can tell the cops."

"What are you talking about?" Aerin exclaimed. "He's obviously talking about my sister. He stalked her on Metro-North! And he worked at Starbucks – that's a *huge* lead! Cops can get employment history and pictures of him on Target's surveillance video."

Target. How many times had Seneca gone in there with her mom? *Do you mind if we run in?* Collette always said. *I need to pick up a few things. I'll buy you a book.* Seneca remembered a particular time mere months before her mom disappeared when she'd perused the fiction aisle at the back of the store, happy a new thriller was in stock. She'd been so engrossed in the first chapter that she didn't notice until fifteen minutes later that her mom hadn't come to check on her. And her mother was . . . at the Starbucks counter? Having a freaking latte with *Brett*? Her stomach heaved.

"Seneca?" Maddox's voice cut through her murky memories. "You still there?"

Seneca made a small sound from the back of her throat.

"What should we do?" Maddox asked. Seneca could

hear the apology in his voice. She and Maddox had been close – they'd even kissed. And, okay, she might have had a few fantasies about him in the months since they'd parted, but things had chilled between them. Still, he understood her. He got that the last thing she wanted to do right now was strategize. All her hunches confirmed. All her worries, her terrors, true. But knowing Brett was truly the murderer felt neither satisfying nor vindicating. It was, instead, like she was getting sucked into quicksand. Like someone had punched her hard in the jaw, sending her brain clanging against her skull.

But then something hit her. Maybe Brett wanted her to feel this way. Numb. Scattered. Ruined. Too hurt to think. Perhaps this was part of his plan.

She straightened up, determined not to fall prey to his mind games. "Brett knows what's he doing. He's given us a clue to where he is, and it has something to do with this missing girl. He wants us to find him. He wants to play a game."

There was a long pause. "So do we?" Maddox's voice wobbled.

The bells to the front door of the ice cream shop jingled, and Seneca heard voices. She placed her head in her hands and considered all she'd just heard. Chelsea – blonde and pretty – fit Brett's type. He had been hiding out, and now he had this girl. The injustice of it, the *brutality* of it, made her curl her hands into fists. But beneath her shock and anger, excitement crackled. Here Brett was, finally. In her crosshairs. And with the new information about her mom, Seneca was even more determined to take him down.

32

"Yes," she decided. "I think we do."

Aerin gulped in a breath. "So we go and find a kidnapped girl? Can we do that on our own?"

"Of course," Seneca said, surprised by the force of her voice. "We've done it before. We found out what Helena was up to. We exposed Skip and Marissa. Even if they weren't the actual killers, it was a lot farther than the cops got. Think about the things Brett wrote about your sister in that letter, Aerin. That he'd followed her. *Stalked* her. You know he broke into the Dakota. You *know* it. Don't you want to avenge your sister's death? Don't you want to wring his freaking neck?"

There was silence. Seneca realized she'd been speaking very loudly, and she was now on her feet, her muscles tensed. She glanced at herself in the mirror. Her skin was blotchy. Her mouth was taut. Her fingers clutched the edge of the sink.

Then Aerin softly exhaled. "Yeah. I really, really do."

"Madison?" Seneca asked. "Maddox? What about you?"

"I totally get wanting to find Brett, you guys," Maddox said gently. "But go to New Jersey? How do we even know if Brett's still there?"

"Because he *says* he is. In his letter."

There were whispers; Madison and Maddox seemed to be discussing it. "We're in, one hundred percent," Maddox said when he got back on the line. "But if we don't find her within a week, we have to go to the police."

Seneca paused. Brett was crazy enough to make good on his threat to kill Chelsea – or perhaps someone else – if they went to the cops. But maybe Maddox was right. If they couldn't figure this out in a matter of days, they would have to go to the police. She was about to agree when there was banging at the bathroom door. "Uh, Seneca?" It was Brian.

Seneca opened the door a crack and gave him an apologetic smile. She pointed at the phone and mouthed, *My dad*. Brian nodded, and she closed the door softly.

She ducked her head and fiddled with the gold *P*-initial necklace she wore every day of her life, the one that used to belong to her mom. This was happening. Really happening. But was she ready to face her mom's killer?

She thought of her mother. The tangy smell of the moisturizer she rubbed on her face every morning. How she addictively applied ChapStick at stoplights and after meals. Over the summer, she'd gotten back into looking through old photo albums; there was one of her mother standing in front of a tree with a square burned into its trunk. She wore a strappy sundress and held a squirming, sticky-faced, three-year-old Seneca on her hip. She was smiling into the camera, and she looked so . . . *innocent*. The kind of person who was so effortlessly happy, she buoyed the happiness of everyone around her.

Had Brett killed Collette immediately, or had he taken his time? Had he *touched* her? Seneca knew it wasn't healthy to obsess over those details, but it was almost like she wanted to prove to herself that she wasn't afraid to look at things head-on. She wanted to prove she had the guts. She wanted to prove she was brave enough to find Brett. To face him. Take him down.

On the phone, they talked about how they would get to New Jersey and what they would do next. It was only after everyone hung up that Seneca stared at herself in the mirror once more. The redness had disappeared from her cheeks, and her eyes looked glassy and vacant. She didn't look angry anymore, she realized.

She looked terrified.

CHAPTER 5

Maddox woke up Monday morning to the wafting scent of J.Lo Glow in his nostrils. Madison stood over his bed, in a red-and-pink dress and five-inch heels. "Why aren't you up?" she hissed.

He jumped to his feet with a start. By the pale whitish light on the window, he could tell it was still early, but he was surprised he'd fallen asleep. All day yesterday, he'd stressed over packing and mapping the correct route and poring over the news. And then for hours last night, his head had swirled with anticipation. A girl was missing. Only *they* knew who did it. And Brett was out there, arms outstretched, waiting for them to come and play.

It scared the crap out of him. It would sound wussy if he admitted how petrified he'd been the night Marissa Ingram had trapped them all in the bathroom at the Easter Bunny party, a shard of glass to Aerin's throat . . . but he *had* been. And Brett was a *murderer*. What if this was a trap? It felt like walking into a shark tank in nothing but swim trunks and a snorkel mask. But he thought again about Brett's letter. The long, heartbreaking silence on Seneca's end of the line after

Madison had finished reading. The determined quiver in her voice when she'd convinced Aerin that they needed to get Brett. He would do anything for Seneca. And also? Seeing her face-to-face, he would finally be able to check in with her . . . *and* tell her how he felt.

Maddox climbed out of bed and pulled on a T-shirt and a pair of shorts. The house was quiet and still; his mother and stepfather were sound asleep in the bedroom at the end of the hall. Madison followed him toward the bathroom, and he gave her a weary glare and half shut the door. "Have you figured out how you're going to explain being away to Mom and Dad?" he asked her.

"How do *you* plan to explain it?"

"I decided to do a couple of days at the track camp in Jersey. It's starting today." Because he'd dominated at the national high school track meet that spring, he'd received several invitations from track camps all over the country, inviting him to attend for free. Leaflets for programs in Florida, Maine, Indiana, and Kansas littered his bureau.

"Well, don't worry about me." Madison tapped a giant hard-shell rolling suitcase. It was the one she'd used for their three-week trip to visit her cousins in Korea last year. "Let's go."

Maddox gawked at the bag. "Do you plan on being away all summer?"

Madison retreated to her bedroom and appeared with yet *another* suitcase, this one only slightly smaller and printed in cheerful pink plaid. "I might want to be a detective, but I don't want to *look* like one." She grabbed the handles of both bags and headed toward the garage. "Let's go!"

* * *

A few hours later, after listening to Beyoncé's *Lemonade* on repeat, they crossed a small bridge that led into the little seaside town of Lafayette. A choppy blue-gray bay gave way to a swanky boutique hotel called the Reeds at Shelter Haven, and then they were spat out onto a main drag lined with surf shops, a saltwater taffy store, and a place called Ralph's 5 & 10 that had boogie boards and inflatable beach loungers displayed on the sidewalk. It was mid-morning, and the street bustled with vacationers. A pancake house had a line out of the door. Maddox spied a sign taped to a telephone pole. *Missing.* It showed a photo of the girl Maddox had stared at last night until his eyes blurred. *Chelsea Dawson. Five feet five, blue eyes, blonde hair.*

Chelsea was a dead ringer for Helena. In the photo, she was cradling a Labrador puppy. She wore a Pandora bracelet containing charms of a horse and a camera. Unlike the racy photos she posted on Snapchat and Instagram, in this one Chelsea seemed like a girl who sang Disney ballads until she was twelve and wrote poetry about boy bands and unicorns. Maddox gripped the steering wheel hard, feeling charged. They were going to save this girl *and* get Brett in the process. They had to.

"So this is what I read about Chelsea," Madison said, following his gaze to the poster. "She's from outside Philly. Her family has a house here and comes every summer. She'll be a senior at Villanova, and until this year, she volunteered at a facility where they do equine therapy for kids with special needs." She made a face. "I don't get horsey girls. What's the big draw of shoveling huge piles of poop all day?"

Maddox felt impatient. "What do you know about the night she went missing?"

"I'm just giving you a full picture. As I was saying, she *was* really into horses . . . but then she started her Instagram account. This girl posts All. The. Time. Mostly selfies. The pictures were pretty innocent at first, but they became sexier and sexier over time. She went from having a few hundred followers to *tens* of thousands. Her account isn't private, and a lot of the comments are pretty pervy." Madison wrinkled her nose. "But I guess she likes the attention."

Maddox bit his thumbnail as they waited for a group of kids to cross the street. "Remember that line in the letter where Brett got kinda judge-y, saying Helena was *deplorable*?" Madison nodded. "What if Brett believes he's doing the world a favor by killing these women? Like he goes after women who he finds morally shameful. Helena because she was with an older man. Seneca's mom because . . ." He trailed off, hating to think of it. "She kissed him and was married. Who knows? Maybe he took Chelsea because he thinks she's a narcissist."

"Maybe," Madison said, her gaze on her phone again. "The last thing Chelsea posted was from the night she went missing. She's half naked, and she practically broke Instagram with it."

"I saw it." It was hard not to stare at Chelsea and her come-hither eyes, pouty lips, and nipples that were visible through her gauzy blue dress.

"The thing is, she looks really happy. I bet she had no clue someone was going to kidnap her in the parking lot later that night."

Maddox shivered despite the warm burst of sun. He thought of the last pictures they'd seen of Helena before she died, quick snaps they'd found on an app called Under Wraps. In the last photo, she looked hopeful, happy, and in love.

She hadn't known anything bad was about to happen to her, either.

The group had arranged to meet at a coffee shop called Island Time, which had a fifties-style sign in the parking lot and a turquoise-painted roof. Seneca had texted Madison about an hour ago to report that she'd already arrived, and as Maddox navigated the Jeep into a space, his chest burned with nerves.

Madison pushed through the double doors, and a bell jingled. A figure sitting at a table at the back of the café looked up. *Don't stare*, Maddox thought, but he couldn't help himself. It felt like a hummingbird had been unleashed in his stomach. Seneca wore the same jean jacket she'd had on when she'd stepped off the train in Dexby the first time they'd met. Her cheeks were adorably pink, her shoulder-length hair was full around her face, and her eyes were bright and stunning. It was jarring being in Seneca's presence after spending so many hours thinking about her. He'd forgotten that she was just as human as everyone else, with ragged fingernails, a Band-Aid on her finger, and an untied sneaker.

Seneca hugged Madison first, and then she turned to Maddox. As she stepped forward, he worried she was going to spread out her arms for a hug . . . and then he worried she *wouldn't*. He wasn't sure which gesture would make him feel worse, so he crossed his arms over his chest. "Hey" was all he could muster.

"Hey," Seneca said back, sounding just as tentative – maybe even defensive. Maybe his *hey* had come out too pitying. Seneca hated being pitied.

Maddox gritted his teeth. *Cut through the bullshit*. Seneca was hurting. Brett's letter was brutal. He needed to tell her he was here for her.

But then the door opened again, and Aerin Kelly breezed in, clad in a flowing maxi dress, round sunglasses, and a bag with two interlocking Cs on the front. She looked tanner, blonder, and even more glamorous than when Maddox had seen her last. "Sorry I'm late," she breathed. "I had to take a train and two buses *and* a cab to get to this place."

"Maddox and Madison just got here, too," Seneca said, and everyone sat down. She eyed Maddox carefully. "Did you have any luck researching Metro-North?"

Maddox rolled his shoulders. Yesterday, he'd looked into how to identify passengers on Metro-North – maybe there was a way to track Brett's train tickets from when he stalked Helena. But it had been a dead end. "When you buy tickets, you don't give your name. And while some of the trains have surveillance cameras, the Dexby line doesn't. Grand Central station has tons of security cameras that might have picked up an image of Brett, but we'd need police permission to access them. And even if we *did* do that, I doubt they saved images from five years ago."

"I looked into his posts from Case Not Closed," Madison said, sounding just as frustrated. "They're impossible to trace."

"Shit," Seneca muttered, biting her lip.

"I'm guessing the Target search didn't go well, either?" Maddox asked uneasily.

41

Seneca stared into her coffee cup. "I called and asked if anyone remembered someone named Brett working there five years before, both by his name and description. Nobody did, no surprise. They also told me they recycle their security footage every thirty days – so there's no chance of Brett on camera. They have a Facebook page, and it goes back five years, but I didn't see pictures of Brett anywhere."

Aerin tapped her nails against the table. "Do you think Brett lied about working at Starbucks?"

Seneca's features brightened for a split second, as if she would love nothing more than for this to be true. But then she shook her head. "I think he's telling the truth – in some capacity. Anyway, then I contacted Darcy on CNC – she goes as TheForceWithin? She helped get some Starbucks records in that case in Missouri where a rapist was targeting women at their local coffee shops. She had a contact in Starbucks corporate. Anyway, I asked if she could look into that particular franchise's employee history. She said she'd try, but it might take a while." Seneca tucked a piece of hair behind her ear. "I'm not sure what good it will do. Brett probably used an alias, with a fake social security number."

"We don't know that for sure," Maddox pointed out. "What if your mom was his first victim? Maybe he'd used his real name, and all his names after that were aliases."

Seneca flinched at the mention of her mom. "Maybe. I also called the hotels he stayed at in Dexby in April. It turns out that the Restful Inn and the Dexby Water's Edge don't have operational cameras. The Ritz-Carlton in New York might have, but they erase their security data after a month."

"What about a credit card?" Maddox remembered how Brett had paid for the suite at the Ritz-Carlton – *and* the big party that had ensued.

"All hotels say he paid in cash." She massaged her temples. "This is like looking for a needle in a haystack, guys. We have to *think*. We don't know Brett's real name. We don't know how old he is, where he's from. Can anyone remember what he looks like, exactly? It's like the more I think about him, the blurrier he gets in my mind."

Maddox stared at the popcorn ceiling. Weirdly, he couldn't remember, either. Brett was one of those guys whose features were so generic he could look different from every angle. Maddox thought of his clothes – those gold sneakers and oversized sweaters at Le Dexby Patisserie, the too-small tuxedo he'd squeezed into at Kevin Larssen's engagement party, the crisp button-down and skinny jeans at the Ritz-Carlton. His style was all over the map. "And none of us have a photo of him?" he checked. They'd had their phones out plenty when they were together in Dexby. He'd certainly snapped enough pictures of *Seneca*.

"Nope," Seneca answered.

"He texted me one once." Aerin scrolled through her phone, then frowned. "But I didn't save it and I got a new phone since we saw Brett . . ."

A blaring sound made Maddox shift his gaze to the TV that hung over the counter. A woman reporter with dark hair and crinkles around her eyes stood at the Hoy's mart they'd just passed with two red-eyed adults. "Investigators are searching for a missing vacationer named Chelsea Marie Dawson," the reporter said. "Miss Dawson was at a party on the night of July 10 but never came home. Witnesses at the party say they saw her leave down a secluded path through the dunes, but no one can say what happened to her after that. If you have any information, please call the number below. Mr. and Mrs. Dawson are desperate for their daughter to come home safely."

The reporter gestured to the man and woman next to her. Chelsea's father made a statement begging for Chelsea to come home – and offered a reward to anyone who came forward with information. Chelsea's mother looked comatose. A few pictures of Chelsea appeared on the screen, including the sweet one from the Missing poster. A lump formed in Maddox's throat, and he looked away.

"It's terrible, isn't it?"

A guy in a Phillies ball cap stood behind the counter, bending a straw back and forth. He had angular shoulders, a five o'clock shadow, and a jutting chin. "I can't believe it happened," he said softly, his gaze on the screen. "She seemed so sweet."

"Do you know her?" Seneca asked.

The guy, whose name tag read *Corey*, kept his eyes down. "Not really, but my manager does." He held up a finger and scurried into the back. Moments later, a petite girl with dirty blonde hair came to the counter. "Hi, I'm Kate. Yeah, everyone's asking about Chelsea today. I didn't know her that well, but I was at that party the other night. The one she went missing from."

Maddox leaned on the counter. "Did you notice anything weird about her?"

Kate spun a silver ring around her finger. "Not really. She was mostly taking selfies. She had this new selfie stick, a motorized

44

thing with a camera." She made a face like she thought that was kind of lame, but then quickly shifted her features back to neutral.

Maddox fiddled with his napkin. "Did you know everyone at the party, or were there a lot of vacationers?"

She shrugged. "I recognized almost everyone. It's a condo complex connected to a private beach club, and there was a guest list. I still can't believe this happened."

The door chimed, and new customers stepped inside. "Corey?" Kate called toward the back room. Corey didn't materialize. Kate rolled her eyes, then smiled apologetically at Maddox and the others. "Sorry, I've gotta take this."

Maddox leaned across the table after she left. "We need to get our hands on that guest list. If it was invite-only, and Brett's telling the truth on CNC about being at the party, then he's been making friends here. Someone must know him."

"Though by a different name, obviously." Seneca drained the rest of her coffee.

Madison looked around the café with trepidation. "Just think. Brett might have sat at this very *table*."

Seneca blotted her lips. "Let's not waste time feeling scared. Let's play."

Aerin tapped her manicured nails against the tabletop. "How?"

Seneca was about to speak, but the news came back on. A big banner that read *Just In* flashed across the screen. "Breaking news from the Lafayette police station," the reporter said excitedly. "Sources say that the authorities have a person of interest in the Chelsea Dawson case. Mr. Jeff Cohen, Chelsea's twenty-one-year-old ex-boyfriend, was brought into police custody for questioning earlier today. Mr. Cohen was the last person to see Miss Dawson before she vanished, and eyewitnesses attest that the couple had been arguing. No one can account for Mr. Cohen after eleven until early the next morning. We'll have more news on this developing situation as we receive it."

A picture of Jeff Cohen appeared. He had thick eyebrows, a square jaw, large dark-rimmed eyes, and wavy brown hair pulled into a little knot at the crown of his head. Maddox twisted his mouth. He so didn't understand hipster hairdos.

Then he realized what this meant. He turned back to the table and, for the very first time, met Seneca's gaze straight on. When Seneca stared back at him, he could feel the connection between them. "That's who Brett pointed to . . ."

"On Case Not Closed," Seneca finished, narrowing her eyes. "Why am I not surprised?" She picked up her phone, tapped the screen, and began to type. After she was finished, she slid the phone across the table for the others to read. Case Not Closed's website was on the screen, and Seneca had accessed the private message part of the site and composed a message to *BMoney60*.

Got your letter, B. We're here. And we're coming for you.

CHAPTER 6

The first thing Brett Grady did when he came into the room, which he'd dubbed Command Central, was make sure the blackout shades didn't show even a millimeter of sunlight. Then he fell into a big leather chair and switched on the monitor.

The Camera A feed shimmered into view. Chelsea lay on the little couch next to the bed. She didn't have a blindfold on anymore – she'd ripped that off shortly after he left her, and then she'd gone to work clawing at the doors and windows, desperate to get out. Defeated, she stared blankly at the ceiling. Her hair was dirty and matted. Smeared mascara caked around her eyes. The bloody scrape from her knees when she'd stumbled – Brett's only mistake – had turned into a brownish scab.

"Hello," he said through the microphone.

Chelsea jumped and looked around. She was wearing the same blue dress she'd had on the night of the party, two days ago.

"Why haven't you changed clothes?" He enjoyed the way the voice-changing software made his voice deeper and more robust.

She glanced fumblingly at the ceiling, the TV, and the walls. "Wh-where are you?" Her frightened tone was very different from the one she'd used when she'd told Jeff off at the party. "*Who* are you?"

"I laid out clean clothes for you in the bathroom. A red dress. Didn't you see it?"

Chelsea blinked as though he were speaking Russian. Then she started to cry. "What do you want with me? Can't you let me go?"

"I really think you should change clothes," Brett said evenly. "And perhaps take a shower. I'm guessing you no longer smell like Aveda Rosemary Mint."

She gasped. Her tears stopped, and her eyes widened. Brett could see the wheels turning in her little brain: *How does he know what shampoo I use?* Was she putting together the pieces?

Whatever. Even if Chelsea did figure it out, even if she had someone to tell, even if she was able to pry open the windows and run away, it wouldn't make any difference. She didn't know who he really was. No one did.

"Why are you doing this to me?" She stared at the television, though he was actually watching her on a camera hidden in a chink in the bookcase. "I'm a good person. I swear it."

Brett thought of the endless conversations they'd had as "friends." The favors he'd done for her. The things she'd confessed. The secrets he'd kept. All her flirty empty promises, and the white lies he'd caught her in. *No, bitch. You're not a good person at all.*

He turned the screen off and slumped back on the chair. He could hear her wailing through the thin wall: "My parents

48

are probably so worried. Hello? Hello! Who are you?" He fiddled with his phone, its bright screen blinding in the absolute darkness. As he scrolled through Instagram, his mouth pinched when he saw all the comments on Chelsea's last picture. There were vigils, too. *Bring her home*, the captions read, under an image of a lit candle. He smiled.

Then Brett logged on to Case Not Closed. There were a few new messages, mostly old-timers weighing in about Chelsea's case. Then he saw Seneca's handle, and his heart lifted. He savored the message slowly. *Got your letter, B. We're here.* This was good. *Very* good.

The last sentence – *And we're coming for you* – gave him a chuckle. That bitch had *no idea* who she was dealing with. Brett's fingers hovered over the keyboard, tempted to tell Seneca exactly what he'd done to her mother, down to the last grisly detail. At the very least he could tell her he'd found a ChapStick in Collette's jacket pocket when her body was still warm. In fact, he'd smeared a tiny bit of it in the letter he sent to Maddox. Little did Seneca know that if she sniffed the paper, a little bit of her mom would be there, still present, still potent.

No, he told himself. He had to keep his head. He had to do everything according to plan. Make her think she had a chance. But maybe there was one small thing he could do to rattle the cage. It was such a good idea that Brett tipped his head back and let out a long, deep laugh.

If those fools didn't know who was boss, they would soon.

CHAPTER 7

"You're in luck, we have two rooms left," Bertha, the proprietor of the Conch B&B, said to Aerin and the others Monday afternoon. "Probably the last in town, am I right? One is the Love Suite. It's got a king bed and a Jacuzzi. The other has two single beds, and it's on the first floor, next to the kitchen."

Bertha was tough to look at without snickering – her hair was perm-fried, and an aquamarine stripe of eye shadow stretched from her lid to her brow – so Aerin peered at the rest of the establishment instead. In the foyer stood a curio cabinet filled with a huge jumble of stuff. It reminded Aerin of one of those I Spy books, where you had to find a tiny yellow ball in a photo amid lots of junk. There was a bowl containing paper clips, dice, and golf tees; at least seven Buddha statues; a whole family of grinning, porcelain apples; a bunch of candlesticks of varying sizes, a ceramic frog wearing a tall yellow crown; and a bottom shelf containing nothing but creepy baby dolls dressed in frilly pinafores. The B&B's foyer opened into a living room done up in poppy-printed wallpaper, crushed-velvet couches, a taxidermied Siamese cat frozen mid-pounce beneath the hearth, and a large tank containing a striped, spiky fish Aerin was pretty sure was poisonous. A scrawny elderly man sat at the doily-covered dining table, eating a bowl of oatmeal and patting a giant Doberman. When the man noticed Aerin staring, he gave her a lecherous wink. The dog spied Aerin and the others and began to bark raucously. Aerin jumped back.

"Oh, that's Kingston." Bertha followed Aerin's gaze. "Best security system in town, but he's harmless once he gets to know you." She shooed the dog into the kitchen and put up a doggie gate. Kingston sniffed the air suspiciously.

Maddox coughed awkwardly and looked at Seneca. "How about you girls take the Love Suite? I'm not really one for hot tubs."

Madison scowled. "How come you get your own room and we have to squeeze into one bed?"

"Two people per room," Seneca advised. "Madison, you stay with your brother."

"I don't want to stay with him! He sleeps in his boxers!"

Maddox sniffed. "*So?*"

Madison pointed at Seneca. "*You* stay with Maddox, and I'll stay with Aerin."

"*I'll* stay with Maddox," Aerin said impatiently – judging by the look on Seneca's face, the idea of sharing with Maddox made her feel extremely awkward. She handed over enough twenty-dollar bills to cover several nights. "Can you please bring a cot to the Love Suite?" she asked.

Then Madison and Seneca headed down a long, narrow hall lined in cat paintings while Maddox and Aerin climbed creaky stairs embedded with sand to the second floor. A door at the end of the hall was painted magenta and had the word *love* stenciled on it in fussy calligraphy. When Aerin opened the door, the scent of roses assaulted her nostrils. In the center of the room was a large heart-shaped bed covered with a quilt bearing the design of a naked man and woman frolicking through the Garden of Eden. A collection of antique mirrors hung on the ceiling, and in the corner was a hanging contraption Aerin was pretty sure was a sex swing. Colin Rooney, who she'd hooked up with last year, begged her to try the one in his parents' bedroom, but she'd vehemently declined.

"Ew," she whispered, wishing she'd chosen the twin room instead.

"It's like a Victorian porno set." Maddox dumped his stuff on the lumpy floral settee. "You're welcome to the bed."

"Gee, thanks. It's probably covered in gonorrhea." Aerin pointed at a large box Maddox had just set down. "What's that?"

Maddox followed her gaze. "Oh. My drone."

She felt a spike of annoyance. "We're not here to have *fun*!"

"I know, I know," Maddox said quickly. "I thought it might come in handy." Then he peered at Aerin guiltily. "How've you been, by the way? I haven't seen you around Dexby."

Aerin rolled her eyes. "It's not like we travel in the same circles," she snapped. But when she saw the wounded look on Maddox's face, she let out a sigh. Sometimes she unthinkingly reverted into her old ways with him, treating him like he was her nanny's quiet, slightly hostile son who sullenly slumped on her family's living room couch. That was before his mom married Madison's dad . . . *and* before Helena went missing. "Sorry. I'm just tense. And scared. And pissed."

Maddox nodded. "Me too."

Aerin stepped into the bathroom, which, to her relief, did not contain a quilted basket of condoms or a crocheted caddy of antique sex toys. A tired girl stared back from the mirror. She tried to fluff her long blonde hair, but it didn't do much good. Her skin was sunburnt from her time on *That's Amore*. Her neck showed a hint of a hickey. Her hands were shaking, but that was because she'd drunk too much coffee at Island Time. Of course it was.

She pulled out her phone and looked at the third text Pierce had sent since she'd arrived. *Miss you, babe. When are you back?* After they'd docked at Pierce's parents' Newport estate, Aerin had called an Uber. She'd slipped away while Pierce and his buddies were playing basketball on the sport court. By the time they came up to the kitchen for Gatorade, she was already at the train station.

She considered not replying, but she didn't like ghosting people – she had enough ghosts in her life. Might as well get this over with. *I'm not coming back*, she wrote simply. Then she blocked Pierce's number.

Sighing, Aerin flung the phone on the sink and pressed the heels of her hands to her eyes. *Brett*. That *letter*. It kept flooding back into her mind. Hearing hints about how he'd stalked Helena brought the nightmare back in nauseating fluorescence. Had Helena and Brett had a drink at the Campbell Apartment in Grand Central? How had he talked her into that? But she knew how. Helena was nice to everyone, even losers. She'd probably found Brett sweet, like Aerin had. An easy guy to flirt with. An ego boost. Aerin shut her eyes, trying to obliterate the memory of Brett's face moving closer to hers at the Ritz-Carlton party. It made her want to get into the shower and scrub her skin until it bled.

But at the same time, there was something satisfying about the sick flare of fury that had grown in her since hearing Brett's letter. She wanted to get this bastard. He needed to pay for what he'd done to her sister. She was going to find him – or die trying.

There was a bump on the other side of the door. She peered into the bedroom; Maddox was gone. The sex swing rocked back and forth. The tassels that hung from the lampshade jingled. The door to the hallway was slightly ajar, wide enough for a body to slip inside. And around the corner, just out of view, Aerin heard rustling.

Her heart leapt to her throat. *Who was in her room?* She thought of Brett's gleaming eyes, his low chuckle.

Heart thudding, she crept into the bedroom. "H-hello?"

There was a footstep, and then another. A shadow appeared on the other side of the bed. Aerin let out a yelp, feeling her knees buckle.

"Wait!" a familiar voice called. "It's just me!"

Spots formed in front of Aerin's eyes, but the rocketing panic eased slightly. She was so disoriented, she figured her brain was misfiring. But when she looked again, she realized she wasn't imagining things.

It was Thomas Grove.

Thomas was taller than Aerin remembered. As he edged around the bed toward her, she noticed how his muscles pulled against his T-shirt. There was a brightness in his eyes, too. He looked settled. Happy. He was probably living an exciting life in New York.

Without her.

"It's really good to see you," Thomas exhaled.

"What are *you* doing here?" Aerin said at the same time, darting away from him, her voice frosty. "How dare you break into my room?"

"The door was open." Thomas glanced at it, and indeed, it was ajar. "I saw the newscast about this girl named Chelsea Dawson. She looks just like . . ." He took a breath. "That's why you're here, right? You're looking for her?"

Aerin felt breathless. "Are you stalking me?"

"No," Thomas said quickly. "I just had a hunch you'd come, and I didn't have anything going on, so I decided to check things out, too. And then when I was driving into town, I saw you and Seneca climbing up these steps. And then, well, I asked the lady at the front desk where you were staying. I said I was a friend." He looked sheepish. "I'm sorry – I just felt like I needed to talk to you, *now*. Do you think that Brett guy has something to do with Chelsea's disappearance?"

Aerin felt the blood leak from her face. She'd forgotten that she'd told Thomas about Brett – it had been months ago, right before they'd gone on their singular date to Sully's Pizza. "You didn't *tell* anyone about that, did you?"

"Of course not," Thomas said. "But I think –"

"Because I'm wrong. It's a crazy theory."

A breeze blew through the open window, and Aerin got a noseful of salt-scented air. All of a sudden, she couldn't breathe. She thought of the disastrous dinner at Sully's. It had been shortly after Marissa Ingram was arrested. All the hubbub about the case was beginning to die down, and Aerin had hoped she and Thomas could settle into . . . well, something.

Listen, Thomas had said. *I liked being a cop but it was always a means to an end. I needed a way to pay for college. A few days ago, I got an acceptance letter for the New School, in the city. It's a partial scholarship, including room and board. I think I'm going to do it. I'd start summer semester.*

Aerin had stared at him. *Wait, you're* leaving?

Not right away, Thomas had said. *Even when I do, you can visit. It'll be fun! And hey, maybe you can go to school in the city next year!*

Aerin had imagined Thomas living in a college dorm. Decorating it with his grandma's afghans and tchotchkes – his parents struggled with addiction, so his grandma had more or less raised him. A pretty girl from down the hall also there for the summer semester would find him adorable. They'd have late-night study sessions in some adorably seedy Greenwich Village diner; one thing would lead to another. By the end of the night, he'd barely remember Aerin's name.

And then it would be over. Aerin could see it all unfurled before her, practically a foregone conclusion. Why endure all that? She'd stood from the table. *Sorry, but I don't do long-distance relationships. Too messy.* Then she'd left. Only when she got home did she slump onto the round nursery-rhyme rug she'd had since she was a baby and let the tears roll down her cheeks. Everyone always left her. Helena. Her parents. Now Thomas.

"Listen, you need to get out of here, Aerin," Thomas said now. "Brett sounds nuts. It could get dangerous."

Aerin jolted at Brett's name, a horrible thought striking her. What if Brett didn't know Thomas was no longer a cop? If Brett saw them talking, he might assume she was telling on him. Chelsea would *not* die because of her. And Brett couldn't slip away.

"You have to leave," she said. *"Now."*

Thomas's brow furrowed. "Huh?"

Aerin glanced around frantically. What if Brett had bugged this room? What if he'd seen Thomas come into the B&B? It all suddenly seemed so likely. "Thomas, get out of here. I mean it."

He crossed his arms over his chest. "Chelsea looks exactly like your sister, and that's . . . weird. Too weird to be a coincidence. Your hunch about Brett might be right."

"You're not hearing me. Leave right now, or I'll scream."

Thomas blinked. "Wait, really?"

She stared at all the junk in the room so she wouldn't have to look at him – the large portrait of a mostly naked half-woman, half-sea creature, a stack of vintage books all with *sex* in the titles. "Yes. Really."

Out of the corner of her eye, she saw Thomas raise his hands in surrender and back into the hall. "Fine," he grumbled. As he turned, she heard him faintly mutter, "Excuse me for being worried."

And then he was gone.

CHAPTER 8

"Oh right," Seneca heard a voice call as she stood over the espresso machine in the B&B's tiny kitchen Tuesday morning. "I forgot about your love of macchiatos. No drip sludge for you, huh?"

Maddox slumped in the doorway, looking sporty – and admittedly cute – in a University of Oregon Nike tee that showed off his broad shoulders, and gray board shorts that accentuated his muscular calves.

"I'm a snob," she said, shooing away Kingston the dog as he tried once again to stick his nose in her crotch – it seemed to be his way of getting to know people. Then she grabbed her cup from under the gurgling milk steamer. "We're taking your Jeep, right? I'm ready."

Aerin and Madison were spending the morning checking out the search party for Chelsea on the beach, so Seneca and Maddox were going to track down Jeff Cohen – aka the police's person of interest. As Seneca climbed into Maddox's Jeep, she looked at her texts. She had two new ones. Brian was cool about her taking a few days off, but her father was proving to be a tougher customer. *Can you send me address where you are staying? Phone #?*

Seneca tried not to jump into defensive mode. It was a miracle her dad was even allowing her out of his sight. Not that she'd told him the truth of why she was here, only that she was going to the beach with Aerin for a few days – it would be a nice vacation. Her dad agreed and even got kind of nostalgic. He said that the family had visited the Jersey Shore area when Seneca was little and really enjoyed it, not that Seneca remembered. She hated lying again – it had been dreadful when her dad had ambushed her in Dexby – but what could she say? *Hey, I think I've found Mom's killer, and I'm going to Jersey to hunt him down?*

She wanted to tell her dad about Brett. *Desperately.* The thing was, Brett's letter held a lot of power, but not enough proof – and her dad needed proof as much as she did. After Collette's body was found, their neighbors, parents from Seneca's school, other accountants at her dad's work – well, they'd all acted sort of strange around her father. Standoffish, definitely, but also kind of . . . suspicious.

Aunt Terri, her dad's sister, had stayed with them for a month after her mom's body found. One night, Seneca overheard Terri murmur something in the kitchen, while drinking a glass of wine. *People aren't going to say they think you did it, but you know that's what some of them are thinking.*

Her father hadn't replied. Aunt Terri had sniffed, like she thought he was being naive.

Seneca had frozen on the stairs, where she'd been listening in. Her father *definitely* wasn't guilty. They were blaming him because he was the husband, and the husband was always the first suspect.

59

Because the murder was never solved, little things in their lives never quite shifted back to normal. From then on, proving her dad's innocence to everyone, *anyone*, was almost as important a reason to solve the murder as finding justice for her mother was.

But while she almost had Brett, she didn't have him *yet*. And until she did, she didn't want her father to know what she was up to. She needed uninterrupted time to look for Brett if she ever wanted a chance of catching him.

"Hear anything from Brett?" Maddox asked.

Seneca shook her head. She'd been checking her CNC inbox like a fiend. "Not yet."

Maddox nodded, then looked at her again. There was a small smile on his chiseled, tanned face. It seemed like he wanted to say something, but he just opened and closed his mouth a few times.

"What?" Seneca finally said.

Maddox's throat bobbed. "I, um, I've been thinking about you a lot. This summer."

Seneca blinked, then became very still.

"About what you must be going through. With Brett, with your mom – I can't imagine it. And, well –" He paused and stared at his hands on the wheel. His face crumpled with misery. "It kills me. But I also realize it might be something that's so big and awful you don't have the words to talk about it. Which is totally okay. But just know . . . I'm thinking about you. And . . . I'm here, in case you want to talk."

Seneca's face felt hot with a mix of gratitude and something else – embarrassment, maybe, because her past made her feel like a freak show on a good day, and Brett had just amped it up another few notches. "Thanks," she said quietly.

Maddox nodded, but by the set of his jaw, she could tell he wasn't done with what he had to say. "I made a huge mistake in Dexby, too. That kiss you saw with my coach, and how you and I left things – I was such an ass. You mean so much to me, Seneca. I've never met anyone like you. And I'd love to be *with* you. No complications. No mixed messages. We just *get* each other, you know? And I just wonder . . . well, if you want to give this a shot."

Seneca made a big deal of adjusting her seat belt, too stunned to reply. On one hand, it was tempting. She missed their old connection, and there was still a part of her that felt *drawn* to him, her gaze resting on his sharp, handsome features and toned body, her nose twitching at his familiar, pleasant smell, her mind cycling through their kiss at the oddest of times. She was touched, too, that he'd felt brave enough to admit he still liked her – looking uncool wasn't Maddox's MO.

But when she tried to process them as a couple, her mind stalled. She swallowed hard and glanced at Maddox. He looked so earnest and expectant that her heart broke a little.

"You're right," she said gently. "There are no words to describe what Brett's letter is doing to my head. But with us searching for him . . . well, it's the only thing I can think about right now. I don't really have any room inside for anything else, you know?"

"Of course you don't!" Maddox said brightly – almost *too* brightly. "You're totally right. We need to focus on the case. No worries."

Then he stared straight ahead, his expression forcibly cheery. Seneca gnawed on her lips. She longed for something to say to erase this awkwardness, but she couldn't come up with anything.

They passed the boardwalk, an arcade, and several huge houses on the beach in silence, neither of them saying a word. Finally, they pulled up to Jeff's address, a white bungalow about half a block from the beach access ramp. The driveway was empty, but a news van was parked at the curb. A reporter and a cameraman stood on the front porch.

Someone answered from inside. A discussion ensued, and the door shut again. The reporter stepped off the curb and trudged back to the truck. Maddox frowned. "So much for that plan."

"Hold on." Seneca waited for the van to pull away, then slid out of her door. She walked up the front path and onto the porch, head held high. When she twisted the doorknob, Maddox caught her arm. "Breaking and entering?" he whispered. "Really?"

"It's already open. We're fine."

The front room was dark and littered with coffee cups, beach towels, bottles of sunscreen, and other random items that indicated whoever was staying here wasn't a huge fan of tidying up. A long floral couch was pushed up against one wall, and the TV seemed to be playing a local public-access channel, because it only showed a shot of the flat gray ocean. There was a Gibson Les Paul guitar propped up against a wooden chair, and a beat-up acoustic lying on the table. She heard voices murmuring in the back room and called out, "Excuse me?"

The voices stopped. "We need to get out of here," Maddox whispered.

"We need to talk to Jeff," Seneca said through the corner of her mouth.

"What if this dude had some hand in kidnapping Chelsea, too? Maybe he helped Brett. Brett doesn't frame innocent people. This guy could be bad news, too."

"Trust me, I've been wondering about that, too," Seneca said. "But I think it's worth it to talk to him, even if it's for a second. We need to see what he's all about."

"Hello?"

A shirtless guy in floral swim trunks appeared in the hall. Seneca couldn't help but notice that his stomach was so toned that she could make out every ab bump. He had a scruffy almost beard, and his wavy dark hair had been pulled into the same bun she'd seen in his picture on the news yesterday.

"Who are you?" the guy finally asked.

Seneca blinked, then stood a little straighter. "I'm Seneca. This is my friend Maddox. Isn't this Sadie's house? We're visiting for the weekend."

The guy shook his head. "That's not us. Try next door."

"Okay, thanks." Seneca counted to three in her head, then widened her eyes. "Wait. You look familiar. Are you the one on the news who –"

"Nice try." Someone appeared behind Jeff. He was shorter, with thick muscles, an enormous neck, and pale, almost-translucent skin that probably turned pink the moment he stepped on the beach, but he and Jeff shared the same square jaws and round, brooding eyes. "Like we just told the news guys, my brother's not answering questions."

63

"Yeah, Seneca, let's go," Maddox said through his teeth.

"Listen, my friend's sister disappeared five years ago," Seneca blurted. Maddox could leave if he wanted, but she definitely wouldn't. "We helped figure out what happened to her. I know the police are questioning you, but I also know you didn't do anything to Chelsea Dawson."

There was a long, pointed silence. Jeff's brother groaned. "Get out of here, or we're calling the cops."

"Wait, Marcus." Jeff walked a few steps toward her. Even in the dim light, his green eyes sparkled. A million years ago, Seneca had gone to a rocks and minerals exhibit in Baltimore with her mom, and though the diamonds and other precious gems were pretty, they lingered at a huge chunk of aventurine – its cool, calm, bottomless celery-green hue put them both at ease. Jeff's irises were the same color. "Do you know what happened to Chelsea?" he whispered.

"No. But I know you didn't hurt her. I think someone is setting you up."

"Who?"

Seneca looked away. "I can't tell you that. But if you work with us, we'll help prove your innocence."

Marcus sighed dramatically. "Just leave, okay? This isn't doing my brother any good. I'm counting to ten."

"Please?" Seneca asked. "Look, I know how this must feel for you. You're worried about someone you care about." She licked her lips, not wanting to say what she was going to say next – but also knowing she *needed* to. "I was in the same situation," she blurted. "My mother disappeared five years ago. She was murdered."

"*Seneca!*" Maddox hissed, giving her a look that said, *Are you* sure *that's a good idea?*

But Seneca didn't take her eyes off Jeff. His lips were trembling; she could tell he was softening. "And if we don't work quickly to find Chelsea, who knows what he'll do to her," she added. "So please. *Please.* Help us."

"I'm counting to ten," Marcus said. "One . . . two . . ."

Jeff fiddled uncomfortably with a black Fitbit on his wrist. Seneca was wearing the same exact one; she knew that the rubber got sticky if you sweated too much. When he met Seneca's gaze again, his Adam's apple bobbed. "Okay," he conceded. "I'll tell you what I know."

CHAPTER 9

Jeff gestured for Maddox and Seneca to sit on the faded couch. As Maddox plopped down, the cushion billowed dustily around him and he could feel stray grains of sand finding their way into his shorts. Seneca chose wisely to perch on the couch's arm, her gaze pointedly avoiding his. He could tell she was shaken. Her voice had quavered when she'd mentioned her mom in exactly the same way it had when she told him there was no space in her brain for anything but finding Brett.

He sucked in his stomach, briefly reliving the supreme awkwardness that had been Seneca's gentle brush-off. He'd never put himself so nakedly *out there* before . . . and he'd never felt so rejected in his life. At least talking to Jeff provided a distraction.

"Do you mind giving us some background information about Chelsea and how you got involved with her?" Seneca asked, her eyes narrowing keenly.

Marcus clucked his tongue. "This is a mistake, dude. Dad's going to be pissed. And Clarence told you not to talk to anyone."

Jeff gave him a tortured, pleading look. "I'm just going to tell them the truth. The same story as I told Clarence."

"So your family is here?" Seneca asked. "And who's Clarence?"

Jeff plucked something from a woven basket by the chair. At first Maddox thought it was a seashell, but as Jeff turned his palm over, it looked more like a pointy red crystal. "My brother and I came down last week, but my parents are on their way from Philly. And Clarence is my lawyer." He squeezed the stone hard, his expression pained.

Seneca pointed to it. "What is that?"

"Red jasper. It's supposed to have centering properties. Give you strength." He stared down at it. "I've been sort of . . . hanging with it. Letting its power seep into me."

He closed his eyes and took a deep, centering breath through his nose. Maddox resisted rolling his eyes. New Age stuff always made him uncomfortable – did Jeff really buy into it, or was this all a weird act? He glanced again at the crystal. One end was dagger-sharp; it could do some damage. With the drawn shades, the tightly closed front door, and Marcus's looming presence, he began to grow uneasy.

"I've known Chelsea for two years," Jeff said. His voice was low. Gravelly. Almost trancelike. "We met here, but we go to colleges close to each other in Philly. She's at Villanova, and I'm at Temple. Things were great for a while . . . we were so connected. Until she got into the whole Instagram thing."

"She posts a lot," Seneca encouraged. "She has a lot of followers."

Jeff opened his eyes. His mouth became small and pinched. "Have you seen some of their comments? It's disgusting."

"So when did you break up?" Maddox asked.

67

Jeff stared at the carpet. "Three months ago."

"Was there a reason?"

He shrugged. "We just . . . drifted."

"Was the breakup contentious?"

"Absolutely not."

"But you were fighting the night of the party," Maddox argued. "What was that all about?"

Jeff closed his fist around the crystal. "I guess you heard about that on the news?"

Seneca leaned forward. "Yes, and there have been posts about you on a website called Case Not Closed, which we're involved with. Someone posted that they saw you and Chelsea fighting at the party. Is that true?"

Jeff rubbed the bottoms of his feet into the carpet in a regular, lulling rhythm. "Chelsea posted a picture of herself on Insta that was so . . ."

He waved his hands helplessly as though searching for a word. *Revealing?* Maddox thought, thinking of Chelsea's see-through dress. He didn't say it out loud.

"Anyway, I made a comment about how I wished she respected herself a little more," Jeff went on. "But that just exasperated the situation."

Maddox pressed his tongue into his cheek, noting Jeff's gaffe. *It's exacerbated, dude.* "Where were you when you had this disagreement?" Seneca asked smoothly.

"On the beach, near the bonfire. She got mad and took off up this path that leads to a parking lot next to the condos."

"Did you follow her to the parking lot?" Maddox asked. That was where the cops found the blood.

"Not right away. I probably waited about twenty minutes. Hung out at the bonfire while I calmed down, got my head together."

Seneca nodded. "Anyone at the bonfire stick out in your mind? Who saw you guys disagree? Who might have posted about your fight on a crime website?"

Jeff looked dazed. "Well, Alistair was there – he's this Jamaican cat I surf with sometimes. And then there was this guy who works at Wawa who everyone calls the Jolly Green Giant because he's really tall. And then this other guy, Cole? Awesome filmmaker from Japan. And the stoners were there, of course. But they were so out of it."

Maddox glanced at Seneca. Was one of them Brett?

"And I can't see those guys selling me out on a crime site," Jeff added, frowning. "What do the cops say about that, anyway? Has anyone come forward saying they wrote the post?"

If only it were that easy, Maddox thought. "I don't think so. I doubt cops even got the tip from the crime site. From my experience, the cops don't pay much attention to our discussions on CNC unless we come up with some hard evidence and go to them directly with it."

"So let's go back to that night," Seneca said. "What time did all this happen?"

Jeff stroked his chin. "I sent Chelsea the text at eleven twelve. I already told the cops that."

Seneca frowned. "Did you give them your phone records?"

He shook his head. "No, my lawyer said they would need a warrant for that. But I let them see my texts from that night."

"And how long after you guys disagreed did you send the text?" Maddox asked.

"Probably like ten minutes. Long enough for me to drink a beer. And then it was another ten minutes before I followed her."

"So Chelsea went down that path at about eleven p.m., more or less," Seneca said.

"And you followed her twenty minutes later," Maddox added, with a sinking feeling. Twenty minutes was a long time. More than enough time for Brett to take her.

Jeff lifted his hands up, then let them fall. "I really cared for Chelsea. Even after we broke up, I tried to protect her . . ." His voice cracked. "What's *happening* to her right now?" His lip trembled.

"I know exactly how that feels," Seneca said gently. "I'm really sorry you're going through this. We're going to do everything we can to find her."

"Do you have any enemies?" Maddox asked after a beat.

Jeff looked surprised. "No way. I'm a pacifist."

"Any secrets?"

A muscle twitched at Jeff's jaw. "I –"

"The cops already asked him this stuff," Marcus interrupted loudly. "I told you, Jeff. This is just a waste of time."

Maddox glanced Marcus's way, wondering why he'd cut Jeff off. "Whose party was this, anyway?" he asked.

"Gabriel Wilton's," Marcus boomed.

"Cool guy," Jeff jumped in. "He's shocked this happened at one of his events."

"Do you think Gabriel would talk to us about the guest list?" Seneca asked. "We heard there was one for the party."

Jeff shrugged. "Probably."

Seneca crossed her legs. "So why did you follow Chelsea? To apologize?"

Jeff smoothed his hair. He looked conflicted. "Yeah. And also . . ." He clamped his mouth shut.

Maddox frowned. "What?"

Jeff ran his fingers over the jasper. "When we were dating, I had this feeling she was cheating on me."

Seneca hitched forward. "With whom?"

"I never knew. But I thought if I went after her, I'd finally see. She was texting someone all night. Or I *thought* she was – I kept seeing her fiddling with her phone, but the cops said they got her phone records already and she hadn't sent a single text during the party." He raised a despondent shoulder. "I just wanted to see who she was into. Who she chose over me."

"So what happened?" Seneca pressed.

Jeff crossed his arms over his chest. "I remember getting to the parking lot, looking around, and not seeing her. And then I took another step . . . and things went black. Next thing I knew, I woke up, and it was morning."

Seneca shifted in her seat. "And you told the police that?"

"I did, but there were no witnesses. Kids were nearby, grabbing rides home, but no one can vouch that I was there. The police just think I was drunk, or that I'm lying about the whole thing."

"*Do* you think you were that drunk?" Seneca's face lit up with anticipation.

Jeff shook his head. "That's the thing – *no*. I feel like something weird happened to me, though I don't know how.

71

It was like all of a sudden, *bam*. Nothing. It was like someone took out my batteries."

Seneca's eyes danced. "You said you had a beer at the bonfire. Were you holding it the whole time?"

Jeff's jaw shifted back and forth. He snuck a peek at Marcus, then looked back a them again. "I don't remember. I *might* have put it down."

Maddox glanced at Seneca. He could tell what she was thinking – could Brett have slipped something into Jeff's beer to ensure he wouldn't look for Chelsea? "The cops didn't do a drug test on you, did they?"

Jeff shook his head. "Was that a mistake?"

"If you'd had a test, it might have showed why you suddenly passed out."

Jeff stood up. "Could I go get a test now?"

Seneca smiled ruefully. "The chemicals only stay in your system for a day or two. It probably wouldn't show anything."

Jeff slumped back to his seat, his expression suddenly breaking. "I can't go to *jail*. I have an internship next year at the Nature Conservancy. And I'm . . ." Sobs overtook him. Maddox tapped his toe. He wanted to feel for the guy, he did. But there was something about his sobs that felt over the top, almost like they were a deliberate display.

"We're going to try to help," Seneca said. "But tell me one more time – at the party, was there anyone there you *didn't* recognize?"

"There were some newish faces, and I didn't know everyone's names, but I'd seen everyone around before." Jeff finally lifted his head from his hands. His eyes were

72

red-rimmed, and his skin was blotchy. "You seriously solved a murder on your own?" He looked at Seneca intently, like he was studying her. Maddox followed his gaze, not sure he liked it.

"More or less," Seneca said.

"I want to help you investigate." Jeff plopped the jasper back into the bowl. "I know everyone around here. I could give you local knowledge."

"Dude, bad idea," Marcus said. "Clarence will kill you."

Maddox bit down hard on the inside of his cheek. He wasn't sure it was a great idea, either – there was something about Jeff that set him on edge, but he was their best point of entry.

Seneca smiled. "We'd love your help. Let us talk to the rest of our group, and then I'll call you so we can meet this afternoon."

When they climbed back into the Jeep, Maddox wanted to crank up the radio so he and Seneca didn't have to speak. But then Seneca said, "What do you think?" Suddenly, Maddox knew this was no time for shutting down on her. They had a mystery to solve and a killer to find, and he needed to put that above his feelings. Translation: He needed to man the hell up.

He shrugged. "About Man Bun? I just couldn't get past that *crystal*." He crossed his arms over his chest. "And why didn't he put on a shirt? I kept having to avert my eyes from his man nipples."

Seneca's gaze was on her phone. "I don't think he had a clue he was shirtless. He's a surfer. Don't those guys walk around without shirts all the time?"

Maddox stared at her. Her cheeks were flushed. Her eyes shone. He couldn't help but wonder if she was flashing back on Jeff's abs. She wasn't attracted to Jeff, was she? No. That had to be the rejection talking.

He twisted his mouth. "If Man Bun were a candy, he'd be something cool, something we're *supposed* to like, but something that's actually not so great. Like those ginger chews they sell at Whole Foods." He was playing their what-candy-are-you-most-like? game. "And did you hear how he said *exasperated* instead of *exacerbated*?"

Seneca snickered. "I *knew* that was going to bother you." When they used to chat, Maddox regularly complained when people confused the two words; posters did it all the time on Case Not Closed. "So do you think he was drugged the night of the party?"

Maddox thought for a moment. "I could see Brett doing that. But I also feel like Jeff wasn't telling us the whole truth about something. I just don't know what."

"Oh my God."

Maddox thought Seneca was reacting to what he'd said, but Seneca was clawing at her chest. "My necklace. The one with my mom's initial." Her hands moved under her shirt. She frantically checked the pockets of her cardigan and leaned over to peer into the foot well. "It's gone."

"What?" Maddox pulled over and put the car in park. "Are you sure?"

Seneca was pawing at the seat. "I don't see it anywhere."

Maddox started to look on his side, too. "I don't see it, either." Seneca let out a small whimper, and he placed his hands on the wheel again. "We'll find it," he said with purpose.

74

"I – I took it off before I went to bed last night and put it on the nightstand," Seneca said. "Now I can't remember if I put it on this morning or not."

"So let's check the B and B. And if it's not there, we'll check the pizza place from last night. Or Jeff's."

The B&B's parking lot was empty. When they pulled into the first space, a black-and-white-striped cat slinked around the front tires. Seneca shot out of the car and hurried to the back door. By the time Maddox crossed the threshold, Seneca was already inside the room she was sharing with Madison. She'd taken everything off the nightstand, but the necklace wasn't there.

Maddox opened a drawer to the bureau. It was filled with silky underthings. He slammed it shut again quickly, then peered under the furniture. Nothing.

Seneca made a beeline for the windowsill. Something small and flat sat on the ledge – an envelope. She pulled it open and made a small yelp. When Maddox pivoted, she was lifting out something on a chain.

"Whoa." Maddox rushed over. The pendant was twisted, the small, flat disk now bent in half. "Shit, Seneca, I'm so sorry. Maybe we can fix it."

But Seneca's eyes were scanning a sheet of paper inside the envelope. Maddox leaned over her shoulder. It looked like it was from the same off-kilter typewriter that had produced the letter he'd received two days before. Blood began to swim in his ears.

I see you when you're sleeping,
I know when you're awake.
Better be more careful, S.

75

"Oh my God." Maddox stepped away. "Brett was *here*? He was –" a horrible image came to mind – "watching you *sleep*?"

And Brett must have watched Madison, too. The single slice of toast Maddox had eaten this morning roiled in his stomach.

"What's going on?"

Madison and Aerin paused in the doorway, looking sweaty and flustered. Maddox shoved the note at them. "Brett's been here. *Inside* this place. He messed with Seneca's necklace."

The color drained from Aerin's face. *"What?"*

"Oh my God," Madison skimmed the note. "He could have killed one of us!"

"No." Seneca's voice was calm. "He wants us here. This is all part of the game."

Maddox rounded on her. "Why aren't you freaking out? Brett was *in your room*. Next to your bed." He shuddered at the thought.

Seneca closed the mangled necklace in her palm, then slowly walked across the room, stood on her tiptoes, and pulled something from the top of the windowsill. "It's exactly what I was hoping he'd do." She held a tiny metal rectangle that looked like a miniature computer motherboard. Everyone leaned forward to inspect it.

"Is that . . . ?" Madison cried.

Seneca pointed to a small window in the middle of the rectangle. "A surveillance camera. I've had it up in my room all summer, just in case. I wasn't going to take any chances here."

Maddox's mouth dropped open. "You bugged the room?"

"Of course I did." Seneca rummaged in her backpack and extracted a laptop. With impressive poise, she inserted a cord

76

from the micro device into the laptop's USB port. A video window appeared along with a grainy image. The room swam into view on the screen. Seneca rewound the video, stopping when a shadow popped up in the corner. The clock at the bottom read 5:42 A.M. Sunlight was just beginning to stream into the room. To Maddox's horror, a figure in a black sweat suit and a face mask stepped into the space. He tiptoed over Madison's huge suitcase. Kicked aside Seneca's Converse sneakers. Hovered over Seneca's bed as she slept.

Maddox's stomach knotted. The person was Brett's height, though it was difficult to tell what his build was under the bulky clothes. Aerin groaned. Madison made a choked gasp. To Maddox's surprise, Seneca grabbed his hand and squeezed hard.

The figure placed the envelope on the windowsill. Then he turned and glanced up at the little camera as though he knew it was there.

"Wait." Aerin stabbed the PAUSE button on the screen. Brett froze in place, gloved hands at his sides. "Those *eyes*," Aerin said, pointing at the two bright orbs peering out of the mask. They flooded back into Maddox's memory: round, very blue, piercing. Nausea roiled through his gut, but after that came an almost disbelieving exhilaration.

"There he is," Maddox said, his voice faint.

"There he is," Seneca echoed, her voice full of determination. "And we're going to find him."

CHAPTER 10

Brett flipped the switch that operated the microphone. "Good afternoon," he said.

Chelsea did her predictable shuffle and spin as she searched for the source of his voice. Her movements were more languid today – she hadn't been eating any of the meals he'd left for her. Her hair hung in greasy clumps, and the bottoms of her feet were dirty. "Don't you look lovely," he said icily.

Her eyes were large and wet. "Can't you just let me go?"

"Now, now. I wanted to let you know that you've gained quite a few Instagram followers. Would you like to know how many?"

She covered her face with her hands. "I don't care about Instagram. I just want to go home. See my family."

"Turn to your left."

Chelsea peeked in that direction. A new full-length mirror stood near the window. Brett had placed it there while she was sleeping last night, finally knocked out from the sedative he'd given her. When she took in her bleary-eyed, withered reflection, she winced and looked away.

"Perhaps that might inspire you to finally shower and change," Brett said gently. "Have you noticed I left makeup in the bathroom for you? And there's a hair dryer in the cabinet, and a curling iron, and some styling products, too. All the brands you like."

Chelsea flung herself onto a pillow. "If you're going to kill me, you should just do it. Get it over with."

"I know you like to look pretty."

She glanced up. Her features sharpened. "If you think I'm going to make myself look good for you, you're insane."

Brett tried not to feel offended. "This isn't for me."

"Yeah right. Who are you, anyway? What do you want with me? Do you think I'm going to have sex with you? Do you watch me sleep and fantasize about what we'd do together? Is that what you do, you sick asshole?"

Brett rolled his eyes. "You're all over the news. Everyone in the country knows who you are. Isn't that exciting? Doesn't that make you want to . . . oh, I don't know, fix yourself up?"

"It's not like they're going to come here for an interview," Chelsea spat. It was a while before she spoke again, but Brett could tell she was mulling something over. "Which news channels, anyway?" she mumbled. "*If* that's not all bullshit."

"All of them. I promise I'm not lying. All the newscasters talk about is how pretty you are. That you're a social media star. Your name is trending on Twitter. Memorials to you are all over Snapchat. Lafayette is teeming with press and police and gawkers. You should be so proud."

Chelsea stared at her lap, the tough expression fading. Something to his left caught Brett's eye. Last night, he'd installed a camera in the entrance of Conch B&B, next to a prince frog statue among all the knickknacks in the curio cabinet. Maddox and Seneca appeared on the screen. He wheeled his chair closer, his nose almost bumping the little monitor. The feed had shown the two entering the B&B a few minutes before, Seneca looking harried and freaked. Surely they'd discovered her ruined treasure by now – *and* his note. Now for the aftermath.

His eyes narrowed at the pixelated image. Seneca's hair bounced. Maddox laughed. They both practically skipped back out the door and onto the porch. Brett felt his lips pucker. Where was the fear? Where was their panic?

He slumped back in the chair, feeling sour and sick. Clutching his cell phone, he checked Case Not Closed. No new messages. Fine. Whatever. *You're hiding it well, but I know this kills you,* he mouthed to Seneca's tall, straight back as she waltzed into the sunshine. *And what's coming next will bring you to your knees.*

"Um, hello?"

On Camera A, Chelsea sat on the couch with perfect posture, staring at a brush in her hand – a brush he'd had left for her on the bedside table. It made a pretty sound as she pulled it through the knots in her hair. "How many new followers?" she said in a quiet, sheepish voice. "If you don't mind telling me."

Brett smiled deliciously, his mood slowly shifting. "Nothing would delight me more."

CHAPTER 11

Aerin, Seneca, Maddox, and Madison stood in the Conch B&B's side yard, talking with a sweaty and flustered Bertha, who'd just returned home from the grocery store. "I've never, *ever* had a break-in," she said, lovingly grabbing the scruff of Kingston's neck. "This guy barks so loud he wakes up the whole neighborhood." The dog let out a phlegmy snuffle.

Seneca shifted from foot to foot. "Well, *someone* got into my room. Maybe it was someone Kingston is familiar with? You said he's friendly once you get to know him."

Bertha narrowed her eyes, seeming to consider this.

"Do you have a dog walker?" Maddox asked. "Someone who does repairs on the place? Someone who stays here a lot?"

Bertha absently stroked Kingston's fur. "I don't have any regular guests except for Harvey, the gentleman you met in the dining room yesterday. He rents by the month."

Aerin exchanged a glance with the others. Harvey had to be about eighty years old. Definitely not Brett.

"I use a few service people," Bertha said. "I keep a list in my office."

"Can we see it?" Seneca asked. "I promise we won't call them and make accusations or anything. I just want to know how my necklace got bent. I'm sure you understand, right?"

Bertha muttered something under her breath, disappeared into the house, and returned with a crumpled list. Phone numbers for plumbers, electricians, a veterinarian, and something called a "paranormal spirit cleanser" stretched to the bottom of the page. Seneca took a photo of it and then everyone stepped off the porch.

After Bertha went back inside, Madison gritted her teeth. "I've called every other hotel, motel, and B&B up and down the coast. Everything's fully booked. Even the local *campground* is too crowded. This is one of the most popular weekends of the summer. Should we sleep in our cars?"

"It doesn't matter where we're staying, Brett's going to find us," Seneca muttered, kicking at some gravel in the yard. "We might as well just stay here."

"We'll have to make sure every window is locked," Maddox advised, peering up at the B&B. "And I think I saw an app that senses movement – we could activate it in our doorways when we go to sleep."

Seneca slumped inside to tell Bertha they were keeping the rooms. When she returned, she said, "Okay, so this is what we know. Brett's still here. Chelsea is still alive. And Brett's definitely been to this inn if the dog knows him."

Aerin tapped a line on the list. "Maybe he's the guy who delivers her groceries? Or the handyman?"

"It could also be someone the dog comes in contact with on daily walks." Madison gestured across the street, where a couple leaned down to pet a passing beagle. "Brett might not be on that list at all."

"We also know that Brett was at the bonfire, overhearing the argument between Jeff and Chelsea," Maddox said.

"And maybe spiking Jeff's beer," Seneca added.

Maddox nodded, though he looked less certain. "Jeff also said Chelsea was cheating on him, and he saw her texting someone all night."

"She might have been communicating with someone," Seneca pointed out as an SUV waved them across the road, "but it wasn't by text. Her phone records show she didn't write a single text all night. They're still checking other social media apps, though."

"We need to talk to all the kids at the bonfire." Maddox sidestepped a big blue mailbox. "And the guy who threw the party."

"Gabriel Wilton." Seneca pointed to the surf shop on the corner. "Maybe someone who works in there was at the party and knows how we can contact him." Then she looked at Aerin. "Did you learn anything from the cops?"

Aerin made a face. "Not really." That morning, she and Madison had checked out the Chelsea Dawson search party on the bluffs near where the party had been held. People scoured the tall grass, and every time one of them found something – a coin, a bottle top, a gum wrapper – they put it in an evidence bag, though Aerin guessed it wasn't evidence at all. They'd asked the cop in charge, Officer Nelson, if he could share investigation details, but he had shut them down.

Everyone headed for the surf shop, but Aerin stopped at an unoccupied bench. "You mind if I hang out here for a little? I need a few minutes to chill."

Maddox looked at her worriedly. "Is it safe to stay out here by yourself?"

"I'll hang out with you," Madison volunteered. "If that's okay."

Aerin shrugged one shoulder. "Sure."

She watched as Seneca and Maddox crossed the street and walked into one of the surf shop's entrances. Then she sat back, tilted her face to the sun, and tried to breathe calmly.

"Just so you know, I'm freaked as hell," Madison murmured next to her. "Want to smoke some weed? That might help."

"Nah." Aerin hugged her chest. "I just can't believe he was in the B and B." Yet, paradoxically, she felt a little disappointed she *hadn't* seen him when he'd snuck in. She had this perverse fantasy of tackling him in the hall and punching him in the face. *I'm not going to let you live*, she would say between blows. Vengeance for Helena would turn her superhuman. Her sheer will would knock him out cold.

But then she thought of Brett's muscular arms and shoulders and felt a wave of hopelessness. She couldn't take him. Maybe she couldn't do this at all. And what if they never found Brett? Or worse, what if he got to them first?

She threw back her shoulders. *Pull it together.* She looked at Madison. "Want to start searching Instagram? Maybe we can find something in Chelsea's account."

"Definitely."

Aerin opened Instagram on her phone and found Chelsea Dawson's last post from the party the night she vanished. Chelsea's resemblance to Helena was uncanny – she was even making the kind of face Helena would have made, a gleeful, happy smile with just a hint of flirtation.

She clicked on Chelsea's profile, and other photos appeared. One was of Chelsea in a red bathing suit lying on her belly on a pool raft; she peered at the camera from over her shoulder, her sunglasses half-lowered.

"Whoa," Madison said, pointing at the post. It had received 60,549 likes. It was an even bigger number than Aerin had seen when she first checked on Chelsea's account.

Monthly, Chelsea did a special "update" video where she talked about what was going on in her life, her favorite makeup finds, and a silly feature called "The Cutest Cat on Planet Earth." Some of the videos took place in a large, airy living room with floor-to-ceiling windows; Chelsea thanked someone named Ophelia at the end for letting her use the space. In the comments section, fans chimed in that they loved BeneFit BeneTint, too, that Chelsea looked gorgeous, and that they wanted to be her. In another photo, Chelsea's hair was pulled into a topknot, her makeup was perfectly done, and she wore a ropy necklace. Aerin pressed the screen to view more comments. *I love you so much*, read one. And, *You're so beautiful*. And, *Girl crush!* Then her gaze stopped on one that said, *Love that dress. If you ever need a shopping buddy, I'm your guy*.

The wording was so familiar. Where had Aerin heard that phrase before?

A light snapped on in Aerin's mind. *Brett*. He'd said that to Aerin in Dexby. She clicked on the poster's account. His name was Barnes Lombardi. All his photos were darkly lit, his face illuminated by candlelight, his eyes wide, almost all whites. She clicked on the first photo; Chelsea's account was tagged on the very first photo. *All I do is think of you, @ChelseaDFab*, he wrote in the caption. *Someday, you'll be mine.*

Chelsea had replied. *I already AM yours.* Barnes replied with a tongue-wagging GIF.

Madison rolled her jaw, reading the comments, too. "So they know each other?"

"Not sure," Aerin murmured.

Barnes had written several other odes to Chelsea, and Chelsea had flirtatiously and cheerfully commented on all – including quite a few comments the night of the party. But there was something overly blatant about her responses, almost like she was pouring it on *too* thick, like it was some kind of game between them.

Madison reached over and clicked on another of Barnes's photos. Aerin could make out broad shoulders and a flat nose. Brett had those features, too. If only the pictures showed his eyes, but most of them were in shadow. Another photo showed a large purple fish swimming in a huge tank. *Shittiest job ever, but at least I get to hang out with this beauty.* The location was tagged at the Lafayette Boardwalk Aquarium. Aerin recalled the poisonous fish in the tank at the B&B. Barnes's name wasn't on Bertha's list, but perhaps she used him to feed the fish when she was out of town?

When she clicked on Barnes's most recent post, she almost dropped her phone. It was of a beach bonfire and a close-up of a beer bottle. *Party hardy*, read the caption. The location was a few blocks away – at the condos where the party had been held.

86

Madison breathed in. "Is this him?"

The sun came out, sizzling the part in Aerin's hair. She stared toward the blue horizon. The boardwalk was less than a mile away. "Should we check it out?"

"I think we have to," Madison said.

Aerin ran her hand through her hair. "I feel so exposed, though. I want to see if it's him . . . but I don't want him to see *us*."

A wrinkle formed on Madison's brow. She rummaged through her oversized purse and pulled out a baseball cap. "Here." She tossed it Aerin's way, then slid on a pair of dark sunglasses. "I'll pick up a hat once we get to the boardwalk."

"Okay," Aerin said, feeling a little steadier. She sent off a quick text to Seneca and Maddox to let them know what they were doing. As she rose, her phone bleated. She expected it to be Seneca's response, but the phone was ringing. The screen read, *Thomas*. Her heart flipped over, but then she felt a surge of irritation. Hadn't she made it clear she didn't want him to contact her? She stabbed at the screen, ignoring the call, then jutted her chin into the air and started toward the boardwalk.

Ten minutes later, Aerin stepped onto the boardwalk. "Grease city," Aerin mumbled to Madison, who'd picked up a tie-dyed baseball cap at a souvenir shop on the way and had the brim pulled down over her face. Aerin wasn't talking just about the brightly painted stalls that sold funnel cakes, French fries, and fried Oreos, either – there was also an obscene amount of sweat glistening on the exposed skin of practically every tourist that passed.

Madison looked around cautiously. "If Brett really works here, where does he grab lunch? Wasn't he always saying his body was a temple?"

Aerin shrugged, feeling too jittery to make simple conversation about the nutjob formerly known as Brett. "Come on. The aquarium is at the other end of the boardwalk."

"But do you really think we're going to recognize him?" Madison hurried to keep up as Aerin ducked around ambling tourists, kids on hoverboards, and a guy enthusiastically aiming a remote control at a drone in the sky.

"*I* will," Aerin said in a steely voice.

They passed an arcade and an ice cream parlor, the sickly sweet smell of waffle cones turning Aerin's stomach. As she edged around a woman walking three large Labradors, someone by the railing caught her attention. A tall, brown-haired guy in a hoodie way too warm for the weather peered across the boardwalk. Aerin frowned. He was setting off every sketchy alarm in her head. She grabbed Madison's wrist. "How do we know that guy?"

Madison stopped and squinted. "I don't think we do . . ."

Aerin's gaze remained on the figure. She'd met him. She could *feel* it. But before she could figure out where, the guy abruptly left the railing and strode quickly toward the parking lot, hood pulled tightly over his head. She watched him for a few seconds, trying to jar her memory, still feeling unsettled, until he disappeared into the crowd.

Madison's phone pinged, and she looked at the screen. "It's an update about Chelsea. The cops found very little, forensically. There were no witnesses in that parking lot where they found the blood. No stray hairs or strange footprints or additional clues. They interviewed kids at the party, witnesses who saw Chelsea. She hadn't been acting strangely beforehand, no one could think of any enemies she had, and her parents didn't have any enemies, either. They haven't received a ransom note."

Aerin recalled Chelsea's parents, a fit, attractive couple in their midforties, scouring the grassy bluffs behind the condos this morning. Chelsea's mother had dark circles under her eyes. Her father looked like he wanted to beat someone up. It had reminded her of her own parents when Helena had vanished.

"What about her phone records?" Aerin asked.

Madison kept reading. "There weren't any texts the night of the party. But they're following up on all her calls from the past few days."

Aerin pushed her hands into the pockets of her shorts and tried to process this information, but she was so addled and frightened by the task at hand, her brain felt like mush.

They ducked out of the way of an approaching tram, then walked down an empty stretch. The ocean was clearly visible over the railing, the tide coming in. Then Madison gave her a pointed look. "So are we going to talk about how you ignored a call from that cute Dexby cop, or is that not important?"

Aerin felt her cheeks sizzle. She hadn't realized that Madison had noticed her screen. "I don't know why he's calling me," she said quickly. "I didn't *tell* him to."

"Is he investigating the case?" Madison widened her eyes. "You didn't tell him about Brett, did you?"

Aerin skirted around a couple holding hands, concentrating on the wooden slats in the boardwalk. There was no way she could tell Madison the truth. "Of course not. And anyway, he's not a cop anymore."

"So what does he want?" Madison had a knowing tone. When Aerin scoffed, she added, "I thought he was your boyfriend, once upon a time."

Aerin jutted her chin high, feeling stung . . . and a little sad. "Thomas decided to go to college in New York a few months ago. So I ended it."

Madison stared at her. The only sound a thrumming techno song spilling from one of the junky T-shirt shops. "*What* school? The priesthood?"

"Of course not. It's the New School. In the Village."

"And for some reason that means you can't be together?"

"It's complicated, okay?" Aerin snapped. Beads of sweat had broken out on the back of her neck.

Madison squinted. "Try me."

A lump formed in Aerin's throat. "Long-distance relationships don't work, okay? It's just a fantasy. My dad moved to the city and was all, *You'll spend every weekend here!* But I see him basically never."

"So this is about your dad," Madison said sagely.

"No!" Aerin practically roared. She slapped her hands to her sides. "Look, Thomas and I are too different – that's why I broke up with him. And I didn't want to talk to him today because he used to be a cop, and I worried Brett might figure it out somehow and get pissed."

"Uh-huh." Madison didn't sound very convinced. Then she pointed. "Is that it?"

Ahead of them was a long stucco building that stretched

90

for a full ocean block and smelled like bleach. *Fourth Street Aquarium*, read a tired-looking banner. *Free to the public*. The lobby was dark and murky and just inside, two tunnels branched to the right and left. Fish tanks glowed eerily. A glassy-eyed stingray flapped past. An angelfish had a huge chunk taken out of its fin.

Madison made a face. "I hope they're giving the fish antidepressants."

Aerin swallowed hard. The seedy vibe wasn't helping her growing fear. She adjusted her cap to make sure all her hair was hidden.

They headed to the right, avoiding the rambunctious kids. Some of the fish tanks were empty, and others were dirty with algae, the creatures only half visible through greenish scum. The farther they got down the tunnel, the colder and darker the air became, almost like they were walking into a giant freezer. Aerin searched for Brett's face swimming up from the darkness, but she didn't see him anywhere. She was grateful for Madison walking next to her, though, and almost reached for her hand several times. She couldn't imagine doing this alone.

"This is a dead end," Madison said once they'd walked past endless tanks. "And I don't see *anyone* working here."

Aerin caught sight of a door in the distance, figuring it was a way out. She headed for it and noticed it was slightly ajar. She pushed it open and hurried through, eager for warm air and light. To her surprise, she found herself in a long black hallway, not the sunny boardwalk she'd expected. She wheeled around, disoriented.

Slam. Suddenly, Aerin was enveloped in darkness.

"Hey!" Aerin lunged for the door handle. It didn't turn. "Hello?" she screamed, banging on it with her fist. "Madison? Get me out!"

"I'm trying!" Madison called from the other side. "It's stuck!"

Aerin heard a small sound from the other end of the dark hallway and stiffened. Her was heartbeat swishing in her ears. *Settle down*. No one had shut her in here on purpose. Right?

"I'm going to get help!" Madison cried through the door.

Aerin whipped around. "No!" She didn't want to be left alone. She clawed at the knob again. "Madison?" she called. *"Madison!"* There was no answer.

Nausea roiled in her gut. She tried to control her breathing, but it was as though she'd forgotten the mechanics. Then she heard the faintest noise down the hall. Someone was there. Goose bumps prickled on her arms. "H-hello?"

Footsteps thudded. Aerin curled her arms to her chest. The air around her darkened, and she could smell a bodily mix of sour sweat and bad breath.

Brett.

Suddenly, he was right next to her. She could feel him crouching down, the fabric of his pants brushing against her bare leg. Aerin whimpered and covered her face. "P-please," she stammered. Was this what Helena felt like, before it was all over? Did time both slow down and speed up? Did she feel a solid, crackling terror in her bones?

Clammy fingers pulled Aerin's hands from her face, knocking her cap off her head. Aerin felt her long hair cascade over her shoulders. She heard a gasp above her, and then whoever it was stepped away.

An overhead light flipped on. A man of Brett's height stood above her, but his nose was wider, his lips thinner, his hair wispier, almost balding. She couldn't see the color of his eyes, but their shape was all wrong – down-turned, puffy. His name tag read *Barnes*, and he wore a bright orange hat with two fins and a fish tail on it. He blinked at her, stunned, but then a look of irritation rolled across his face. "Who the fuck are you?"

"I . . ." Aerin had no idea what to say. She cringed when Barnes moved toward her, but he was just inserting a key into the locked door and opening it. He was still staring at her like he'd seen a ghost. "Get out of here," he hissed.

Aerin scurried into the aquarium, tears in her eyes. When she reached the sunny boardwalk, she wanted to kiss its sticky ground and embrace every tourist that passed. When she saw Madison, pulling on the arm of an aquarium worker, she ran for her and fell into her arms. And then she started crying, hot, scared tears, her whole body shuddering. She felt so childish. Where was her vicious, snarling courage? She wanted to be able to handle this, but she suddenly realized how terrified of Brett she really was. If he got close to her, she wouldn't be able to fight him.

She might shatter to pieces.

CHAPTER 12

Maddox and Seneca stood in Quigley's Surf Shop and Boutique, a warren of rooms containing everything from beachy rompers to motivational DVDs on how to become one with the waves. The place smelled like a mix of surf wax and patchouli, and a jam band Maddox recognized from track parties blasted through the speakers. They were standing in the shoe area, talking to an employee named Kona, a compact, bearded guy with swimmer's shoulders and a tattoo of a bunch of Japanese symbols on the back of his hand. He had been at the party the other night.

"Chelsea seemed happy, excited," Kona said in a lazy drawl. "All she could talk about was how her Instagram account was blowing up and how she'd met some really interesting people lately and had really cool stuff on the horizon."

"Did she name the people she'd met?" Maddox asked. "Were they at the party?"

Kona straightened a display of plastic sunglasses. "It sounded more like they were big shots. Hollywood people who could make her a social media star."

"Who was she hanging out with at the party?" Seneca asked.

"Guys, girls . . . everyone. I kept seeing her with her ex Jeff. Which was weird, because someone said they had a rough breakup."

Maddox narrowed his eyes. "What do you mean?"

A second employee, Gwen, a petite brunette whose eyelashes were either freakishly long or fake, strode up. "Well, they were the it couple, you know? But then something . . . happened."

"Jeff couldn't handle her fame," Maddox guessed.

"Chelsea was cheating," Seneca said at the same time. She shot Maddox a look. Maddox shot her one back.

Kona and Gwen looked from Maddox to Seneca. "Wait, *Chelsea* was cheating?" Gwen said. "Because I thought . . ."

"We don't know if it's true," Maddox said quickly. "Jeff could be lying."

Seneca cocked her head. "Why would he lie?"

"Because he's sketchy, Seneca. I don't know."

Gwen's smile wavered. An invisible problem by the register caught her attention. "Uh, I need to take care of this." She hurried away. Kona gave them a sleepy smile and went to help some customers who'd just walked in.

Seneca put her hands on her hips and looked at Maddox with amusement. "What are you doing, Sherlock?"

Maddox avoided her gaze. "I'm just asking questions."

"This is about *exacerbated*, isn't it?"

"No!" Maddox cried, though he felt his cheeks flush. Was she making fun of him? He jutted his chin in the air, determined not to dwell on it. "It's *not*," he insisted. "I just want to make sure we're fully informed."

95

"Well, we're wasting our time asking about Jeff," Seneca argued. "We need to figure out who else was at that party. Who *Brett* is."

Kona returned. "I've got to get back to work. You guys need anything else?"

"Yes," Seneca said quickly. "Do a lot of people who were at the party work in town?"

He nodded. "Definitely. In shops, as Uber drivers, lifeguards – you name it. Almost all of us have summer jobs."

"Can you think of anyone who was at the bonfire for most of the night?"

Kona stared at the ceiling, which was decorated with old surfboards covered in yellowed wax. "It's usually stoners down there. A kid named Rex? And this guy J.T."

"How about someone named Alistair?" Seneca asked, referring to the guy Jeff mentioned. "Do you remember seeing him after Chelsea left?"

"I got a ride home with him, actually."

"You don't by any chance have the number of the guy who threw the party, do you?"

"Gabriel? Sure." Kona scrolled through her phone, then sent Seneca the contact. Seneca's fingers flew as she texted, and within moments, she got a reply. She examined the text, then smiled. "Looks like we've been invited to lunch at Gabriel's place – which is perfect. We can talk to him *and* check out where Chelsea was last seen. I texted Aerin and Madison to see if they want to join." Then she shot Maddox a pointed look. "I've invited Jeff, too. So be *nice*."

* * *

96

Twenty minutes later, Maddox and Seneca pulled up to a big structure with a sign that read *Ocean Sands Beach Club and Condos*. With its marble-white exterior, enormous balconies off each condo, swanky valet service, expansive lobby, and private cabanas lining the beach, the place definitely looked nice enough. The parking lot was roped off by yellow police tape, with a single officer on guard.

He walked ahead of Seneca down the sidewalk, then up a set of stairs to the second floor, where Gabriel's place was. Someone was whispering on the landing, and he froze. He caught sight of Jeff's man bun bobbing as he paced back and forth. "Listen, it's not *worth* it," he said quietly into the phone. "Back off, okay? I can handle this. I can handle *them*."

Maddox felt a crawling sensation over his skin. When he cleared his throat, Jeff peered over the stairs, widened his eyes, then slipped the phone in his pocket without saying good-bye. "Hey," he said, his gaze on Seneca, who had just appeared behind Maddox. Jeff's hair was wet, he was unshaven, and he wore a burlap-like white hoodie with ragged sleeves, striped board shorts to his knees, stretched-out, filthy Etnies sneakers, and a pair of Maui Jim aviators propped on his head. He looked like a homeless pirate. A *sketchy* homeless pirate.

"Who were you talking to on the phone?" Maddox asked loudly.

Jeff's features hardened. Seneca stepped between them. "Thanks for coming," she said evenly. "We appreciate it."

Jeff murmured a thank-you, his gaze still on Maddox. Maddox stared back coldly. He was all for including this guy in the investigation if Jeff could get them closer to Brett. But how could they be sure he was on their side?

"So this is where the party was?" Seneca gestured to the pool down the stairs.

"Yep," Jeff said. "The party was all outdoors." He continued up another staircase to a set of three doors. Knocking on the left-most one, he said, "This is Gabriel's. He'll tell you more."

After three knocks, a bleached-blond guy in aviator sunglasses and with a scruffy beard pulled the door open. "Hey," he said, grinning.

"Hey, Gabriel." Jeff gave the guy a fist bump. "These are the people I was telling you about. Seneca and Maddox."

Gabriel nodded at them. "Gabriel Wilton," he said, extending his hand. "Good to meet you." The guy's skin glowed golden with a tan. A tattoo on his arm showed a guy doing a trick on a skateboard. "Come on back. We're on the patio."

They walked through the condo, which was filled with bright, almost-blinding sunlight and decorated with comfy off-white couches, Navajo blankets, and a large leather beanbag chair. Three surfboards were stacked in the corner, a ginormous flat-screen showed an X Games rebroadcast, and black-and-white photos of ocean waves marched across the walls. Maddox nodded approvingly. He wouldn't mind having a beach pad like this.

Gabriel slid back a glass door and stepped onto a small patio that contained a bistro table laden with sandwiches, chips, and drinks. Sitting on one of the chairs was a tall man with warm brown skin whose hair was buzzed short. He wore a pair of mirrored Ray-Ban Wayfarers, and Maddox caught sight of his reflection in the frames. "This is Alistair Reed," Gabriel said.

Alistair said hello as well, the word bent with a Jamaican accent, then slapped Jeff's back. Maddox slid into a chair, admiring the unobstructed water view. Waves rolled steadily to shore in the distance. A few spattered clouds drifted casually though the sky. Three drones hovered over the ocean, their operators squinting up at them.

"Thanks for all your help," Seneca said to the guys, sitting down next to Maddox.

"It's no problem at all." Gabriel settled into a chair with a plate of food in front of it. He took a big bite of a sandwich. "We want to figure this out. We cared about Chelsea, too. I can't believe this happened. But I *definitely* don't think Jeff is responsible, and I'll do everything in my power to prove that."

Jeff looked grateful. "I appreciate that." His gaze flicked to Maddox again. The look seemed loaded.

"So the party was at the pool and on the beach, right?" Seneca asked, grabbing a sandwich from the platter.

Gabriel nodded, pointing out the pool – they could see the very tip of it from the patio. "Yep. Pool was packed. We had drinks, food, music, the works. And then people were down at the bonfire, too."

"Was anyone on that patio?" Maddox said, pointing to a large raised terrace just next to the pool. A few people were leaning over the railing, staring at the ocean. Just underneath the terrace was a rather ugly undeveloped square of property littered with spare boards, cardboard boxes, and several Dumpsters.

Gabriel shook his head. "The building management asked that we keep the parties only at the pool so that people staying at the condos who didn't want to come could use the terrace.

That's the way most of my parties work – they're either at the pool or on the terrace, but not on both. But like you already know, the party spilled over to the beach. The bonfire was just over the dunes."

Maddox followed his finger to a bunch of burnt-looking logs beyond the cabanas. He suddenly shivered. Had Brett lingered down there, listening in?

He turned back to Gabriel. "Did you talk to Chelsea that night?"

Gabriel nodded. "I said hi. But I didn't keep track of her."

"Did she seem . . . okay?"

Gabriel shrugged. "I guess so. Pretty much the same as always."

"I hung out with her a little bit," Alistair volunteered. "I was even down at the bonfire just before she blew up at Jeff. But I wasn't paying much attention."

"He was stoned," Gabriel explained, giving Alistair a wry look.

"You can't remember who else was at the bonfire?" Seneca asked Alistair as she poured herself a glass of lemonade. "Someone who might have posted something about Jeff on a crime-solving chat site?"

Alistair shrugged. "Lots of people were down there all through the night. But isn't it possible that someone told someone else about the fight and that was who posted about it on the website?"

Maddox and Seneca exchanged a glance. "Maybe," Maddox said tentatively.

"Was everyone at the party interviewed by the police the next morning, when Chelsea was reported missing?" Seneca asked.

"Most were, yes," Gabriel said. "They talked to me, Alistair, our pal Cole, a bunch of the lifeguards, this group of girls who have a house on Ninety-Fifth, and a few of Chelsea's friends."

"And was anyone unaccounted for around the time Chelsea vanished?"

"Well, according to the police, Jeff was the only one." Gabriel looked uncomfortable. Jeff shifted in his seat. "But the party was so scattered. Everyone was all over the place. From my perspective, *lots* of people were unaccounted for . . . it's hard to know."

"Do you have a guest list we could take a look at?" Maddox asked. "We think Chelsea's kidnapper stopped by your party for a little bit."

"I'll text it to you now." Gabriel pulled out his iPhone, and in moments, Maddox felt his pocket buzz.

Gabriel's gaze was on his phone still, and suddenly, his brow wrinkled. "My freaking boss. I gotta jet. "

"Now?" Seneca sounded disappointed.

"Yeah." Gabriel drained the rest of his water. "There's an emergency at the office."

"Where do you work?" Maddox asked, thinking, *surf instructor, obviously.*

"I'm a realtor-in-training." Gabriel pulled a beanie onto his head. "Mostly I handle gripes from renters about how the toilets don't function properly." Everyone else stood up to go, too, but Gabriel gestured for them to sit back down. "Stay. Finish eating. Take a look around the grounds, anything that might help find Chelsea."

101

Seneca looked uncertain. "A few other people are supposed to meet us here." She glanced at Maddox. "Have you heard from them yet?"

Maddox nodded. "Madison texted. They're okay, but she didn't give details."

"Tell them to come on up," Gabriel offered. "There's enough food for everyone. Just toss everything in the trash once you're done. Oh, and the door locks automatically behind you, so just make sure you grab all your stuff when you leave. And, hey, you'll come to my Bastille Day party tomorrow, right?"

Jeff shook his head. "I don't think so, man. I'm not sure I can do the party scene right now."

"Understood," Gabriel said. Alistair rose, too.

"One more thing," Seneca said, catching the guys as they headed back through the condo. "Can you think of anyone Chelsea might have been dating this summer? Or last summer, for that matter?"

Gabriel looked surprised. "You mean besides Jeff?"

"Yes," Seneca said. Maddox peeked at Jeff. He had his head down, looking miserable.

"No," Gabriel said slowly. The question seemed to blindside him. Alistair looked just as surprised. "But do you want us to ask around? Maybe her friends know something?"

"Sure, and we'll get on it, too," Seneca said. "Thanks so much, guys."

Alistair said he had to jet as well, stuffing the rest of his sandwich in his mouth and grabbing his bag. The guys strode away, their gaits powerful and athletic. When they'd gone, Seneca looked at Jeff. "Are you sure it's fine if we stay for a bit?" she whispered. Gabriel's place *was* a much nicer HQ than their creepy rooms at the B&B – plus it was private. The last thing she wanted was to be discussing the case in public and for Brett to accidentally overhear.

"Totally." Jeff nodded. "He's very *mi casa, su casa*."

"And is he really throwing another party so shortly after Chelsea went missing?"

"It's because the town is French," Jeff explained. "The party is tradition around here. I'm going to skip it, but you guys should go. You'll get a good sense of who was at the other party."

"Hmm," Seneca said, mulling it over.

They sat back down. Jeff gazed out at the water, suddenly looking contemplative. "You guys ever surf? Catching a wave brings the dopamine rush to a whole new level. You'll never get the same kind of buzz."

Seneca chuckled. "Don't expect to get Maddox out there. He's afraid of sharks."

Maddox glared at her. Seneca raised her hands playfully. "What? Don't pretend Shark Week last year didn't happen." She looked at Jeff. "In every email he wrote to me, he said he'd had another dream that he was being attacked by Megalodon."

Maddox snickered. "As I recall, *your* nightmares were about being attacked by your high school's cheerleading squad."

"Doing complicated tumbling moves and knocking over my carefully arranged stacks of books." Seneca shuddered. "Which is *way* scarier than a megashark."

Jeff chuckled halfheartedly, but it was clear he didn't get the joke. Then he turned to Seneca. "Well, *you'd* be great at surfing. You have the shoulders for it."

Seneca looked surprised. "You think?"

"Totally. You're ripped, girl. And you have to be majorly strong to surf."

"Not as strong as you have to be to run a sub-thirty 10K," Maddox grumbled under his breath.

Seneca glanced at him for a moment, then at her bare, freckled shoulders. "You know, I've always thought surfing sounded fun."

"It's beyond fun," Jeff said. "I'll teach you, if you're ever interested."

"Can we focus?" Maddox interrupted, hating that Jeff had something to offer her that he didn't. "Don't we have a guest list to investigate?" he continued.

Seneca blinked, her pink lips parting. "Yes. You're right." She stood and pushed the chair back with a scrape. "Actually, I'd like to check out the place where Chelsea was last seen."

"Absolutely." Jeff rose, too.

Maddox heaved himself up, but Seneca shook her head. "You stay here, Maddox. Start going through that guest list."

Maddox's mouth fell open. "Wait, really?"

"Aerin and Madison are coming. Gabriel said the door locks automatically behind us, so someone needs to stay behind to let us back in. I'll take pictures in case I find anything sketchy, okay?"

Maddox tried to protest, but she'd already marched through the apartment and into the hall. Jeff trailed behind her, his man bun bouncing. Halfway through the door, he turned and glanced back at Maddox, their eyes meeting. There was a look of triumph in Jeff's eyes.

Maddox rolled his jaw. He didn't want this to feel like a rejection. He didn't want to feel any emotion about Seneca at *all*.

Distraction, distraction, distraction, he chanted to himself. And then he opened his phone and studied the guest list, determined to put her out of his mind.

CHAPTER 13

As they shut the door, Seneca realized the pleasant smell inside Gabriel's condo – a mix of sandalwood and cleaning products, like something a boutique hotel would use – did not extend to the hallway, which reeked of warm beer. Wrinkling her nose, she opened the guest list Gabriel had texted and began to peruse the names. Jeff cleared his throat as they walked down the steps to the first floor. "So . . . are you and Maddox together?" he asked.

She glanced over her shoulder. "No. Why would you say that?"

Jeff shrugged. "Your auras sort of match, if you know what I mean."

Seneca felt a knot of guilt. Maddox had looked so crushed when she'd told him that now wasn't a good time for them to try to be a couple. Had she been too harsh? But Maddox was acting fairly normal now. He seemed over it. Why, then, did she feel like she'd done something wrong?

On the wall leading down the stairs to the pool was a flyer for the Bastille Day party decorated with a large rainbow peace sign on the top. Seneca noted when the party started – should they check it out, or was that a waste of time?

They reached the bottom of the stairs. To the right was the swimming pool, where the party was. To the left was a vacant lot she'd noticed from the terrace, filled with Dumpsters and trash. "Let's cut through here," Jeff said, leading her through the pool area, saying it was a shortcut to the beach.

He guided her past a bunch of bistro tables scattered around the pool, and his arm brushed against Seneca's. She pulled away, giving him an awkward smile. Then her phone beeped. It was Aerin. *On our way*, it said. *Oh, and Barnes isn't Brett, but there's something creepy about him all the same.*

A shiver ripped through her. She called up the guest list Gabriel had sent them, noting that Barnes's name was on it. She cleared her throat. "Do you know Barnes Lombardi?" she called out to Jeff.

Now it was Jeff's turn to stop abruptly, next to the diving board. His face clouded. "Definitely not a fan. He has a major thing for Chelsea."

"And he was at the party, right?"

Jeff's eyes widened. "Wait. I remember seeing him around the bonfire. Why? Do you think . . ."

Seneca felt jumpy. Was Aerin *sure* he wasn't Brett? Should she follow up on Barnes herself? Maybe Barnes was involved in the kidnapping in another way.

They continued out of the pool and through another gate. Down the beach was an empty tiki bar and a few volleyball courts on the beach. Most of the area was surrounded by police tape, though a few condo residents sat inside blue-and-white-striped cabanas closer to the shore. "That's where the bonfire was," Jeff explained, pointing at a circle of logs. "Chelsea and I were right about there when we argued."

Seneca squinted at the unremarkable stretch of sand. "And then where did she go?"

Jeff turned and gestured to a path through the dunes covered over with tall grass. "This leads all the way to the public parking lot, but you have to cross over a bunch of dunes. It's kind of a sketchy path, to be honest. Had I been less mad, I would have told her not to take it."

"Let's check it out," Seneca said, starting toward the path.

Jeff stared at her. "But it's blocked off."

Seneca shrugged. She didn't see any cops here now. She started up the embankment, but her strappy sandals shifted in the sand, and she began to slip. Jeff grabbed her hand to steady her.

"Thanks," Seneca said, pulling away when she had her footing. Her cheeks were warm. Jeff's touch felt protective, and . . . deliberate. She snuck a peek at him, unsure about his intentions, but Jeff's head was turned away.

She climbed up the dune, ducked under the police tape, and started down the path. Tall wild reeds jutted up on either side. The path wound behind the houses and was so rutted at times that it dipped low in the earth, concealing a traveler from someone sitting on the beach. Sticks, spiky sand spurs, and spiny weeds littered the path; sometimes the vegetation was so thick on all sides that the tall grasses engulfed her almost completely.

The path spat them out into a wide parking lot that was half-full with cars and golf carts. Seneca ducked under the police tape once more and shook some sand out of her shoes. "This is where they found the blood." Jeff pointed at a spot adjacent to a bike rack. If Seneca squinted, she could see the outlines of a dark splotch there. "Maybe there was a struggle. But there's no blood anywhere else."

Seneca scanned the lot, noting there were no surveillance cameras that could have recorded what might have happened here, so she had to try to piece it together from evidence and conjecture. The blood was in the parking lot, which meant Brett had accosted Chelsea here and not on the sidewalk by the street. So he'd gotten to the parking lot as quickly as Chelsea had. Maybe he was waiting here for her all along? But Brett hinted on CNC that he'd overheard the argument. Had he followed her right afterward, grabbing her in the reeds?

She looked at Jeff. "Is it possible someone overheard you guys talking at the bonfire, jumped up, and followed right behind her?"

Jeff narrowed his eyes. "It's possible. I did grab a beer, but I feel like I would have seen someone go past."

Seneca gritted her teeth. "Is there another way to get to the parking lot that's just as fast?"

"You could go back through the beach club, but it takes much longer."

Seneca made a mental note to question people at the party if they'd seen anyone running like hell through the beach club, but she doubted that was the answer. Brett hadn't gone that way. It was too visible.

Then she noticed a large pipe next to the steps to the beach. "What's that?"

She padded over and peered in. The pipe was hollow and filled with a shallow pool of slimy-looking water. It pointed straight out to the beach. "Drainage," Jeff said. "Something to do with erosion. I'm not sure."

Seneca tapped her lip. "Do you know where this comes out?"

"I think near the bonfire."

Her heart quickened. "Maybe *this* is how he got to the parking lot so quickly."

Jeff made a face. "People don't crawl through those things. Could a person even fit inside?"

Seneca ducked down and peered into the tube. She could just fit. If Brett had climbed through here, it meant he'd slimmed down since they'd last seen him. She shut her eyes, adjusting her mental picture of the person they were looking for. It felt like another piece to the puzzle.

She glanced around in the darkness. The tube smelled like salt and plastic. The sides were very smooth and slick. If Brett had crawled through this, it was doubtful he'd left evidence behind – even if he had, the ocean water had probably washed it away by now. But maybe she should check it out to be sure . . .

Jeff pulled her sleeve. "*Don't*. Sometimes those things flood. You could get really hurt."

Seneca's heart thudded steadily as she climbed back out. If Brett was at the bonfire, this could have been how he'd gotten to the street without anyone seeing.

She scanned the rest of the lot. "Where did you pass out?"

Jeff pointed to a spot just inside the path, on the sand. "Right about there."

"I can't believe no one saw you." It was secluded, but not *that* out of the way.

"I know. A lot of kids got picked up in that lot. The beach club driveway is for valet service only – they get really pissy about random cars waiting for passengers."

Seneca stared out at the ocean. A single head bobbed on the water, and when a wave came, the man rode it all the way to the shore. "You know, if you *had* been drugged, the same person who'd done it also could have seen you fall. And then he or she could have positioned your body so that it was hidden in such a way that no one noticed you."

Jeff's eyes widened. "You think?"

It certainly *sounded* like Brett. Seneca tried to picture how Brett had pulled it off. She could buy that he'd planned to spike Jeff's drink – he'd probably carried crushed up pills or some such in his pocket in case he needed them. As for positioning Jeff's body out of sight, was that premeditated, or did he react on the fly? If only they could get a better idea of how that night unfolded. A video or something. Even a picture. Too bad Chelsea didn't post *this* on Instagram.

Then something occurred to her. "Wait," she said. "What about a PhotoCircle?"

Jeff looked at her. "Huh?"

"I'm sure Chelsea wasn't the only one taking pictures that night. We have everyone's email addresses and phone numbers on the guest list. We could contact them and ask them to join our PhotoCircle, and they'd upload their pictures from that night. We can say it's our own initiative to help find Chelsea. A digital search party." Seneca reached for her mother's necklace

111

at her throat, which she always did when she was thinking through an idea. It wasn't there – she didn't have any tools with her to bend the pendant back into place, and she wasn't quite sure she wanted to wear something Brett had touched, anyway. "We might be able to fill in some of the blanks. There might even be proof of you passing out in the grass in the background of a photo someone hasn't yet noticed."

Jeff's eyes widened. "Wow." His mouth quivered. "Thank you."

Seneca met his eyes, then looked away. He was staring at her so intensely. "It's no problem," she mumbled.

"No, seriously. You don't know what this means to me. To everyone else, I'm enemy number one. But then you believe in me, and it's just . . ."

"There's no reason *not* to believe in you," Seneca assured him, giving Jeff a friendly but guarded smile. She wasn't 100 percent sure, but it seemed like an alarm in her head was going off. Did Jeff *like* her?

Not wanting to draw a circle around that, she texted Maddox about the PhotoCircle idea and asked him to start emailing people to join. "So," she said as she finished, "want to head back up to the condo? I wouldn't mind another glass of lemonade before we leave."

"Actually?" Jeff's voice cracked. He suddenly looked a little gray. "Do you mind if we stay out here for a minute more?"

Seneca peered at him worriedly. "You okay?"

"I just need to breathe." Jeff collapsed on the stone wall alongside the condos. He looked a little piqued, like rehashing all this had physically drained him.

112

"Sure," Seneca said softly. After all, she couldn't just leave Jeff here. And she understood what it meant to be overwhelmed. Hadn't she felt like this a million times after her mom vanished?

Jeff smiled shakily. "I just want to talk about something else other than Chelsea for a second. Like what about you? Where are you from? I don't even know. Connecticut?"

"No, my friends are," Seneca said cautiously. "I'm from Maryland."

Jeff smiled. "I've got a friend who goes to the University of Maryland."

"I went there, too."

One eyebrow shot up. "You graduated?"

Seneca leaned on the wall. The stones were rough against her back. "God no. I ended up not going to any of my classes freshman year, so they kicked me out." She winced. It still felt shitty to say that out loud. "It was a disaster."

"Really?" Jeff looked astonished. "What are you going to do?"

Seneca sighed. It was a subject she'd avoided thinking about. "Um, I reenrolled, but I'm not psyched about going. I don't know what I want to do with my life."

Jeff touched her arm. "That sounds really hard."

At first, she felt a spike of annoyance – she hated pity. But then her shoulders sagged. It *was* hard. She might as well face that.

"So what's your lawyer like?" she asked Jeff, deciding to change the subject.

Jeff wrinkled his nose. "Totally unfriendly."

"Is he okay with you helping us look into this?"

113

Jeff stared at a line of seagulls flapping overhead. "He'd rather I didn't, but he says as long as I don't do anything crazy or dangerous – or, like, tamper with any evidence – I'm not breaking any laws." He fiddled with his Fitbit on his wrist, unhooking it and letting it fall to his lap. Then he gave Seneca a cagey look. "You believe I didn't hurt Chelsea, right?"

"Of course!" Seneca cried, startled at the question.

Jeff set his jaw. "I'm not so sure about Maddox."

"Maddox . . . well, he's . . ." Seneca brushed sand off her thighs. "He'll come around."

The wind gusted. A kite whirled on the beach, and they watched it for a moment. Seneca could feel Jeff looking at her, maybe waiting for a clue about Maddox. That same alarm in her head beeped. She decided to veer the conversation again. "What about your family?" she asked. "Is it just you and Marcus?"

"I have a sister, too, but she's a flight attendant," Jeff said. "I barely see her. My parents are cool, though. And my brother and I are really close. We used to beat on each other as kids, but now we look out for each other."

"I wish I'd had a sibling," Seneca admitted. "It got so lonely sometimes."

"Siblings definitely pull you out of your own freaky head. When Chelsea and I grew apart, I was really down. Marcus was a huge help. He forced me to tell him what was going on. It probably prevented me from becoming a total hermit."

Seneca sighed. "I need a Marcus this summer."

"Why is that?" Jeff cocked his head.

Seneca thought about the map on the inside of her closet. The obsessive Brett stalking she'd done on Case Not Closed.

The notebooks she'd filled with theories about who he was and what he'd done. The only people she'd talked to this summer were Brian at the parking authority – and that was because she had to – and Madison, Aerin, and Maddox, though those weren't exactly deep conversations.

And what did she have to show for it? She hadn't found Brett. He'd found *them*. Maybe she'd hid from the world because it was easier. But it was so lonely, too. All of a sudden, she thought of Maddox's emails to her. And how he'd said how much he was thinking about her this summer. *Had* she pushed him away? Had that been a mistake?

She took a deep breath. "It just gets hard sometimes. About my mom."

Jeff's face fell. "I'm so, so sorry. I can't even imagine." After a beat, he slid closer and gave her a hug. Seneca shut her eyes, smelling his coconut sunscreen. His bicep was hard against her shoulder.

They pulled back, and he gazed at her tenderly. A gentle breeze lifted the ends of her hair. Jeff inched his face closer, and she knew what he wanted next. She ducked her head, feeling awkward. "Um," she said.

Something caught her attention above. A tall, athletically built figure peered at them from one of the condo decks. It was almost certainly Maddox. Did he see her? Seneca's stomach turned over, and she pressed her lips closed and jerked away.

"I don't . . ." She pushed a lock of hair behind her ear. "We should probably check on everyone."

Jeff shot to his feet. "Um, yeah. Of course."

He hurried away as though escaping a fire. Seneca almost stepped on his Fitbit – he'd dropped it in his haste to get away. She sighed and slipped it into her bag. She felt so exhausted all of a sudden. So . . . *heavy*, like everything in the world was too complicated to sort out. As she headed back along the creepy path to the condos, she concentrated only on her footsteps through the soft sand. Moments after she stepped, the wind whisked away the evidence, as if she'd never been there at all.

CHAPTER 14

Maddox was a third of the way through the guest list – emailing leads, inviting people to the PhotoCircle, cross-referencing faces on Instagram – when he heard someone pounding on the condo door. His sister and Aerin stood on the other side. He opened it without speaking, but the frustration was all over his face. "What's wrong with *you*?" Madison snapped instantly, her eyebrows raised in suspicion.

"Nothing," Maddox snapped. "I just can't believe how hard it is to find a guy we already *know*." It was like that dream he sometimes had where he was winning a cross-country race, the finish line in view, and suddenly, his legs turned to Lego blocks. He no longer had knees. His limbs were brittle; one by one they fell off. Racers passed him, and he could do nothing about it, just lying there on the ground, a Lego torso and head.

After oohing and aahing over Gabriel's condo – "Can I marry this guy? He has a *Vitamix*!" – Madison and Aerin padded to the terrace. She spied Seneca and Jeff against the wall of that parking lot immediately, then whipped around and looked at Maddox with wide eyes.

Maddox balled his fist. "She's just trying to crack the case. Jeff has a lot of intel."

Madison sipped her drink, which smelled more like vanilla flavoring than coffee. "Okay," she said, watching him carefully.

Seething, Maddox grabbed his phone and started tapping. "A little help here? This guest list is mad long." The last thing he wanted was for Madison to feel *sorry* for him. He'd successfully managed not to think about Seneca for forty-five minutes. He didn't want to break that streak now.

Maddox, Madison, and Aerin sat down at the table on Gabriel's deck and kept searching Instagram, the guest lists, and the PhotoCircle Seneca had just set up. One by one, people joined the photo group, uploading their pictures to the public circle. Maddox stared at the app, his gaze flicking through pictures of strangers' faces. Kids were dancing, laughing, posing, trying to look sexy. People splashed in the shallow end in their clothes. A guy with a scruffy goatee named Rob Dalton had posted a picture of Jeff walking a slack line tied to two trees. Next to him was Chelsea, head down, scrolling through her phone. Maddox tried to zoom in on her screen – what was she looking at that was so interesting? – but it was too blurry. He searched for an image of Barnes Lombardi, whom Madison had told him was a total creeper, but Madison couldn't spot him in any of the pictures.

A girl named Hailey Garafalo uploaded pics of pretty blonde girls singing into a karaoke machine, a montage of people's feet, and Gabriel giving a speech. The pictures were time-stamped between 9:05 p.m. and 9:14 p.m., hours before Chelsea went down that path. They waded through more, finally coming to a picture of the bonfire at 10:45 – around the time Jeff said he and Chelsea argued. Alistair provided a photo of three guys sitting on a log, holding their beers up in a toast. One of them was photo-tagged *J.T.* While most of his face was in shadow, there was something reminiscent about his posture. He was about Brett's height and weight. Maddox felt a chill.

"Has anyone talked to him?" Aerin murmured, her gaze on J.T., too.

"He hasn't uploaded pictures yet," Madison murmured. She found his number on the guest list, called, and put it on speaker. Everyone was silent as the phone rang. Maddox heard a sleepy voice answer. Madison introduced herself as a friend of Chelsea's who was trying to figure out what went down the night of the party. "We're putting together a PhotoCircle. If you want to share anything –"

"I didn't take any pictures," J.T. interrupted, his voice flat. "And really, I don't understand how another PhotoCircle is going to help anything."

"We're just trying to put together the pieces of the puzzle," Madison said smoothly. "Do you at least remember Jeff and Chelsea fighting that night?"

"Yeah. They were near the dunes. She seemed pissed."

"And then she ran away?"

"Yep. Down the path."

"Did anyone follow her?"

"Not that I remember." J.T. let out a yawn. "Except for Jeff."

Madison picked impatiently at her fingernails. "Do you remember who else was sitting with you at the bonfire?"

"Not really."

The silence felt desolate. Everyone exchanged skeptical glances. "Well, thanks anyway," Madison finally said. She hung up and looked at the group, clearly at a loss.

"He sounded stoned," Aerin grumbled.

"Or he could be lying," Madison said. "Maybe *he's* Brett." Her fingers flew. She typed J.T.'s full name into Google. A Periscope account came up. At first, the video was of a shaky ride down a street in midtown New York City, probably filmed on a GoPro. But then J.T. turned the camera on himself and started narrating. With his olive skin and wide-set eyes, he didn't really look like Brett. Then Madison pointed at the date that popped up on a digital scroll snaking around the outside of NBC Studios. It was April 19, a few months ago.

"Even if this guy *did* look like Brett, he can't be Brett," Madison concluded. "On April 19, we were in Dexby, at Kevin Larssen's engagement party. Not even Brett can be two places at once."

"So he's telling the truth," Maddox said. He was about to ask if they'd gotten anything useful from J.T. when a knock sounded on the door. Madison opened it, and Seneca and Jeff strode in. They weren't walking very close together, but their posture was friendly and relaxed. "Hey." Seneca's gaze drifted to Maddox for a split second. He looked away quickly, then scolded himself and gave her a small smile.

"Good idea about the PhotoCircle," Madison announced. "People are sending in a lot of pictures."

Everyone sat down on the couch and flipped through more images. At the end of a long stream of pictures from a girl named Brianna Morton of the same four friends sitting on a chaise, a blurry photo popped up. It seemed Brianna had taken the shot accidentally, her hand slipping on the shutter. "Huh," Seneca said, stopping on it anyway. Maddox leaned in. The shot showed a view out of a window of the intersection in front of the condos. It was time-stamped 11:02 P.M.

Seneca pointed at a figure in the upper right corner, half-hidden behind a parked car. Though he was in the distance, the image was clear. The guy seemed tall and lanky.

Aerin gasped. "It's him." She looked at Madison. "That kid we saw on the boardwalk. The one I swear we knew from somewhere."

Jeff squinted. He made a face. "I think it's . . . Corey."

Seneca scrunched up her nose. "Why do I know that name?"

Jeff's eyes darted. "I doubt you've met him. He keeps to himself. He wasn't invited to the party as far as I know. People . . . talk about him."

"What do they say?" Madison asked.

"Someone told me he brought a gun to his high school in Delaware a couple years ago. Got expelled immediately." Jeff rubbed his temples. "He always comes to parties and just sits on the chair with a beer. Stares. It makes some people uncomfortable."

Seneca widened her eyes, and Maddox knew they were thinking the same thing. He looked at the time again. 11:02 P.M. If Jeff's timeline about that night was accurate, that was right when Chelsea walked down the path. Why was Corey standing on the street by himself? Was he trying to crash the party?

"Was this kid at the bonfire?" Maddox asked.

121

Jeff shook his head. "I don't remember seeing him, but . . ."

Seneca suddenly had a light in her eyes. "Does Corey work at the Island Time Café?"

Jeff nodded. "I think so."

Maddox's mouth dropped open. "He *talked* to us." He tried to remember the few moments they'd had with the kid their first afternoon here. He'd jumped right in on their conversation about Chelsea. It felt like a slap. Had Brett been practically the first person they'd met here?

"That café allows dogs," Madison said, amazement in her voice. "Bertha has an Island Time magnet on the fridge that says so. Maybe she goes there with Kingston? That could be how the dog knows him."

Seneca glanced at Jeff. "We've figured out that whoever took Chelsea also has a reason to get into the B and B we're staying at. It's a long story."

"And maybe he was following us to the boardwalk," Aerin said. "It's such a strange coincidence that he was right there, in the crowd . . ."

"Jesus," Seneca said, pressing her hand to her forehead.

"That dude took Chelsea?" Jeff's voice was hoarse. *"Him?"*

"We have to call the girl who posted this," Seneca said. "Make sure she didn't see anything."

"I doubt she realized she took this photo at all," Maddox murmured.

Jeff exhaled sharply. When Maddox looked over, the guy had turned pale. "Whoa," Maddox said, jumping to his feet and catching Jeff just before he crumpled to the ground. "Take a breath."

"Sorry," Jeff said shakily. "This is just so . . . *intense*. I mean, I know that guy."

"Get him inside," Seneca said, quickly pulling the sliding door open.

Maddox walked Jeff into the condo and deposited him on Gabriel's white couch, where he collapsed into a heap. Moments later, Seneca returned with two cool glasses of water. Jeff drank his down quickly, sending her a grateful smile. "I'm going to go back outside and look through the PhotoCircle," she said. "Maddox, can you stay with him?"

"I'm fine," Jeff insisted. "Really."

But Maddox nodded at Seneca, and she returned outside. He focused on Jeff again. Pieces of hair stuck to Jeff's sweaty forehead, and he'd stripped off his sweatshirt and now had on a sleeveless Billabong tee. His eyes were glazed and unfocused – it seemed as though he'd had a full-on panic attack. Maddox changed the channel on the TV, worried that the program he'd been watching about hurricanes might stress Jeff out. But as soon as he saw what was on the screen – a Philly news broadcast of Chelsea's disappearance – he winced and changed the channel again. SpongeBob appeared. Hopefully that was harmless enough.

"Just relax," Maddox said awkwardly. "We're all shaken up."

"Yeah." Jeff's voice was strained. He picked at a frayed hem in his shorts. "Um, you asked who I was talking to on the phone. It was just this girl I know from school. A friend. She's kind of a drama queen. Freaked out when she saw me on the news. I tried to calm her down, but she was going crazy, and I was getting frustrated at her."

Maddox wanted to ask *why* Jeff hadn't just said that from the start, but the guy was looking at him so beseechingly that he decided to let it go. Jeff probably wasn't worth wondering about. There's no way he was Brett, and it was clear he hadn't kidnapped Chelsea, either. "No worries," he murmured.

The cartoon cut to a commercial about water balloons, and Maddox shut his eyes. The notion that Brett might have been right there, practically the first moment they'd set foot in Lafayette, shook him. He felt a sense of urgency, like they needed to call out this Corey guy *right now*. But he shouldn't jump to conclusions. And they had to play it cool. Alerting Brett that they were onto him might make him do something rash.

"It's pretty amazing that she figured this out," Jeff said in a croaky voice. "I mean, without her? I'd probably be going to jail."

Maddox turned his head with a start, at first not understanding whom Jeff was talking about. Jeff had a wistful smile on his face, and his gaze was on the patio, where Seneca was pacing around. Maddox swallowed awkwardly, all at once very aware of what was going through Jeff's head. He *thought* he'd picked up on something.

He cleared his throat. "Yeah. Definitely. But, um, just so you know, she's kind of off the market."

Jeff shifted on the couch. "Huh?"

Maddox studied his knuckles, feeling slimy for talking about this – but, hey, he might as well spare Jeff the pain. "I mean, she doesn't have a boyfriend or anything. But all she cares about is this case. She has no room for anything else right now. Especially . . . relationships."

Jeff's jaw twitched. "Oh?"

"I'm not trying to be an asshole. I just . . ." He laughed sadly. "I know it firsthand."

Jeff pushed his toe into one of the perfect vacuum lines on the carpet. "Huh. Well, good to know." Then he stood, pulling his sweatshirt back over his head. "Um, I'm going to jet."

Maddox frowned in surprise, taking in Jeff's ashen pallor. "You still look pretty weak, man."

"I'm fine." Jeff avoided eye contact and made a big production of putting his shoes on. "I should get back to my family. I'll see you later, okay? And thanks for everything. I mean it."

"Okay," Maddox croaked, hoping he hadn't misstepped. He'd thought telling Jeff would help him, not destroy him further.

Once Jeff slumped out the door, Maddox collapsed in his spot on the couch. SpongeBob came back on the TV, but he stared at the screen without absorbing the story.

When the door to the patio slid open, he jumped. Seneca stood on the carpet, her eyes searching the room. "Where's Jeff?"

"He . . . had something to do. Why?"

Seneca hurried into the condo. There was something about her movements that seemed antsy and troubled, not angry. "What is it?" Maddox asked, propping himself up.

She sat next to him on the couch. Her proximity both excited him and made him horribly nervous. "We found another photo," she said in a low voice.

"Of Jeff?"

"No. But something from that night." Seneca showed her phone to Maddox. It was another out-of-the-window shot, time-stamped shortly after the first. But this time, there were two figures. The girl stood with her arms crossed and her body arched away. The guy – gaunt, gangly – bent toward her, his arms outstretched menacingly.

"It's Corey," Seneca said. "With *Chelsea*."

CHAPTER 15

Brett sat under a beach umbrella and peered through binoculars at the condo's balcony. Jeff and Maddox had just gone inside. Their shoulders were squared. There was an air of seriousness about them. Were they off to have a conversation, too, something like the one Jeff and Seneca had had earlier? Not that Brett had been able to hear everything, but he knew parts of it had been deep. He'd also heard a little bit about a PhotoCircle. *Look through as many photos as you want. Knock yourself out.*

Just as he was getting a good, long look at Seneca, Aerin, and Madison on the balcony – Aerin had no idea that he could see a little down her shirt when she leaned over – static crackled on the iPad on his lap. An app showed a closed-captioned feed of Camera A. Chelsea stood in front of the full-length mirror, admiring her reflection. "That's right," he murmured. It was incredible what a shower and new clothes could do for the psyche. Even prisoners wanted to look pretty for their last meal.

A Bruce Springsteen song he loved lilted through the air from a nearby radio, and he lay back on his elbows and tilted his head to the sky. Some days, it was really good to be him.

But he only allowed himself to enjoy a few self-congratulatory moments before peering at the condo again. He could just make out Jeff and Maddox through the windows in the living room. They were sitting close together, talking. After a moment, Jeff rose and left.

Brett scowled. Why did they all think Jeff was such a gem? He thought of all the times Chelsea had come to him last year, crying, distraught, insecure. *Jeff never compliments me. He says my beauty is beside the point.* Once, Jeff wrote a song for Chelsea where he compared her to an African elephant, the strongest and most beautiful matriarch on the savanna. *A goddamn elephant! He thinks I'm fat and disgusting!* And then there was the day three months ago when she told him the secret Jeff had finally confessed. Brett had demanded to know why she still hung out with him – she should cut him off, then and there. Chelsea had shrugged. *He knows what I think about him – it's why we broke up. But we have a long history. It's complicated.*

Then she'd leaned in and fluttered those pretty lashes, and Brett knew what she wanted. And he was more than happy to give it to her.

Brett noticed a familiar figure starting down the beach with a surfboard under his arm and flinched. *Speak of the devil.* He hurriedly shoved the iPad, remote, and binoculars into his bag and zipped it up in the nick of time.

"Hey," Jeff said, suddenly above him. He looked surprised. "What are you doing here?"

Brett laced his hands behind his head and gave him a friendly smile. "Just enjoying a little me time. You?"

"Yeah. Same." Jeff stared at him. Brett tried not to bristle, but suddenly, Jeff's gaze felt . . . *intrusive*. Almost like he knew that tucked inside his bag was a camera feed of his precious ex-girlfriend. *Could* he know? Brett didn't blink, thinking innocent thoughts. Though Jeff waved and turned a second later, heading for the water, there was something distracted about his walk, as though he was thinking something through. Seneca and the others didn't have all the pieces of the puzzle, but Jeff almost did – it was one of the reasons Brett planted the seed of Jeff's guilt. And now that he was working with Seneca, he might put the pieces together even faster. Maybe something more needed to be done.

Pulling out his phone, he logged onto CNC and looked at Seneca's message thread. Chuckling softly, he thought about the new message he would send . . . and what he had in store. It was perfect. And it was going to blow them all away.

CHAPTER 16

At a few minutes to six the next morning, Seneca stood with
the others at the locked front door of Island Time Café. A mild
wind whipped her hair. She felt eyes on her back, but when
she turned, the only people she saw were an elderly couple
vigorously power walking on the path across the street that
paralleled the ocean. Kate, the woman with a blonde ponytail
they'd met the first morning they'd arrived here, padded
through the café's front room, setting up for morning customers.

Seneca glanced again at the photo of Corey they'd found
yesterday, standing next to Chelsea. The true focus of the
picture was Brianna and her four friends, all holding up
drinks in a toast; Corey had no idea he'd been captured in the
background. They'd called Brianna about the picture, though
they suspected she had no idea what she'd caught on camera.
Trouble was, Brianna hadn't yet called them back.

The guy in the photo was definitely Brett's height, and
though his hair was cut differently and she didn't remember
his face being so angular, this lined up with their theory that
he had lost some weight. If she looked hard enough, she could
almost see it.

As a large clock in the center square struck six, Kate leisurely strolled over and unlocked the door. "Hey," she said sleepily to the group as she let them in. The room smelled like espresso beans, and the only sounds were the pop radio station turned on low and the burbling of the coffee percolator. Magazines were neatly fanned out on the low coffee table by two large orange couches, and the muffins behind the glass at the counter stood in perfect, even lines.

"What can I get for you?" Kate asked as she strolled back behind the counter.

Seneca cleared her throat. "Actually, we're here to ask about Corey Robinson."

Something flickered across Kate's face. She focused on a slip of paper by the register. "Corey doesn't work here anymore."

A jolt went through Seneca. "What?"

"He quit yesterday." Kate pushed a register button, and the drawer shot open. Her voice was flat, guarded. "Just walked out."

"Do you know why?" Aerin asked. "Or where he went?"

"He didn't say. Sorry." She shot them a tight smile.

Seneca sank into her hip. "He didn't give you an excuse?"

Kate kept her eyes down. "He seemed to be in a hurry."

"Where is he from?" Seneca was desperate for anything, even if it was one of Brett's lies. Moments before, they'd felt so close.

"Delaware, I think." Kate's gaze was cold. "Did you guys want to order or what?"

Everyone looked at each other. Seneca tapped her lip, trying another tack. "Can you show me the application he filled out to work here?"

131

Something fluttered across Kate's face, but it submerged quickly. "That's private."

"You can block out his social security number. All we're looking for is the address he listed."

"Uh, unless you're the police, I don't have to –"

"Look," Aerin blurted. "Chelsea's been missing for three days now. We think Corey might know something. Be a good person here."

Kate's gaze was steady and challenging, but not exactly surprised. "You mean he's a suspect?" she demanded.

"Maybe," Aerin said.

Kate put her hands on her hips. "Can I see some sort of proof?"

There was a brief stare-off, but then Aerin pulled out her phone and called up the picture on the feed. "See?" She pointed at Corey next to Chelsea. "This is right around the time Chelsea was last seen. They're *together*."

Kate glanced at it, but she seemed unimpressed. "I'm sorry. I can't give out his address. If you aren't going to order anything, you can't be here."

Seneca spun around and tramped out of the café. Everyone followed. Once they were on the sidewalk, she glared at Kate through the glass. "I think she's hiding something."

Maddox cocked his head. "Me too."

Seneca nodded. "She looked freaked when we mentioned Corey's name. What does she know?"

"If Corey is Brett, then maybe he charmed her – or manipulated her." Madison lowered her voice as a jogging couple passed. "But maybe she senses there's something off about him. Maybe she even has *evidence* . . . but she's too afraid to talk."

132

Maddox cleared his throat. "Maybe there's another way we can get information. MizMaizie should be able to help."

Seneca pinched the bridge of her nose. MizMaizie posted on CNC and, being a former Seattle cop, still had access to basic records like driver's license information. She'd helped with Helena's investigation, trying to figure out where Heath Ingram had disappeared to the winter after Helena vanished. Seneca scrolled through her phone for the number and was surprised when MizMaizie wrote back quickly. *No Delaware driver's license for Corey Robinson.*

Seneca asked for her to check other states, but after another beat, the only Corey Robinsons that came up were much older, or of a different ethnicity, and one was female. Maddox frowned. "That's weird."

"Not really," Seneca said. "He could be using an alias."

"How could we figure out where he's staying?" Aerin asked.

"We could call Gabriel," Seneca suggested. "Maybe the realty company he works for rented his family his vacation house." But then she looked at the time. It was 6:30. She doubted Gabriel was up yet.

Aerin raised empty palms to the group. "Now what?"

"I have an idea." Madison pointed at a truck that had just rolled up to the curb. *Peace, Love, and Donuts!* it read, featuring a smiling donut as its logo. A sleepy-looking worker wearing a Grateful Dead T-shirt slid out of the driver's seat, ambled around to the back, and opened the doors to reveal boxes of freshly made pastries.

"Excuse me?" Madison strolled over. Her eyes twinkled, and she'd put on her most winning smile. Her head bent close to the guy, and after a moment, Seneca saw him nod, hand her his cap, and lift a box of food into her arms. He pointed to a back alley that ran behind the shops, and Madison started off.

Seneca caught her arm. "What are you *doing*?"

Madison grinned. "I told this guy I'd give him all my indica weed if he'd let me deliver the donuts to my friend inside. I'll set the donuts on the counter and grab that application."

"Madison, I don't . . ." Seneca started, but Madison was already skipping off.

Seneca shifted nervously on the sidewalk, half expecting Madison to dart out of the café with Kate chasing after her. She glanced around, once more feeling the sensation that someone was watching them. A garbage truck lumbered down the road. A Jeep carrying surfboards passed. A few joggers galloped by, but no one even glanced in their direction.

Aerin tapped her foot impatiently. Maddox cleared his throat. "I wish we had a getaway car. If that Kate girl comes flying after my sister, Madison won't be able to outrun her. Did you see the shoes she's wearing?"

Seneca smirked. "You'll have to carry her on your back."

He scoffed. "Yeah right."

She cocked her head. "But I thought runners were, like, the *strongest* athletes ever." Maddox's face reddened, and she nudged him. "Kidding."

Madison strolled calmly from around the corner. She tossed the delivery guy his hat, popped an unidentifiable bundle in his pocket, and returned to the group, her cheeks pink with excitement.

"What happened?" Seneca whispered, hurrying over to her.

Madison held up her phone. She'd taken a photo of an open file cabinet with an application sticking out of a manila folder. Corey Robinson, it read on the top. And an address: 49 Ninety-First Street. Seneca looked at the street sign: They were on Ninety-Sixth. "This isn't far."

Maddox pivoted on the sidewalk. "Let's go."

"Are you crazy?" Seneca pulled on her sleeve. "We can't just show up at his house. It's six thirty in the morning, for one thing. And for another, if this *is* Brett, what are we going to do? Ring his doorbell, and . . . ?" She trailed off, suddenly unable to speak. The idea of coming face-to-face with Brett made her shrink down in terror. They needed to think this through more. They needed a better plan.

Maddox turned from the curb. "If we don't want to go there in person, we could check it out with my drone. See if he's there. Make sure it *is* Brett."

Madison gawked at him. "You *didn't* bring it."

"He did." Aerin smirked. "It's in our room."

"Drones are nerdy and weird!" Madison hissed. "Only stalkers use them! We're trying to keep a low profile, not draw attention to ourselves!"

"Actually, a drone isn't a bad idea," Seneca said. "Have you seen how many people are flying them on the beach? Brett won't know which one is ours." She smirked at him. "Let me guess. You're amazing at flying it."

Maddox grinned. "I didn't play hours and hours of *Top Gun* on Xbox for nothing."

They headed back to the B&B, though after some discussion, they decided to wait a few hours to fly it, when there would be more drones on the beach and Maddox's would blend in. Finally, around eleven, Maddox pulled the box into the B&B's

135

driveway. He assembled the large, flat flying device, turned it on, pressed a few buttons on the remote, and the drone lifted into the air. He managed to fly the thing over the trees and houses without bumping it into a single branch. His features relaxed into something very intelligent, and admittedly very handsome, and Seneca felt an unexpected tingle. Maddox glanced up at her and raised an eyebrow. She gave him a thumbs-up.

Everyone stared at the iPad synced to the drone's progress. Madison used a map on her phone to tell Maddox where to turn. Finally, the drone hovered over the address Corey had used on his application. There were no cars in the driveway, but there was a bike propped against the garage and a light on inside. Maddox flew the drone a little lower. "Watch it," Madison hissed. "Don't crash it into a window."

They studied the screen on the iPad. The drone hovered across the street to get a view inside the front windows, but there weren't any signs anyone was there – the TV wasn't on, and there were no shadows moving behind the glass. The house was on a public street, too – Seneca doubted Brett was actually holding Chelsea hostage inside.

She leaned back on her heels, feeling frustrated. When her phone started to buzz in her back pocket, she almost ignored it. But then she pulled it out and gawked at the screen. "Look," she whispered to the others. She'd received a new message on the CNC boards from BMoney60.

Hope to see you at the Bastille Day party. I've got a killer surprise for you . . .

CHAPTER 17

Aerin stared at the message on Seneca's screen. Her throat felt dry. Her fingers tingled. She could practically hear Brett's voice. *Taunting* them.

"Okay." Seneca's voice was steady, and her shoulders were squared. "So Brett's either going to be at the party . . . or close by, watching. Which means we're *definitely* going, too."

"We're going to *face* him?" Aerin cried.

Seneca looked at her like she was crazy. "We can't just stay home! But I'm thinking we'll just be on the lookout. We need to figure out who he is. Maybe he's Corey . . . or maybe he's someone else. We'll have to think outside the box."

"What if we *do* spot him at the party?" Madison asked. "What's the plan?"

Kingston, the Doberman, barked loudly from inside the B&B, making Aerin jump. "I think we play it cool," Maddox whispered. "We don't know where Chelsea is, and we don't have any hard evidence we can give the police that Brett has her. That's what we need tonight. If Brett thinks we haven't found him, he might get cocky and give away something about where he's hidden Chelsea . . . or else bail on the party and

137

lead us straight *to* her. So we act oblivious. Pretend we don't see him."

"Agreed," Seneca said. "We just track him. Don't go up to him. Don't *look* at him. Pretend nothing's out of the ordinary."

Aerin swallowed hard. The idea of keeping a cool head in the face of her sister's murderer sounded impossible, but if there was anytime to rise to the challenge, it had to be today. "What do you think he means by a surprise?" she asked, pointing to that part in Brett's note.

Seneca shifted from foot to foot, her expression darkening. "I don't know. But we need to keep in each other's sight at all times. And we'll put the cops on speed dial, just in case." She pulled Madison over and took Aerin's hand. "Now I need to check out your suitcases."

"Why?" Aerin asked.

Seneca gave her a half smile. "I didn't exactly bring clothes for a party. But something tells me you guys did."

Six hours later, after trying on multiple dress-and-shoe combinations and having multiple freak-outs, Aerin and the others stood across the street from the condos in front of a mini golf course called Zoo Adventure. Even from a half block away, they could hear music floating out from the pool area and a few loud hoots of laughter. Aerin took a deep breath, feeling like she might puke. As they stepped onto the sidewalk, she slipped her hand into Seneca's. Seneca squeezed back, but it didn't help much.

The sun had set over the buildings, turning the sky a mix of pink and yellow. Heat still radiated off the sidewalks, but the breeze felt cool and refreshing. At the condo entrance, the music had grown louder, and so had the crowd. A tall, thick-necked man standing at the gate straightened as they approached.

"Name?" he asked, eyeing them coolly.

"Aerin Kelly," Aerin said in almost a whisper. She looked around, wondering if Brett was close, listening.

The man checked a list on his phone, then nodded and let her through. Seneca, Maddox, and Madison gave their names as well. Aerin watched as Seneca peeked at the bouncer's phone screen, clearly searching for Corey's name. But the bouncer gave her a suspicious look and dropped the phone into his pocket.

They walked through the gate and into the huge pool space, where the party was taking place. It held a wide expanse of tables, several long grassy nooks, a bar area, a DJ booth and dance floor, and, of course, the enormous, glittering, open-to-the-sky-and-beach-beyond pool, complete with water slide, diving boards, a swim-up bar, and a battalion of rafts. A number of kids were in the pool already, and the space smelled like a mix of chlorine and tiki torches. As Aerin scanned the crowded deck, she suddenly had a horrible thought and grabbed Seneca's hand. "What if Brett brought a gun?" she whispered. "What if *that's* his surprise?"

Seneca frowned. "Doubt it."

"What makes you so sure?"

"Brett strikes me as someone who thinks he's better than weapons. Like he can outmuscle everyone with his brain."

They pushed into the party some more. The pool area was decorated with French flags, statues of militiamen on horses, and banners that read, *Happy Bastille Day!* The food spread seemed to consist mostly of French bread, wheels of Brie, baskets of fries, a huge cauldron of mussels and clams, and a large chocolate cake iced with *Let them eat cake!* There were at least ten people dressed up as characters from *Les Misérables.* In the corner, past the water slide, was a large bounce house; someone had written in black ink on one of the turrets *Storm the Bastille!* Everyone jumping inside waved cardboard swords and shields.

"Let's fan out," Seneca murmured in Aerin's ear.

Aerin's heart thumped double time. She didn't want to be separated from the group even for a second. Seneca added, as if reading her mind, "Just stay where I can see you. It'll be okay."

Then Seneca crossed the patio. Madison took a spot near the pool. Maddox headed toward the dance floor. Fearfully, Aerin stepped near a bunch of kids lounging on oversized outdoor beanbags, figuring there was safety in numbers. She glanced around hesitantly, fearful of what she might see. So many people were wearing hats, eye masks, sometimes complete *face* masks. Was Brett lurking under one of them? She felt eyes on her across the room. She jolted up, but all she saw was a seagull sitting atop the fence.

She moved jerkily, glancing over her shoulder every few seconds, until she was near the bounce house. A song by Demi Lovato played at deafening volume, making it difficult to think straight. The bounce house shook wildly, stuffed with people. Behind it, a couple made out against the wall, their arms and legs entangled. Aerin squinted hard – the guy's eyes were shaped like Brett's, and a big beard covered his face like a disguise. He caught her staring, and she noticed a big nose, wide-set eyes. Her Brett radar didn't flash.

Eyes, faces, bodies. Hats, masks, costumes. She scanned each party guest thoroughly, but the twinkling fairy lights combined with the dark, moonless sky cast confusing, obfuscating shadows. A few of the *Les Mis* characters were now singing a song from the show, which gave Aerin a pang – Helena always used to love *Les Mis*, often choosing songs from its sound track to sing in their garage karaoke booth. She'd enjoy this party, actually. She'd probably get up there and sing, too.

Across the patio, Seneca sipped a drink, coolly surveying the pool area. Madison was stationed by the snacks, talking to a girl in a corset. The hair on the back of Aerin's neck prickled again, and all at once, she felt a watchful presence. She turned slowly, nearly getting mowed down as a knot of laughing, tipsy kids hurried past. A cackle rose through the crowd, high and sharp. A tall head bobbed above the others – someone in a pirate hat. Aerin looked right and left, her thoughts splintering. Then someone pulled her backward.

"Hey!" she cried, staggering in her high wedges. She scanned the area for the others – did they see this? Were they watching? But she couldn't see Seneca or Maddox anymore, and Madison's attention was elsewhere. Whoever had grabbed her pushed her into a dark corner and then spun her around to face him. Aerin breathed in, stiff with fear, gaping into a rubbery mask of a man with a pageboy haircut and a silky goatee. Her heart lurched. She was about to scream when the masked man's hand clapped over her mouth.

"*Shhh.*" His voice was muffled. "Don't make a scene. I just want to talk to you, Aerin."

The scream stilled in Aerin's throat. It wasn't Brett's voice . . .

141

but she knew it all the same. And when he lifted the mask up just so, revealing full lips and a square jaw and those familiar soft green eyes, she was certain.

Thomas.

The party thrummed and shimmered around them. Kids splashed down the water slide. Someone called, "Limbo!" Aerin was astonished the world could continue so happily apace despite what was happening to her.

Hastily, Thomas loosened his grip, but he still held on to her wrist as though he feared she might bolt. He faced the party again. For a moment, they stood silently side by side, like strangers on a curb waiting for the light to change. "I think I know why you've been avoiding me," he finally murmured. "Brett told you not to tell anyone, right?"

Aerin swallowed hard. Her blood felt like ice in her veins.

"But if you think I'm going to just sit back and watch this happen without helping, you're crazy."

"Thomas, you need to go," Aerin said frantically. "This isn't safe – for any of us."

"He's here, isn't he? That's why *you're* here."

Aerin's jaw twitched. "Have you been spying on me?"

The mask bobbed, and for a moment, Thomas didn't speak. "No. Okay, maybe. Okay, *yes*. I've been watching you all day, and all yesterday, too. And I overheard Seneca say something about Brett sending her a *message* earlier. Are you guys communicating with him?"

"*Shhh*," Aerin said, feeling uneasy. Come to think of it, she *had* felt paranoid someone was watching them this morning . . .

but she'd chalked it up to nerves. She glanced over her shoulder, wondering who *else* could be listening now. Every shifting body, every lurking presence in a mask filled her with paralyzing dread and fear. On instinct, she moved a little closer to Thomas. As complicated as she felt about him being here, she needed protection. All of a sudden, she weakened. How bad would it be if she told Thomas everything? He'd already practically figured out the whole story on his own anyway, and he wasn't taking no for an answer.

She sighed. "Fine. He's here. But keep your voice down. He said that if we went to the police, Chelsea would die. You're *ex*-police, so . . ."

"Got it," Thomas said, his voice full of vindication.

As briefly as she could, Aerin filled Thomas in on some other details – Brett's letter, the CNC posts, and their suspects thus far. "Brett said he'd be here tonight – with a surprise," she added. "But I don't see him yet."

Thomas peered around the party. To an onlooker, he just seemed like a guy in a mask standing next to a pretty blond girl in a sundress, trying to figure out how to talk to her. Aerin noticed Seneca reappear, look her way, and frown. She could tell Seneca was about to come over, but she waved in an I'm-okay gesture.

The party had swelled in size in the past half hour. A horde of surfers chatted in the corner. A few girls who'd complimented Aerin's purse earlier that day waved from the beer keg. She noticed Gabriel Wilton, the party host, wearing a large Napoleon-style hat that completely engulfed his head and a heavy-looking blue blazer with gold tassels on the epaulets.

He stood next to a guy who wore a towering, powdered Marie-Antoinette wig, no shirt, and a French flag wrapped around his waist like a sarong.

"I sort of remember what Brett looked like, but I don't see anyone like him," Thomas said.

"He could be in a mask. Or maybe he's not here yet. Promise me one thing, okay? If we *do* see him, don't do anything rash."

Thomas nodded again. After a beat, he cleared his throat. "So how are you?"

Aerin glared at him. Did he really expect her to answer?

"It's a party," Thomas reminded her. "We should act like we're having a good time."

Aerin rolled back her shoulders. "I'm fine," she said begrudgingly. "Great, in fact."

"Good," Thomas said. "Me too."

"Great," Aerin snapped, though she felt a dip of disappointment. Of course Thomas was happy in his new life.

But then Thomas's chin tilted down. "Oh, what am I saying? New York is crazy. It's so crowded, and it smells, and there are people *everywhere*."

Aerin bit her lip, suddenly guilty that she'd wished for Thomas's misery. "But you like school, don't you?"

"It's . . . okay."

A few new kids had streamed in, whooping loudly. Though some of them were in masks, no one matched Corey's height or weight, and none of them looked like the old Brett, either. Aerin's gaze flicked to several kids typing frantically on their phones. They seemed jittery, and they kept looking cautiously around the area. What if Brett had some sort of network, and these guys were warning him that she and the others were here?

"This must be really hard for you," Thomas broke the silence.

Aerin stiffened. *"What?"*

"Diving back into this investigation again. It's like the nightmare that never ends."

The corner of her mouth twitched. "Yeah. Good times."

"You should have called me. I'm always here to listen."

"I'm fine," Aerin said frostily. She stood on her tiptoes, pretending to be interested in a guy who'd just jumped into the pool.

"I wouldn't be fine."

Aerin clamped her lips together. The party felt too crowded and close. Or maybe *Thomas* felt too crowded and close, his questions too intrusive. Did he really think he could march back in here and take the same old spot in her heart? "Maybe we should mingle," she said. She shot him a tense smile and began to cross the patio.

Thomas caught her arm. *"Aerin.* Please. Don't walk away from me."

She didn't turn. "I don't want to arouse suspicion. We need to circulate."

"Wait." Thomas's muffled voice cracked beneath the mask. Reluctantly, Aerin stopped, her shoulders tense. "Why do you hate me?" he asked. "I'm the same person, and I'm not going anywhere. I promise."

"Except to New York." Aerin wanted to take it back as soon as she said it. The hurt was evident in her voice, a chink in her armor.

Thomas went still. The whole party seemed to still, actually – Aerin was suddenly aware of all the space around them. Floating above them was the fragrant, summery smell of grilled burgers and hot dogs. She lingered on the sensation for a moment, letting it fill her. If she shut her eyes, she could almost imagine standing in her own backyard on a summer evening six years ago, before Helena was gone, before her parents split up. Her father was grilling on their three-tier deck. After they ate, she and Helena were going to retreat to the garage, where they'd sing into their karaoke booth for hours. A fresh wave of sadness cascaded over her.

Thomas's shoulders rounded with hurt. "Y-you're mad I went to New York?"

The lump in Aerin's throat grew larger. "It doesn't matter."

"But New York isn't even far. It's a quick train ride. We could have visited each other every weekend."

Aerin was clenching her jaw so tightly that it ached. "I said it doesn't matter. None of it matters."

"Stop pushing me away. What do you want, Aerin? What can I do to make this better? For you to talk to me again?"

Aerin opened her mouth, but no words came. She stared across the glittering surface of the pool.

"I didn't even think you *cared* I went to New York," Thomas said.

Aerin let out a surprised laugh. "Why?"

The mask didn't move. Aerin wished she could make out his expression. "Because you didn't react," he finally answered. "You just . . . shut down. I figured I wasn't that important to you."

146

Aerin curled her toes. "It's not that. But I also wasn't going to try to talk you out of it. You had no future in Dexby. You needed to get out."

"But I did have a future in Dexby. *You.*"

It was unbearably sweet, exactly what she longed for him to say to her, and yet she felt the urge to run. Not just across the room, either, but out of the party, out of this *town*. All of this was just too much. Facing this. Rehashing it. Asking for something she needed. It just wasn't something she could do.

She was pushing Thomas away – *again*. He was about the millionth person she'd pushed away since Helena vanished. But what did she gain from it? Okay, it kept her safe and sealed, free from hurt. The flip side of that, though, was her crushing loneliness. Which she suddenly felt so acutely, it was almost an ache.

She let out a shaky breath, wondering if she could, just once, ignore her instincts. "Okay, I didn't want you to leave," she said in little more than a whisper, barely audible over the loud techno that was now blasting out of the speakers. "Are you happy now?"

"I . . . *am*," Thomas said immediately. "And . . . well, I've been thinking. I want to come back to Dexby. I miss it there. I miss my grandparents. And I miss . . . you."

She gave him a sidelong glance. "Don't just come back because of me."

"I wouldn't be. I've looked into colleges right around Dexby, and they have the same programs I was interested in at the New School. But without the crowds in New York . . . and with you."

Aerin turned to him. There were so many things she wanted to say – things maybe she *could* say. Because Thomas would listen. She knew he would. Who else would have followed her all the way to Lafayette just because he was worried? Who else would have risked so much to approach her at this party? Who else would wear such a horrible mask to remain incognito?

He cared. Really, really cared – and maybe she could let herself care, too. It was the most incredible feeling of freedom, even amid all this turmoil. Slowly, she inched toward him until their shoulders were touching. Their fingers brushed together. Thomas caught her pinkie and curled it into his palm. Aerin felt a swoop in her stomach and shut her eyes.

All at once, he was pulling her close. At first, she felt the rubbery mask against her cheek, but then it gave way, lifting off his face. His breath was warm and sweet, and she could just make out his twinkling eyes. Her heart rocketed as he gently touched the edge of her lips with the tips of his finger. And then, unable to stand it any longer, she pressed her lips to his, savoring the rush and the release of the kiss.

CHAPTER 18

Seneca stood next to the pool and coolly assessed the scene. Girls in boho dresses were already so tipsy they were having trouble walking in their wedges, guys in board shirts and tees were cheering at a very competitive game of ladderball that had started up, and some people in complete Francophile regalia, including face masks, traipsed around affecting drunken French accents. The people in the masks were maddening. Was Brett right in front of her, hiding in plain sight? Was *this* his surprise? Whenever someone jostled her, she jumped and turned around, on high alert. She kept expecting Brett to grab her, hurt her . . . but the party seemed so innocent. It was *buoyant*, in fact, almost like a caricature of a party. The guests' mirth was heightened and exaggerated, as though they were laying it on thick *because* Chelsea had been taken a few days before and they wanted to show whoever had done it that they weren't broken, that they were stronger than ever.

She fiddled with the strap on her shoe and eyed Aerin across the pool. She was still with that guy in the mask; she'd been worried, but Aerin signaled that she was okay. Maddox, on the other hand, stood at the edge of the dance floor, trying to blend in with the other partygoers by halfheartedly bobbing back and forth to the beat. When he noticed Seneca watching, he stopped moving, and a blush crept from his neck to his cheeks. Seneca smiled wryly – *Gotcha!* But then she remembered how nervous she felt and frowned again.

"Hey!" Kona from Quigley's Surf strutted up next to her, giving Seneca a start. "What's up?"

Seneca swallowed awkwardly, reaching for the cup of beer she'd filled a half hour ago and hadn't taken a single sip of. "Just getting my party on!" she chirped, realizing how insane she sounded.

Kona waved at someone by the bounce house. Seneca turned and recognized Alistair, Gabriel's friend who'd come to the condo. He wore a blue blazer, a silly-looking two-cornered hat, and a French flag as a cape. "Hey!" he called back, then merged into a knot of *Les Mis*-costumed girls.

As Kona bounded away, Madison appeared, clutching a completely full wine cooler and looking frustrated. "Any luck?" Madison asked.

Seneca shook her head. "No. Nothing."

"Me neither." Madison held up a copy of a New Jersey newspaper. On the front page was a headline: *Police May Have Evidence to Hold Cohen in Chelsea Dawson Abduction Case.* "But I did find this crumpled up in the bathroom."

The paper crinkled in Seneca's fingers. "What evidence could they be talking about?" she said faintly.

"It says they got another anonymous tip about how Chelsea and Jeff's relationship was violent." Madison leaned against

150

a nearby table. "What do you want to bet it was from Brett? But I guess Chelsea's parents are glomming on to anything, and they're talking about how possessive Jeff was."

"But it's not true," Seneca said quietly.

"They're bringing him in for questioning tomorrow morning." Madison widened her eyes. "You know, I saw on *Dateline* that these cops kept this kid awake for seventy-two hours, drilling him and drilling him until he confessed to a crime he didn't commit. What if they do the same to Jeff?"

Seneca's stomach clenched. "We have to try to figure out a way to prove his alibi. The faster the cops stop focusing on Jeff, the faster they might turn to the *real* person who did it."

"Agreed."

Seneca squared her shoulders and scanned the crowd again. Still no Corey. Still no one else that could be Brett. Aerin had vanished from her post across the pool. The guy in the mask wasn't there, either, but then she spotted both of them walking casually toward the food table. Had Aerin seriously picked up a date? By the dance floor, Maddox had gone back to surreptitiously dancing. Seneca giggled, despite herself. Maddox was kind of getting into the rhythm.

Madison groaned. "Would you two just get together already?"

"Huh?" Seneca blinked.

Madison gave her a knowing smile. "You heard me. You've been staring at my brother nonstop since we got here."

"I have not!" Mortified, Seneca averted her gaze from the dance floor and pretended to focus intently on a few people passing by. A guy in the third Napoleon costume she'd seen. Four girls with pink stripes in their hair. They were all wearing the same brand of fitness tracker, too. One girl's tracker lit up, proclaiming she'd achieved her step goal for the day. It was a wonder the trackers all didn't ping at once, the friends synchronized in every way.

Then a switch snapped on in Seneca's head. She looked at Madison. "Jeff's Fitbit. Oh my God."

"Huh?" Madison asked.

Seneca started to riffle in her purse, and her fingers clamped around the rubber bracelet at the bottom. She pulled it out triumphantly. "I've had this since yesterday. Jeff took it off while we were talking outside the condos, and I slipped it in my bag. I forgot to give it back."

Madison cocked her head. "So?"

Seneca plunged her hand into her bag again. The USB cord for her own Fitbit was nestled in one of the pockets. She untangled it, plugged it into her phone, and connected it to Jeff's Fitbit. "A Fitbit tracks when you move and when you sleep. I saw pictures of Jeff from the party – he had the Fitbit on. The data from the device should show us when he stopped moving – when he fell asleep. It should also show us when he started moving again the next morning. We could get GPS data from it, too – proving he stayed in that one spot."

Madison's mouth made an O. "Which proves he couldn't have done anything to Chelsea."

"Exactly."

The Fitbit app launched, and Seneca tapped the screen to import Jeff's data. As it loaded, she suddenly felt eyes on her back. She turned slowly. From behind the gate, the security guard glanced up from a game on his phone. A seagull pecked

152

at a spilled piece of food on the pool deck. The place was crammed with people, but no one was watching her.

Information popped up on the screen. Seneca scrolled back to July 10, the day Chelsea disappeared. Jeff had walked 13,492 steps and had gotten 56 minutes of cardiovascular exercise. She inspected the data from later that evening, and her heart leapt. The Fitbit tracked Jeff walking steadily from 8:00 p.m. to about 11:10 that night – a step here, several steps there, the typical behavior of someone milling around a party. But at 11:23 p.m., after walking a quarter of a mile – the distance down the grassy path to find Chelsea – the Fitbit recorded no new steps. For seven hours. Based on his heart rate, the device reported that he was in a deep REM sleep by 12:03. GPS data backed up that he was right by the parking lot, nestled in the grass. He didn't take the device off all night.

"Oh my God." Seneca squeezed her phone. "I need to call Jeff. He needs to see this." She quickly sent off a text. Within a few moments, Jeff replied, *That's incredible. Was on my way over anyway. I've got something to tell you, too.*

Seneca couldn't wipe the huge smile off her face. *Score one for me,* she thought. This would throw a wrinkle into Brett's plan; if Jeff was exonerated, the cops would focus on someone else – maybe *him.* Suddenly, she felt ready for anything he might throw her way.

Full of glee, she stood on her tiptoes and peered across the room for Maddox, who, sure enough, was still bobbing to the beat of some techno song. She waved her hands, and he headed over. Her lips stretched even wider with a smile, and all of a sudden, as she watched Maddox weaving through the crowd, his jaw set, his eyes bright, his body quick and athletic, Madison's words flashed back to her. *Would you two just get together already?*

She watched Maddox continue to make his way toward them, feeling a sense of brief lightness settle over her, despite danger lurking so close. Maybe Jeff was right. Maybe her and Maddox's auras *did* match up. Maybe they were a good match, in fact.

And maybe, just maybe, she should own that she felt the same way he did.

CHAPTER 19

Aerin didn't want to stop kissing Thomas, but she pulled away regardless, remembering the task at hand. She needed to remain vigilant. They might not have spotted Brett yet, but maybe that was because of their location. Moving around might help. "Come on," she said, taking Thomas's hand. "Let's grab some food."

They walked to the table overstuffed with snacks. Aerin felt a mix of nervous giddiness and wasn't in the mood to eat, but she grabbed a couple of pretzel rods anyway. She wasn't sure what made her look over her shoulder, but when she did, she noticed a flutter off to the left. She jolted back, doing a double take. A figure lurked behind one of the large concrete posts across the pool. He wore a black mask that concealed most of his face, but when his head turned just so, she got a look straight into his eyes. They were bright and round; if she'd been closer, she was sure they'd be blue.

They were *his* eyes. *Brett's.*

Aerin dropped Thomas's hand. "What?" Thomas asked, pulling the mask back over his face. "What's going on?"

"Quiet," she hissed, her throat tight. She could feel the heat in her cheeks. Sweat prickled on her brow. *Holy shit*, yelled one voice in her head. This couldn't be happening. It *couldn't* be him.

You need to play it cool, yelled a second voice. *You need to pretend you didn't see him*. But how long had he been standing there? Had he seen her? Had he seen *Thomas*? Finally, when she thought enough time had passed that it no longer seemed so obvious, she glanced at the concrete post once more. Brett was gone.

She took off across the pool deck. Thomas was on her heels. "Aerin," he murmured. "Tell me what's happening!"

"*Shhh*," Aerin murmured out of the corner of her mouth. "I think . . ." Then she froze. The figure in black – *Brett* – had reappeared by one of the exits.

Thomas seemed to spy him at the same time. He grabbed her wrist. "Is that . . . ?"

Aerin squeezed his hand. "*Don't look directly at him.*"

The figure in black was just *standing* there, blending into the high bushes that acted as a natural barrier around the pool. Every few seconds, his head jerked this way and that – he seemed to be searching the crowd. *He didn't see them.*

Aerin folded in her shoulders to make herself smaller. She was desperate to signal Seneca, but she didn't want to make any sudden movements that gave her position away.

"You don't know how badly I want to go over there and bash that guy's head in," Thomas murmured quietly.

"Please don't," Aerin urged. But Thomas had brought up a good point: It was insane that they were just *standing* here, just a few yards from a mass murderer, but they couldn't do anything about it. She considered the words in his message again: *I've got a killer surprise for you.* What could it be?

There was a sudden shift out of the corner of her eye, and Aerin stiffened, instantly on alert. The figure in black was now staring at a phone screen, its tiny LED light illuminated against his mask. Aerin's fingers clamped around her phone – maybe she could snap a photo of him. Suddenly, he turned sharply and headed toward a small break in the bushes. He moved quickly and with purpose, his head ducked, his shoulders hunched. In mere seconds, the darkness had swallowed him up.

Aerin glanced at Thomas. "Let's go."

They elbowed their way toward the exit. Aerin glanced over her shoulder once more for Seneca but couldn't see her through the crowd. Anxiously, she elbowed around a knot of kids doing group tequila shots and peered into the little corridor. Tiny tea lights lit the path, and the air temperature, free from the crush of bodies, had dropped at least ten degrees. Not a single person was around.

Aerin listened for footsteps, breathing, *anything*, to indicate Brett was close, and though she heard nothing, she was almost positive someone was close by. What if this was a trap? She glanced at Thomas. What if Brett was watching? What if he was furious Thomas was with her?

"Hello?" she whispered. A wave crashed in the distance. Someone splashed loudly into the pool.

"Up there?" Thomas pointed to concrete steps to their right that led to the condo's lobby through a set of double doors. Aerin nodded, and they took the stairs two at a time. At the top of the stairs, she looked around. The lobby was empty. Two elevator doors stood open. Even the front desk was eerily unoccupied.

Frowning, she stepped out of the lobby and walked down the stairs. To her left, perpendicular to the stairs and opposite the pool, was a chain-link fence. Beyond it was a vacant grassy stretch of sand that sat directly under the building's expansive terrace. Aerin squinted into the dark lot. Maybe that was where Brett had gone? All she could see were some weeds, some trash, and a Dumpster. She looked up. The terrace loomed above, awfully high. It seemed empty.

It might be a perfect place to hide.

"Come on." She grabbed Thomas's hand and pulled him through a gap in the fence and into the lot under the terrace. She bumped her bare ankles against spare boards strewn about. The area was dark, and there was a strange chemical smell emanating from the earth. Every time Aerin took a step, she kicked against more trash and debris.

She heard a whimper and turned her head. It was just the wind, swishing the grass back and forth – right? But suddenly, as she stepped around a Dumpster, something new rose up in front of her, a dark, uncertain shape on the ground that turned her limbs to stone. Her breath froze in her throat. The moment seemed to stretch out for years, but finally Aerin dared to peek more closely at what it was: a crumpled, lifeless male body, half-hidden among the trash and the reeds.

She started to scream.

CHAPTER 20

Head throbbing from standing too close to the DJ's speaker all night, Maddox was grateful when Seneca and Madison motioned him over. "Any news?" Seneca asked when he got close enough to hear.

"Nope," Maddox said. He gazed around uneasily. "It's aggravating, with everyone in masks. He could be right in front of us, and we wouldn't know."

Seneca bit her fingernail. "I know. But listen, Madison and I figured out a way to clear Jeff. His Fitbit shows that he was sleeping between eleven thirty p.m. and six a.m. the night Chelsea vanished. That can prove that he didn't abduct her."

Maddox blinked. "That's great." Of course Seneca had figured out how to exonerate him. She was amazing.

"Jeff's on his way here. After I fill him in, he can go to the police." Seneca lifted to her tiptoes to see over someone's very tall, feathered hat. "Actually, where *is* he? It's been at least ten minutes. He said he had something to tell me. It sounded urgent."

"Speaking of not being able to find people, has anyone seen Aerin?" Madison piped up. She had her hands on her hips and was squinting at the food table.

Maddox frowned and pivoted in the direction where she was staring. "Isn't she right there?" But Aerin had vanished. "Huh," he said softly, feeling a nervous frisson. "Maybe she just went to the bathroom?"

A wrinkle formed on Seneca's brow. "Someone should text her. Just in case."

Madison scrambled for her phone and sent a text. When Aerin didn't reply, she rolled back her shoulders. "I'll do a lap. I'm sure she's okay." But as she said it, her voice wobbled. Maddox's stomach clenched.

Madison's dark hair disappeared into the group, and Maddox and Seneca were alone. Seneca jiggled on her heels. "If only we could just message Brett and say, *Okay, we're here. What's your big surprise?*"

"I know." Maddox ducked out of the way of a group of girls trailing large helium balloons behind them. "Maybe his surprise is that there *isn't* a surprise?"

Seneca twisted her mouth. "Doubt it." Then her phone beeped. Madison. Maddox leaned over to view the message. *Think I see her heading toward the exit. She looks okay.*

Maddox breathed out. Then he watched Seneca scrolled through her phone some more, noting the time. "Where is Jeff?" she asked, annoyed. "I would have thought he'd drop everything to come here, considering what we discovered."

Maddox felt a lump in his throat, recalling his conversation with Jeff yesterday – especially the look of extreme disappointment on Jeff's face. "I think he'd drop everything just to see you, *period*," he said softly.

Seneca's head snapped up. "Huh?"

He let out a stifled, sheepish laugh. "Well, the guy's into you. I thought you noticed."

Seneca's mouth made a line, and two bright spots appeared on her cheeks. "Whatever," she said, gazing into the middle distance. "It doesn't mean I'm into *him*. Not like that."

"Because you're not into *anybody* right now," Maddox stated.

Seneca's head jerked toward him, and her eyes narrowed. Maddox could feel her watching him, sliding her gaze over his features. He was about to apologize – he hadn't meant the statement to sound accusatory; he was just stating facts. But when he peeked at her, she had a strange smile that seemed to be so many things at once – tentative, sad, but also . . . nervous. Jittery. Call him crazy, but he'd seen that look on her face before – he just thought he'd never see it again.

His stomach suddenly swooped. "Am I wrong?" he asked.

She turned to him head-on. Her expression had changed to something sheepish, uncertain. She coughed awkwardly into her fist. "I know this isn't the time or place for this, but I feel it needs to be said. It, well, it sucked not having our normal conversations for the last three months." She was speaking so quietly, Maddox had to lean closer to hear her. "I felt totally rudderless. I made bad decisions." She caught his gaze and lifted her chin. "I joined the Annapolis Parking Authority, for God's sake."

Maddox tried to laugh, but it came out choked. "That *is* a bad decision. I would have talked you out of that one."

In the distance, the bass thrummed. Someone laughed loudly. Seneca suddenly feigned intense interest in her thumbnail. "I wish we would have talked, period," she mumbled. "I wish . . . a lot of things."

161

She looked so timid and unsure of herself. Maddox's breath caught. Was it *possible*? He felt the corner of his lips wobble into a smile. Seneca smiled nervously, too. They both laughed, and a butterfly flapped its wings inside Maddox's stomach.

There were goose bumps on his arms as Seneca slowly took his hands. He reached out and pushed a sprig of hair from her eyes. She smiled at him crookedly, and his heart squeezed. He was going to kiss her. Pull her to him. Whirl her away from this party and . . . forget, even just for a moment.

Then they heard the screams.

They shot apart. Maddox followed Seneca as she ducked haphazardly around partygoers through a small hedge archway at the perimeter. They found Madison standing in front of a chain-link fence. "It came from there," she cried in a wobbling voice, pointing inside the vacant lot. "I think . . . I think it's Aerin."

Seneca ducked clumsily through a ragged hole in the fence. Maddox and Madison followed, blinking in the sudden darkness. When another scream rose up, his heart leapt to his throat. It was coming from somewhere very close by. He looked right and left. The patchy grass, jutting out of the gritty sand, quivered in a gust of wind. Aerin emerged in front of them, ghostlike, her eyes wild, her mouth open in a silent wail.

"What?" Seneca said, grabbing Aerin's shoulders. "What's going on? What did you see?"

"Brett?" Maddox whispered, daring to say his name out loud.

Aerin's mouth opened and closed, and she struggled to get sound out. Eyes popped wide, she gestured behind her. *"There,"* she whispered.

They pushed through the grass, bypassed some abandoned cardboard boxes, and rounded a Dumpster. Aerin stopped and pointed again. Maddox looked down. Something incongruously lumpy lay twisted on the ground. It had volume. Hardness. Angles. Seneca breathed in sharply and backed away. Maddox's eyes adjusted, but it took him a moment to understand what he was seeing. It was a hand. A human hand.

"Oh my God!" Seneca screamed. "Someone call an ambulance!"

Maddox kept looking. Connected to that hand was an arm, a shoulder, a broken neck . . . and a head. The face was in profile, the skin an ashen gray, the lips slightly parted, a mass of long, thick hair cascading around the shoulders. Maddox took in the sharp nose, the chiseled chin, the enviable cheekbones. He clapped a hand over his mouth. The world started to spin.

It was Jeff.

CHAPTER 21

The next thing Seneca really remembered, beyond the woozy backpedaling into the grass, beyond the sounds of the sirens, beyond the EMTs screaming that Jeff had no pulse, beyond Jeff's mother hysterically crying and climbing into the ambulance with her son, beyond the hand on the small of her back, guiding her and Maddox into a cigarette-stinking police cruiser with sticky backseats and non-working seat belts, was standing in the hallway of the police station next to a water fountain. The walls were white cinder block, and the air was chilly. She pressed the lever, and a stream of water made an arc near her mouth. It reminded her of an ocean wave, which reminded her how Jeff had said that she'd love surfing because she had good shoulders. And for some reason that reminded her of her mother sometimes straightening her shoulders, saying, *Don't slouch. You're such a tall, strong girl.*

It was so obvious Brett had done this to Jeff. *I've got a killer surprise for you!* And none of them had seen it coming.

"Seneca."

Aerin, who had come in a separate police car with Madison, was heading down the hall toward her. Her cheeks were stained, as if she'd been crying. Then Seneca noticed the guy standing next to her. He was tall and clean-cut, though he had the same shocked expression Aerin did. He held a Guy Fawkes mask at his side. She instantly recognized him. It was Thomas, the cop from Dexby who'd helped with Helena's case.

That sobered her up fast. "What's *he* doing here?" she snapped.

Aerin looked stricken. "I-it's a long story. But Thomas was with me when I found Jeff. He's here to help."

"We both saw Brett tonight," Thomas added. "He was at the party."

Seneca stared at Aerin, her whole body gone cold. "He knows about *Brett*?"

Aerin pushed her hair out of her round, frightened eyes. "I told him ages ago, before Brett sent that letter. But then we broke up and I forgot about it."

"I came to find Aerin in Lafayette. I demanded to be part of the investigation. Don't blame her for any of this," Thomas said.

Aerin let out a tormented whimper. "I feel like this is all my fault. I'm afraid Brett saw us talking, and he did something to Jeff."

Thomas looked pained. "I never meant for anyone to get hurt."

"But someone *did* get hurt!" Seneca roared.

"We know." Aerin covered her eyes. "We're so sorry."

Seneca bit down hard on her lip, trying to calm down. She gazed at Thomas. His skin was pale, there were circles under his eyes, and he looked drawn. It was so obvious that he'd only wanted to help. The guy had practically been the first person

165

on the scene when Marissa Ingram had accosted them at the Easter Bunny party, and he'd personally made sure each and every one of them was okay afterward. Her anger, she knew, wasn't at Thomas – it was at Brett.

"No, I'm sorry," she said wearily. "I didn't mean to snap. But I have a feeling this had nothing to do with Brett seeing you guys together." In her mind, Brett had killed Jeff because of Jeff's text to her: *I have something to tell you, too.* Maybe Jeff *had* figured something out. And maybe Brett knew.

Then she realized what Thomas had said. Her heart started to rocket. "Wait. You saw Brett was at the party? Are you sure?"

Aerin nodded. "He was all in black. I could only see his eyes – but that was enough."

"Why didn't you tell us?" Fresh despair rolled over her. Brett had been close, and she hadn't known?

"He disappeared so abruptly," Aerin explained. "I wanted to keep him in my sights, so I followed him. But when I saw Jeff in that lot, I forgot about him completely." She clapped her hand over her eyes. "I'm sorry. I ruined everything."

Seneca bit down hard on her lip. "It's not your fault," she said, her voice choked. "It's mine. I took my eye off the ball. I should have seen Brett, too . . . but I didn't." It made her feel so weak, all of a sudden. So vulnerable.

"Excuse me? Can you come in here, guys?"

A young cop with reddish hair and a smattering of freckles leaned halfway out an open door down the hall. He reminded Seneca of Woody from the Toy Story movies, earnest and friendly and a little bowlegged, though he'd said his name was Officer Ethan Grieg.

Officer Grieg gestured for the group to enter the room, which was empty save for a circular wooden table and chairs. He dropped a plain spiral-bound notebook on the table with a slap, then pushed a Coke can toward each of them. Seneca stared at the one in front of her, then shook her head, feeling too sick for sugary liquid.

"Sorry to bring you guys in." Grieg sank into a seat. "We just needed you to make a statement about what exactly happened when you found Mr. Cohen. Think you can do that?"

"Is he . . . dead?" Aerin blurted.

Grieg's gaze dropped to the table. "It's been confirmed," he said stonily. "His neck was broken, seemingly from a fall. I'm very sorry."

Seneca blinked hard, trying to process this. *A fall.* She thought about the terrace above the junkyard. Had he fallen from there? Or more accurately, had Brett *pushed* him?

Maddox briefly met her gaze, then looked away. His handsome features were muddled with torment. Seneca considered the swell of emotions she'd felt for Maddox only an hour ago but then quickly put them on a high shelf. Part of the reason she hadn't noticed Brett at the party was because she'd been dwelling on her feelings for Maddox. The price for that distraction had been Jeff's life.

With gulping breaths, Aerin and Thomas began to describe how they'd come upon Jeff in that vacant lot. Aerin must have drilled it into Thomas's head that they shouldn't mention Brett, because they both awkwardly mumbled that they'd simply been on the stairs and heard a strange noise. Seneca listened only halfheartedly to their words, instead thinking about what had just happened. Once again, Brett had done something awful, and once again, he'd gotten away.

Her blood boiled. Her hands curled into tight fists. She was so *sick* of this. She wanted justice for her mom but not at the expense of lives. She was done with Brett's game. This was about more than her now.

She looked up into the cop's bleary eyes. "It's Corey Robinson."

Grieg held his Coke halfway to his lips. "Pardon?"

"Corey Robinson. He did this to Jeff. You need to find him."

"*Seneca*," Maddox hissed from across the table.

Seneca leaned toward the cop. "We think he abducted Chelsea Dawson, too. We have a photo of them together outside the night of the party, around the time Chelsea went missing and right around where her blood was found. Jeff knew all this. Maybe he was getting too close to the truth, and Corey had to shut him up."

The only sound in the room was the rattling of the air-conditioning through the vents. Grieg sat back in his chair and crossed his arms over his chest. "First of all, it's too early to classify Mr. Cohen's death as a murder. He fell from the terrace – it could have been an accident or even a suicide, but . . . Okay. You know all this how?"

Seneca licked her lips. "We've been looking into the case. As a group."

A scowl crossed Grieg's lips. His freckles had disappeared, and his eyes darkened. "Can you tell me this kid's name again?"

Seneca repeated it. She also told him about Island Time and Kate, who'd seemed uncomfortable answering questions about Corey, and then rattled off the address he'd put on the job application. After scribbling this down in his notebook, Grieg gave Seneca a steely stare. "Don't move."

His footsteps rang through the hall. Once they faded away, Thomas cleared his throat. "Are you sure that was a good idea?"

Seneca opened her mouth, almost wanting to tell him that he didn't have the right to an opinion. But maybe she was overreacting. Brett hadn't killed Jeff because Thomas was a cop – he'd meant to do it way before he knew Thomas was even around. "This isn't a game anymore. They need to find Brett before he does something worse."

"I know, but what if telling the cops *makes* Brett do something worse?" Maddox said.

"I'm sick of Brett's stupid threats." She could feel the desperation rising in her, an almost palpable heat just beneath her skin. "This guy killed Aerin's sister. My mother. Jeff. Brett has to be stopped, *now*. It's time to end this."

The fluorescent bulbs flickered. It was so quiet in the room, Seneca could hear the carbonated bubbles in Grieg's can of Coke rising and popping. Seneca lay her head on her arms and closed her eyes, suddenly bone-weary.

When the door opened again, she jumped frantically, banging her knee on the bottom of the table. Grieg rushed in. There were a few papers crinkled in his palm. "This your guy?" he asked in an annoyed voice, slapping a photo on the table.

Everyone peered at the grainy security image. The familiar fifties lettering of the sign outside the Island Time Café was in the background. The guy in the photo was the same one

169

from the PhotoCircle – and the same one Seneca remembered at the café. The ball cap was pulled low. His head was bent. He was medium height with broad shoulders and a skulking posture.

"Yes," she said. Everyone else nodded, too. "Was he at the party?"

Grieg crossed his arms over his chest. "Corey Robinson left town with his parents yesterday – his grandfather unexpectedly passed away from a stroke, and they had to attend the funeral. And I don't think this guy kidnapped anyone. He's fifteen years old. Can't even drive."

Seneca blinked. "Wh-what?"

"Fifteen?" Madison said at the same time.

The cop sighed. "Kate Ruggio, the manager of the Island Time Café, wasn't lying to you about this guy being a criminal – she was uncomfortable about you asking questions about Corey because she'd hired him to do a forty-hour-a-week job when, as a minor, it isn't legal. She thought she was going to get in trouble. She says Corey was quiet, hard-working. Well-behaved. Just wanted to save up money so he could go to a survivalist camp next summer."

"He's not well-behaved," Maddox blurted. "We were told he brought guns to his school. Had to go to juvie."

Grieg glowered at them. "There's no record of guns or juvenile detention – we checked. You guys need to do your homework a little better."

Seneca ran her tongue over her lips. "But what about the picture of him and Chelsea together on the sidewalk outside the party? How do you explain that?"

"Mr. Robinson didn't come clean about being there earlier because, again, the kid's fifteen – he was scared about what his folks would say about trying to crash a party where there was alcohol." Grieg stacked his notes neatly. "I'm not happy that he didn't come forward sooner, but that's beside the point. He remembers briefly saying hi to Chelsea Dawson, but she was distracted. Said she was texting someone. Barely paid him any attention. Corey left shortly after. Didn't see anything weird. His father can vouch when he came home to the beach house, and a buddy of his at Wawa who sold him a Mountain Dew can place him there at eleven fifteen p.m. And as for tonight's events, Mr. Robinson wasn't even in town, so his involvement is out of the question."

There was a cold, hollow feeling inside Seneca, as though her stomach had been scooped away with a large spoon. "Oh." It was so obvious. Brett set this up. *How*, Seneca wasn't sure. But he must have.

"We're really sorry to have wasted your time," Maddox croaked.

The cop snorted. Seneca hated the pitying, condescending way he was staring at them. "Look," he said as he stood, "this is police business, okay? Take your little crew and go home, and leave the rest of this to us. We wasted forty-five minutes following up on a fifteen-year-old kid because of you guys."

There was nothing to do but leave. The blood felt hot in Seneca's veins as she stood. Someone put a hand on her shoulder, and as she turned, she realized it was Thomas. He looked pained. "As a former cop," he said in a low voice, "I can honestly say the dude that just questioned us is a major asshat."

Tears prickled Seneca's eyes, and suddenly, she felt so weary. "As a former cop, feel free to join us," she offered. "It looks like we need all the help we can get."

"I'm in," Thomas answered.

Then Seneca ducked into the bathroom at the front of the station. There was a cop in one the stalls, and she shot Seneca a tight, knowing smile as she dried her hands. Maybe everyone knew, Seneca thought. Everyone in town thought she was an idiot. She stared at her reflection in the mirror, keeping her expression neutral until the woman left. Only then did she let her composure crumble. She stuck her whole head under the faucet, though it did little to cool down her blazing cheeks.

She doubted anything would.

A squad car dropped everyone off at the gates of the B&B. Before the vehicle pulled away, Madison asked the officer if it would be dangerous if she ran to Wawa, which was only a block to the east. The officer, a youngish guy who seemed to perk up whenever Madison spoke to him, said that he'd escort her, and so she slid back into the front seat, taking Wawa orders. But Seneca couldn't fathom eating anything. Her stomach felt like a numb, hollowed-out pit, too ravaged for food ever again.

She closed the door of her room and stood on the rug. In some ways, she was grateful for the temporary solitude. After locking the windows and checking on the surveillance camera, she walked over to the minibar in the kitchen, slid in some cash, and wrenched it open. The mini bottle of Stoli burned her throat and brought tears to her eyes and unfortunately didn't make her feel much better. She pulled out another bottle and drank it just as fast. Then she returned to her room, crawled to the bed, and stared dizzily at the ceiling.

Her heart beat strongly and loudly in her chest. Her limbs felt exhausted, and all she wanted to do was sleep, but whenever she closed her eyes, the only thing she saw was Jeff being covered with a sheet and loaded onto that stretcher. Why had Brett gone after him? What had Jeff found out? Would she ever know the answer?

The door creaked open. Seneca squinted, figuring it was Madison, when suddenly she felt her mattress shift. Had Madison climbed into the bed with her?

A large, rough hand pushed her down. "Don't you dare move."

Seneca's veins turned to molten lava. She knew that voice. *Brett.*

His dark shape loomed above her. Seneca couldn't make out any of his features, but she knew without a doubt it was him.

She pivoted on her side, desperate to switch on a light. Brett clamped down on her wrist. "You move, and you're dead. You scream, and you're dead. Got it?"

Seneca let out a shaky nod. She glanced toward the vague outline of the door to the hall. *Please, someone hear.* Maddox. Bertha. That damn, ineffective dog. But the little B&B remained still. Quiet. Dark. Disinterested.

"So listen." Brett's breath was hot, and he had a familiar tangy smell about him. Bug spray, maybe. Lemon. "I'm surprised *you* haven't figured me out yet. You thought I was a fifteen-year-old kid? Really?" He sucked his teeth. "It just goes to show who's the real mastermind."

Seneca shifted her weight, and Brett moved right with her, digging his nails into her wrist. "But the game's taking too long, okay? So I'm going to speed it up. That bitch is still alive, but you have to find her by noon on Friday. After that, she's dead. I'll even help you – I'll give you some clues. Your time starts now."

His body lifted away. Seneca sprang up instantly, but Brett pushed her back to the bed. She let out a surprised squeal.

"Noon on Friday," Brett hissed. "Thirty-six hours. See you on the other side. Or not."

His footsteps creaked away. Seneca sprang up again, but the adrenaline was zooming frantically through her veins, and she felt light-headed. Her knees buckled, and she grabbed onto the bedpost to steady herself. By the time she was on her feet, it was too late. Brett had bolted into the night.

CHAPTER 22

Aerin had just gotten into bed, but she jolted up at a loud sound. *Someone was pounding on the door.*

Details from the night pounded at her temples. Thomas in the mask, begging that she speak to him. Jeff lying lifeless in the weeds behind that Dumpster. That weird scene at the police station. Being wrong, *so* wrong, about Corey.

Brett still being out there. *Killing* again.

Someone jolted up from the floor, and Aerin realized it was Thomas, who'd crashed with them instead of heading back to his motel a few towns over. Across the room, Maddox leapt from the divan and threw on a T-shirt. He peered through the peephole, then relaxed and pulled the door open. Seneca burst in mumbling hysterically. Madison followed her in tears. "I came back from Wawa and Seneca was lying in a ball and I didn't know what else to do!" Madison cried.

Aerin scrambled over the bed to Seneca, who was looking at all of them with wide, glazed eyes. "Seneca, what happened?"

Seneca's lips twitched. And then, to Aerin's horror, she uttered a single word: "Brett."

Aerin felt her heart go still. *"What?"* Thomas whispered.

"H-he was here." Seneca crawled to Aerin's bed. Her hands were shaking. "In my room. He threatened me. He said we had thirty-six hours to find Chelsea, or she was dead."

Aerin exchanged a spooked look with Maddox and Madison, then turned back to Seneca. "Oh my God," she whispered.

"What did he look like?" Maddox asked at the same time.

Seneca shook her head. "I couldn't tell. I didn't see *anything*. But it was his voice."

"I got the surveillance camera down from the window," Madison said, opening her palm and showing off the tiny device. "But it seems . . . disabled, somehow. The green light isn't flashing."

Seneca sounded so dazed. "I was so out of it when I was in my room. If he knew where it was, he could have reached up and switched it off before climbing into my bed."

Maddox winced. "Jesus," Thomas whispered. Aerin was grateful for his strong fingers entwined with hers. They made her feel – well, not safe, exactly, but at least they kept her from fainting.

"We have to tell Officer Grieg, right?" Aerin said shakily. "Maybe Brett slipped up and left a fingerprint. Maybe someone saw him come in."

"But the cops already think we're crackpots," Maddox grumbled. "If we call them now, they'll think we're crying wolf."

Madison shut her eyes. "Can we at least leave this B and B?"

"We should definitely leave," Seneca agreed. She ran her hands down the length of her face. "You guys, who *is* Brett? We were so close to him tonight. He isn't Corey, but there are still other things we know. Like his eye color. And he's connected with the B and B somehow. And *Jeff* figured out who he was – it's why Brett pushed him off that terrace. So who does that leave?"

Aerin hugged her pillow tightly. "Do you think Jeff told anyone else what he suspected? Maybe we could text one of his friends?"

"But what if the friend we text *is* Brett?" Seneca countered. Then she looked at Aerin. "At the party tonight. Can you think of who was around when you saw Brett? That will at least rule out who he *isn't*."

Aerin tried to think, but her brain felt mushy and slow. "That girl named Gwen," she said slowly. "And . . . and maybe Alistair? And some girls who liked my bag?" She looked at Thomas hopefully, but he just shrugged. "I don't know anyone's name," he said. "All I remember is that there were a few Napoleons wandering around."

"Great." Maddox sounded frustrated. "Anyone who was Napoleon *isn't* Brett."

"I'm sorry," Aerin protested. "I'm trying to think . . . but it all happened so fast, and . . ." She waved her hands helplessly, frustrated at all she couldn't remember, irritated how everyone's eyes were on her, waiting for the answer.

Shrugging, Maddox reached for an iPad from his bag and tapped an app. "Maybe we need to go back to the beginning. I bet by tomorrow we can set up a PhotoCircle from tonight's party, but until then, we have the last party – the one Chelsea was at. Brett was there, too. Look through these faces, Aerin. Tell us who you saw at the same time you saw Brett and who you *didn't* see."

The PhotoCircle popped up. Aerin scrolled through the images, pointing out various girls and guys who she was pretty sure weren't on the scene the moment Brett's dark shape had appeared – but even so, her memory felt muddled and unreliable. Coupled with the crushing exhaustion and edgy, buzzing adrenaline, she wasn't sure what was real anymore and what was a dream. Wearily, she swiped to the incriminating photo of Brianna Morten posing with her friends. Unbeknownst to Brianna, there was Corey and Chelsea, lurking out of the window. Aerin stared at it a moment, glassy-eyed and tired, and then swiped once more. Then her mind caught. She scrolled back and squinted, suddenly sure of something. "There's something weird about this picture."

Maddox leaned in. "What?"

She pointed to the smiling girls in the foreground, then Corey and Chelsea out of the window. "Everyone is in focus. Most cameras can't do that."

Thomas leaned back. "Most . . . or all?"

"I think a trained photographer can make everything in focus, even at different depths. But a camera phone can't handle it. And certainly not a person at a party handling a camera phone. It's doubtful, anyway. I wonder if this was Photoshopped."

Madison's eyes were large. "How?"

Aerin leaned in. She'd hooked up with a kid from the local arts school last year, and it wasn't like she'd wanted a lesson in photo retouching, but he'd gone straight back to his Mac post-kissing, and she'd been bored. "Someone could have taken a picture of Chelsea and Corey on the street and dropped it into Brianna's photo, making it look accidental. Someone could have even taken a photo of Corey and Chelsea *separately*, then put them together in Photoshop making it *look* like they were talking. I'm not even sure the photo of them was taken from this same window. The perspective seems a little weird."

"So theoretically," Maddox said slowly, a skeptical look on his face, "Brett could have taken a photo of Chelsea, or even of Chelsea and Corey, from somewhere else – wherever he was hiding. But then dropped it into *this* photo, which matches our timeline and incriminates Corey."

"Exactly," Aerin said.

"But it says the picture is from Brianna's phone," Madison argued. "How could Brett have gotten access to her pictures?"

"It can be done," Thomas piped up. "I've seen savvy hackers do all kinds of things."

"Maybe he was watching photos pop up on our stream." Seneca shifted on the bed, making the springs creak. "When he saw this shot, he grabbed it, dropped in Corey and Chelsea, and figured out a way to post as her."

Maddox made a face. "That seems too coincidental. Brett would have had to freeze time, practically, to find just the right photo, do Photoshop magic on it, and hack into our stream to make it look like this was coming from Brianna's account."

"But the more I look at it, the more I'm sure it was Photoshopped," Aerin said, staring at the images until her vision blurred. "So how is that possible?"

Madison looked up. "Wait. When we called J.T., he mentioned another Photo Circle, didn't he?"

Seneca narrowed her eyes. "Who?"

"You're right." Aerin filled Seneca in on the call with J.T., which she'd missed because she'd been outside with Jeff. "J.T. sounded annoyed, like this was wasting everyone's time. Maybe the cops – or another friend – asked for a PhotoCircle before we did. And everyone joined *that* PhotoCircle, uploaded their pictures. Is it possible?"

"No one else mentioned another PhotoCircle, but it doesn't mean there wasn't one," Seneca said. "We should take a look. I bet Brianna's picture is in that one, too. And maybe Brett saw that photo and realized he could use it to set Corey up. I don't know how he broke into her account again and slipped the doctored photo in her camera roll, but he might have had days to do that, not minutes. That seems more likely, right?"

Maddox laced his fingers across the back of his head. "So you're saying Brett planned to set up Corey from the start, then?"

Seneca shifted on the bed, making the springs creak. "I think so. For other reasons, too. When I pointed Corey out to Jeff, Jeff had a rumor ready about him – about the guns. But the cops said it wasn't true."

Aerin felt her heart start to pound. "That rumor threw suspicion on Corey – for us and everyone else. Could Brett have started it to set up Corey?"

Maddox squinted. "We need to figure out who started the rumor, then. Because if we do . . ."

"It'll lead us to Brett," Seneca finished.

Aerin grabbed her phone, suddenly feeling energized. "Who can we ask? Alistair? Kona? Gabriel?"

"What about Jeff's brother?" Seneca asked. "Jeff knew the rumor – Marcus probably does, too. I have his number."

"I don't know?" Aerin asked uneasily. "His brother just *died*."

"This could lead to his brother's killer," Seneca urged. "Though, good point. Maybe just send a text? And if he doesn't reply, we can try someone else?"

Seneca scrolled through her phone and found Marcus's name. Aerin listened to the double *ping* of the message zinging into the ether, then stood and pulled up the shades. The sun was just rising, streaking the sky with whitish-pink clouds. A few seagulls stood in the front yard, pecking at something on the grass. Two joggers passed, shoes cheerfully slapping against the pavement.

"Wait a minute," Seneca said suddenly.

Aerin turned. Seneca's brow was knit in concentration. Her hands lay calmly in her lap. "When Brett attacked me tonight, he mentioned that we thought he was a *fifteen-year-old boy*. But we never said Corey's name out loud at the party. I can't see how he'd know what we said to the cops in that interrogation room unless he bugged the police station. The only other place we talked about him freely was at Island Time – but I didn't see anyone around there watching. It was so *early*. But we did talk about Corey a lot when we were first looking through the PhotoCircles. Where were we?"

Madison frowned. "At those condos. On Gabriel Wilton's back deck."

Seneca nodded, like she already knew. "And did you notice any cameras there? Microphones?"

Madison laughed nervously. "Why? Do you think the place was bugged?"

"Why would Brett bug a random kid's condo?" Maddox asked.

Aerin suddenly understood where Seneca was going. Was it *possible*? She shuddered, then glanced over her shoulder, fearful Brett was standing there, watching. It wasn't so unimaginable, maybe. After all, he'd been in front of them all along.

Seneca's phone buzzed. She scrambled to wake up the screen. "Marcus," she whispered, and then looked at the text. Her eyes widened. Wordlessly, she turned the phone around for the others to see. But Aerin didn't have to read it. She already knew.

I remember exactly who told me those rumors. Gabriel Wilton.

CHAPTER 23

"*Shit.*" Seneca stared at the text. "We should have seen this coming."

Maddox swallowed shakily. "Gabriel bugged his condo. That's probably why he offered for us to hang out there all day. He wanted to know what we were talking about and how close we were to figuring out who he is. He probably heard us talking about Corey."

"Do you think this is what Jeff figured out?" Aerin whispered.

"Probably," Seneca said. She felt so frustrated. How was it possible they'd been in Brett's home . . . and she'd missed it? And if Jeff had figured out the truth, why hadn't he just texted his suspicions? Why was he waiting to see her face-to-face?

Unless he wasn't sure he was right. Gabriel was a friend, after all. *And* he'd said he was standing behind Jeff's innocence.

Aerin paced around, deep in thought. "So Gabriel – *Brett* – planted those rumors about Corey in the same way he planted rumors about Jeff on Case Not Closed," Aerin added. "Anything to direct our attention away from his identity."

Madison hugged a pillow tightly. "But people *know* Gabriel. *We* know Gabriel. Does this even make sense?"

183

"We don't *really* know him," Maddox scoffed. "We met him for a few minutes, and then he left. I didn't get a vibe he was Brett, but he had on sunglasses, and he had different hair, and his voice was so surfer dude . . . not like Brett at all."

"Thomas and I saw him at the party, but it was from far away," Aerin said. "He was dressed up. And Brett was all in black. Why would Gabriel go to all the trouble to change if he was already fooling us?"

Seneca's eyes lit up, the answer suddenly so obvious. "Unless he wanted you to see him, Aerin. He knew you'd focus on a guy in black. He knew you'd follow him when he ran out. It's obvious – he wanted you to find Jeff. He *led* you there. It was part of his surprise."

Aerin ran her hand over her chin. "Brett did take off kind of suddenly," she said in a shaky voice. "And he went straight to that vacant lot."

Seneca stood again. The sludgy, dirty feeling from having encountered Brett had faded, and now she felt refueled and buzzing. "Okay. If I were to do a timeline, I'd say Brett knew he was going to kill Jeff way ahead of time – that's why he sent us that *killer surprise* message. He must have figured out a way to get Jeff to come. And who knows? My message about the Fitbit might have helped, too." She felt guilty suddenly, like she'd been unwittingly pulled into Brett's murder plot. "At the party, Brett put in an appearance as 'Gabriel,' the host. But when he realized Jeff was on his way – which I'm not sure how he figured out, except maybe he was tracking Jeff's phone, somehow?"

"That's possible," Thomas interrupted. "There are apps that spy on phones."

"Right." Seneca nodded. "Anyway, after Brett realized Jeff was coming, he ducked out of the party and met him at the condo's entrance. Took Jeff to the terrace. Found a shadowy spot and pushed him into the vacant lot. Then he changed into his black hoodie and reappeared at the party as this anonymous creeper, waiting for one of us to spot him."

Everyone paused for a beat, taking this in. Thomas reluctantly nodded. "Whoa," Madison said, looking stunned.

Maddox cleared his throat. "And doesn't 'Gabriel' work at a realty place? Bertha told us she has a regular renter – that old guy, Harvey. Perhaps his company manages renters at this B and B, too. Maybe that's how the dog knows him."

"Also, living at that condo gives him easy access to the scene of the crime," Seneca added. "He knew of a private path and parking lot where he could grab Chelsea. He probably knew of a spot where he could plant a getaway car. He also knew of a secluded terrace where he could kill Jeff. It all fits."

Thomas paced the room. "So what do we do now?"

"Let's check out the condos," Maddox said. "The cops are crawling all over the place there, but we might get lucky. Brett might have left us a clue."

Seneca nodded, crackling with adrenaline. "Bring it on."

The sun was just coming up as the group pulled up to the condos. Some of the building was swathed with police tape because of Jeff's attack. Quite a few cops stood out front, hands in pockets or tucked around coffee cups, their postures slumped and weary. Seneca and the others discussed a strategy about getting into the condos without a keycard, but it ended up not being an issue – one of the gates stood wide open. Maddox slipped through. "I guess they forgot to close this after the party last night?"

"Or else Brett is laying a trap for us," Madison said warily.

Seneca's stomach flipped. Could that be true? What if Brett anticipated their arrival? But then she straightened. No. The cops were here.

They passed the pool area, which was still messy with overstuffed trash cans, beer bottles, and colorful napkins strewn like confetti over the deck from the party. The deflated bounce house lay on its side. At the stairs that led to Gabriel's condo they paused. "Look, it's likely that Brett's gone," Seneca whispered. "He's too smart to hang around the scene of the crime with all these cops. But maybe we can get into his place. Dig up some clues to where he went."

Aerin bit on a thumbnail. The last thing she wanted was to be inside the place where Brett slept *again*. One time was enough.

A crack sounded through the air, and everyone froze. Seneca pulled the group under the stairs. Footsteps creaked to their left, then above. Someone was walking on Gabriel's landing.

Aerin turned to Seneca, fear in her eyes. Maddox clamped down hard on her wrist. They might be smushed into the stairwell, but their bodies cast long, overt shadows on the pavement. If Brett came down here, he would see them immediately.

When a second crack boomed, everyone tensed. Next came a loud bang. "Open up!" a voice shouted. Seneca peered up the stairs. Two figures in black stood on Gabriel's deck. Police officers?

A cop opened Gabriel's door, which appeared to be unlocked. "Mr. Wilton?" Both men disappeared inside the condo. "Mr. Wilton, it's Dalton County Police. Please come out. We'd like to ask you some questions."

Seneca looked at the others in alarm. "How do the cops know it's him?" she whispered. Everyone looked just as blindsided as she did. Maybe they were just asking Gabriel questions because it had been his party? Because he'd been Jeff's friend?

Suddenly, a *bloop* sounded on her phone. It was an alert Seneca had set up for the Chelsea Dawson thread on Case Not Closed. *Chelsea Dawson, Lafayette, NJ, has a new post!*

She clicked on it. As she read the post, she frowned. This had to be a joke. Aerin studied her. "What?"

Seneca's eyes scanned the message. *"Always said I was a master,"* she read aloud, her voice faltering. *"Turns out Chelsea's cell provider's records aren't too secure, and I found out she's got two phone lines, not one. I don't think friends and family knew of the second line, though. Did a little digging into that second phone: lots of pics. Sexy ones that were way too explicit for Instagram – maybe she was hoping to upload them somewhere more hard-core that Mom and Dad wouldn't know about. And she talks to only one person on this phone: someone named Gabriel. Anyone know who he is? Looks like her last text to him was moments after she fought with her boyfriend at the party. But she blows him off. I smell a motive!"*

Maddox looked stunned. "Who posted that?"

Seneca's lip twitched. A hot, slimy feeling crept over her bones. "BMoney60."

Aerin burst out laughing. "Yeah right."

"It's true."

The freaked-out smile faded from Madison's face. She peered up at Gabriel's condo, then back at them. "Wh-why would Brett set up himself?"

"Is there a chance Brett *isn't* Gabriel?" Maddox whispered.

Another crash sounded over their heads, and everyone jumped. The cops tramped out of the condo, guns lowered. Seneca craned her neck, desperate to see Brett, but the men were empty-handed. They looked frustrated. "There's nothing here," one of them boomed. "We have forensics coming, but I bet they won't be able to find a single print. It looks like the whole place has been wiped clean."

A tempestuous wind kicked up from the sea, bringing with it a blast of cold, unsettling air. Seneca suddenly understood. Brett was definitely Gabriel . . . but this was all part of his plan. This was all just a distraction. Brett was gone, and he'd already become someone else.

She watched as the police hurried away, then stared up at the door to the condo. It was ajar. "Come on," she whispered, heading up the stairs.

"Why?" Maddox called after her. "Cops just said it was free of prints, and now you'll get yours all over the place."

"I just want to check it out. I won't touch anything, and it'll just take a minute."

She slipped through the open door and into the space. The condo still smelled of sandalwood and cleanser, but as the cops pointed out, it was immaculate. The pillows were arranged just so on the couch. Everything gleamed from the refrigerator handles to the buttons on the microwave. Without touching anything, she peered into the sink and found no dishes – obviously, because that would leave DNA. She peeked into the bathroom. The mirror was spotless. The sink shone a bright white. Brett hadn't left a toothbrush, a bar of soap, or a comb. The shower didn't contain a single hair. The toilet looked unused. Pulling her sleeve over her hand, she tipped open the medicine cabinet, hoping to find Rohypnol or something like it – a drug that could have knocked Jeff out the first time he was Brett's victim, the night Chelsea vanished. A single bottle of Advil stood on the top shelf. Of course Brett was too smart to leave anything incriminating behind.

She walked out of the bathroom, feeling uneasy. The others had gathered by the door, ready to bolt. Seneca wasn't sure why she doubted the cops' assessment of the place – she just had an odd feeling a stone had been left unturned. Suddenly, she spotted it: There, lying just inside the door, was a piece of paper. She ran and scooped it up. It was a flyer made of light, slick paper. Parts were crumpled, and the edges had greasy, food-stained fingerprints, but when she saw something in the corner, she gasped. "Holy shit," she whispered.

Maddox crouched down and looked at it with her. "*Sushi Monster,*" he read off the front of the flyer. "So?"

"*Look.*" Seneca pointed with shaking hands. In the corner, in faint pencil, were her initials: *SF.*

Brett knew they were going to come here. He knew they were going to figure him out. And he'd left this here . . . for her.

She just didn't know why.

CHAPTER 24

Brett stood in the empty room and peered out of a gap in the dusty wooden blinds. The cops strolled out of the condo and climbed into their vehicles, looking dejected and puzzled. Moments later, he saw his ragtag bunch of pals slip upstairs. Brett felt a smile spread across his lips. *Bingo.* It was good to be back on track.

Yesterday, things had almost derailed. He knew Jeff had figured him out – through tracker software, he'd found that Jeff had checked out "Gabriel's" social media accounts thirty-two times in the past day. He'd seen Jeff's car passing by the condo *three* times between early yesterday morning and noon. When he called the realty office, his boss said that "that tall kid who's been on the news" had been in to see him. He and Jeff weren't *that* close. He wasn't visiting for friendly reasons.

So Brett had gotten to work quickly, organizing his next steps, sending that message to Seneca about the killer surprise, convincing Jeff to come to the party after all. But he'd been so caught up in his plan that he'd made a critical error: He'd left Jeff to stew in his suspicions. Jeff could have spilled the beans to Seneca – or even the cops – before the party. Thankfully, he hadn't . . . but Brett was astounded at his oversight. He was usually so calculated about every last detail. This could have been a disaster.

But he'd been spared. Everything was *fine*. And really, he'd only made a teeny, tiny mistake – barely a blip on the radar. He'd be more careful from now on. He was ready, and he was thrilled to ratchet up the game. *Bring it on*, he murmured silently to the group, watching them pause in the doorway of his condo. And then he paced through the empty house across the street, opened the front door, and locked it neatly behind him with his realty-office key. That was the nice thing about working there. He had access to all sorts of places all over town. Instant hideaways, whenever he needed them.

Later, instead of heading into Command Central, he unlocked Chelsea's room and walked in. The air smelled fragrantly of lily of the valley. So she'd been burning the candles. Spritzing perfume.

The toilet flushed noisily. The door to the bathroom opened, and she stepped out dressed in the gold empire-waist minidress he'd left hanging for her in the open closet while she slept. Their eyes met, and she froze. Her brows pinched together, and for a moment, she smiled hopefully. But something in Brett's face must have given him away, because she suddenly seemed to understand he wasn't her knight in shining armor. The corners of her mouth went slack.

She turned an odd shade of yellow. *"Gabriel?"*

"It's nice to see you," Brett said, taking a step toward her.

Chelsea cowered back, hands curled at her chest. "D-don't come any closer."

Brett pointed. "I really like that dress. The color looks great on you."

She opened her mouth, but no sound came out.

"And you've fixed your hair. It looks so nice, don't you think?"

Chelsea's bottom lip trembled. When Brett took her arm, she let out a pained whimper. Her forearm felt boneless. "I thought you might like to see what's going on in the world." He led her over to the chair closest to the TV. "Here. Sit."

Chelsea sat slowly, cautiously, seemingly understanding that he wasn't to be disobeyed. She was spasming with fear, her knees jumping, her fingers twitching. Brett hovered over her, breathing in the herbal scent of her shampoo. He turned on the TV. "You're everywhere now. You're such a star." On CNN, her picture popped on the screen. Her parents appeared next, looking haggard, like they hadn't slept in years. Chelsea let out a choked wail and covered her eyes.

"I can't believe it's you," she whispered behind her hands. "Wh-why would you do this to me? I thought we were friends."

Friends. That word was like a branding iron on his skin. Friends confided in each other. Friends didn't lead each other on. Friends weren't users.

Brett clucked his tongue. "Has it really been that bad? You've had food. Shelter. Makeup. I've noticed you admiring your new clothes in the mirror. I bet you really want to take a selfie."

Then he slipped the phone out of his pocket. Chelsea's eyes widened at its shiny pink case. Brett bet she was trying to figure out which phone it was – the one everyone knew about, or the one only he did. He remembered the day he'd bought the second device for her. *Guys get jealous,* he'd said. *If*

Jeff finds out we're friends, if he knows we talk so much, he won't be happy. This'll be our secret. Trust me on this one.

"I saved it for you," he cooed.

"C-can I see that?" Chelsea reached for it. "Can I tell my parents I'm okay?"

He held the phone aloft. "Out of the question. But I'll take a picture of you." He held it to her face, super close, and on cue, she gave a small, weak smile. He looked at the screen. "Not your prettiest. Let's try again."

Chelsea swallowed back tears and dutifully smiled. Brett nodded – much better. Then, after a moment, she seemed to gather her courage again. Her eyes darted over his features. Slowly, she licked her trembling lips. "I'll give you whatever you want. Anything to make you happy. I know you think I'm hot. Well, here's your chance. We can be a couple in real life. We'll tell everyone. Would that make you happy?"

Brett snorted. Didn't she realize that was exactly why he'd chosen to punish her? Because she thought everyone loved her. Because she thought her beauty could afford her – and forgive her of – anything and everything. It was despicable.

He uncurled her fingers from his skin. "It's too late for that."

Chelsea's face crumpled. Then something caught her attention on TV, just past him in her line of sight. Jeff Cohen's face swam into view. *Suspect dead*, read the caption.

Chelsea's mouth dropped open. "Jeff's . . . *dead*?"

Brett turned away. He rankled at the pain in Chelsea's voice. "Why do you still care about him?"

Something new appeared on the screen. *Second Suspect in Dawson Kidnapping Case AWOL*. In the photo, Brett's hair was longer than he liked. His beard was almost unbearable to look at, almost comical. Thank God he was shedding the look today. Because now, like the newscaster said, everyone was looking for Gabriel Wilton.

Chelsea stared at the screen, then at him. Her eyes showed a mix of vindication and fear. "They've got you," she said in a small voice.

Brett snorted. "No, they don't."

He stood. Chelsea was staring at him in confusion, her pretty mouth hung open. All of a sudden, it was as though she was made of something extremely delicate – flour, maybe, or sand – and if he touched her, if he flicked her just so, she'd collapse to nothing.

"There, there," he soothed. "No need to worry. It will all be over soon." And then he patted the girl on her head, turned on his heel, and left the room, locking it tight.

CHAPTER 25

At 10:00 a.m., Maddox and the others stood on the main drag between a pancake house and an office called Golden Shores Realty. The pancake house was a bright space, painted in cheerful shades of yellow and orange; tourists were eating stacks of waffles and fluffy, buttery omelets. But the mood was fraught – there were three cop cars on the sidewalk, and the crimes that had rocked Lafayette were on everyone's lips as they waited in line for a table. Maddox had heard the name Gabriel Wilton from at least three different groups – the news had broken this morning that Gabriel was a "person of interest" in the Chelsea kidnapping case. As the news told it, an anonymous tip on a crime website revealed evidence of a second phone line in Chelsea's name, and after some scrambling, the cops were able to track it down and look through its records. Apparently, Gabriel and Chelsea texted nonstop, including the night of the party. His flight from his condo without warning was very incriminating.

Seneca breathed in sharply and pointed out an overweight bleached-blonde woman wearing too much pink lipstick walking quickly into the real estate office. *"There."* It was Amanda

Iverson, Gabriel Wilton's boss. They'd been waiting for her to show up to work all morning. Seneca hurried over to the woman. Maddox followed.

"Mrs. Iverson?" Seneca trilled.

The woman looked up cautiously. Her gray eyes narrowed. But before Seneca could say more, a reporter elbowed past her. "Mrs. Iverson! Can we get a few words?" The reporter shoved a microphone in her face. "How well did you know Gabriel Wilton? Did you ever suspect he might be a kidnapper?"

Mrs. Iverson fumbled to push her keys into the lock. "No comment."

"Do you know where he might have taken Miss Dawson? Has he ever seemed violent to you?"

The woman finally got the door open. Her keychain, a large pink rabbit's foot, swung merrily from the lock. "I've told the police everything I know." She hurried into the office and slammed the door shut. The reporter pounded on it, and she pulled down the shade. Shrugging, the man retreated to the sidewalk, then stopped a passerby. "What do *you* think about the Chelsea Dawson abduction?" he asked smoothly, microphone at the ready.

Thomas glowered at the reporters. "They're like vultures."

Madison was studying a report on her phone. "According to this, the cops can't link Gabriel Wilton to a bank account – he paid for everything in cash. Also, it says his Prius is missing. He took things from the condo. No one has seen him anywhere."

Maddox sank down onto a wooden bench next to the street. "That's because he isn't *Gabriel* anymore. He's someone else. And I'm sure he ditched that Prius somewhere it'll never be found."

196

Then he caught sight of a TV broadcast on the set over the counter at the pancake house. A reporter stood in front of the local hospital. He knew they were talking about Jeff Cohen. He was about to turn away when an image caught his eye: a simple selfie of an unsmiling Jeff on Instagram. Below the picture, highlighted for clarity, was a simple, horrifying sentence: *Sometimes it's all just too much.*

His jaw dropped. He grabbed his phone and called up Jeff's account. The post was there. It had uploaded yesterday at 9:08 p.m. – around the time Seneca had hinted that she was into him.

"Seneca," he said sharply, motioning her over. Her eyes widened as she read the post and the comments beneath it, which said things like, *Wish we'd have talked more, man*, and *A life cut short*, and a number for the suicide prevention hotline.

Seneca's eyes darted back and forth. "Do we know what happened to Jeff's phone?"

Maddox nodded. "Cops found it smashed near his body. They figure it was on him when he fell."

She gritted her teeth. "Or the person that pushed him could have tossed it over after posting his suicide message on social media."

"Exactly." It felt like another big point scored for Brett.

Seneca slapped her hands to her sides. "Well, there's nothing we can do about it now. But we have to get Brett. We *have* to." She held up the Sushi Monster menu they'd taken from "Gabriel's" condo. "This has to mean something."

A couple in a golf cart whizzed by down the main street. Someone was blasting a thrash metal song out of an open car window. Maddox studied it carefully. "Maybe it's something on Instagram? Have we searched Sushi Monster on her account?"

"Searched on her account, searched for the hashtag in general – there isn't much," Aerin grumbled. She showed everyone her phone. A Chelsea video from a few months ago was playing. Chelsea's face flooded the screen, her smile white, her eyes glittering. "Hey, everyone! I just want to say first that I am thrilled that all of you followed me. Thank you so much for the love! And now, because I know you've been waiting, here's what I've been up to this week . . ."

Aerin and Madison studied Instagram some more, though there were no sushi references. Thomas loitered in front of the realty office, perhaps waiting for Mrs. Iverson to pop back outside. Seneca retreated to Maddox's bench, her leg bumping against his as she sat. He smiled, but she looked away quickly and anxiously jiggled her foot.

"So," he said, his voice cracking. He so badly wanted to say something about what had happened between them at the party. Part of him wondered if it even *had* happened, it had been so fleeting. But it was like that Seneca had disappeared again, swallowed up by Crime-Solving, I'm-Going-to-Get-Brett Seneca. Now definitely wasn't the right time.

She held the sushi menu in her hands, folding it back and forth over the well-worn creases. "He left this deliberately. I can *feel* it."

"Maybe this is Brett's favorite take-out place?" he posited, but he felt so stymied. They'd been staring at this crazy menu for hours and it just looked . . . well, like a menu. But suddenly, something caught his eye, and he leaned in. Beams of sunlight

198

illuminated the shiny paper, giving it a slight iridescent sheen and sharpening all its blemishes. Invisible before, he now noticed a few light pencil marks around certain menu items. Edamame, Krab Stick, and the First Date roll were circled.

He pushed it to Seneca. "Look."

Her eyebrows shot up, and she brought the menu closer to her face. "Maybe it's the first letter of each dish. E, K, P? Or maybe First Date is significant?"

"Or maybe it's their numbers." The first dish was number nineteen on the Appetizers, the second nine on the sushi nigiri menu, and the third was three on sushi rolls. "Nineteen, nine, three," he said aloud. "A locker combination?"

Seneca stood and stared across the street at a large, decorative sign. When there was a break in the traffic, she hurried across; Maddox loped behind. It was a cartoon map of Lafayette. The pancake house they were standing at was drawn at the top of Ninety-Fifth Street, Hoy's was at the bottom, and it showed the surf shop, the fudge place, the ice creamery, and the Wawa. Spiraling out from the main drag were the other streets, and at the very bottom of the map were abstract swirls that represented the sea.

"What if it's an address?" she whispered.

They exchanged a glance. Maddox raised his eyebrows. The corners of Seneca's mouth pulled into a nervous smile. They waved over Madison, Aerin, and Thomas, saying they needed to get going.

"Go where?" Madison asked warily.

"We'll explain on the walk," Seneca said. "Come on."

* * *

The house at 19 Ninety-Third Street had three different vehicles with Fraternal Order of Police bumper stickers in the driveway, and at one point, a burly, rugged, strong-looking roughneck appeared on the patio and glared. One Ninety-Ninth Street led to a ramshackle building next to a marina, and it didn't have an apartment 3. But there was a 1993 Yellowtail Drive, which seemed promising, as yellowtail was an item on the sushi menu, and maybe that was a link.

They drove up wearily, desperate for a lead. The house on Yellowtail Drive was a large yellow Victorian with four second-story decks, three quaint gables, and a fish-shaped wind sock blowing on the front porch. The front offered a view of the town's public water tower, and Maddox could hear the roaring ocean a block away. When he was younger and it was just him and his mom, his mother used to pin pictures of beach houses just like this one into a scrapbook, saying someday they'd get to vacation somewhere like here.

The house was quiet, and there were no cars in the spaces on the street. There was a big sign out front that proclaimed the house was managed by a local rental agency – the agency, in fact, that Brett, aka Gabriel, worked for – but it didn't seem like anyone was renting it for the week. Madison curled her hands around the wrought-iron gate. "Do you really think she's in there? All the windows are huge, and nothing's covered. We can see right in."

"Maybe there's a basement?" Aerin asked.

Seneca peered at the foundation for small windows that indicated a lower floor. "I don't think there's one." She started to walk around the perimeter. Her sneakers crunched in the white-gravel yard. "What are you looking for?" Maddox asked as he trailed behind her.

"I'm not sure." She stooped to pick up something under a pebble, but it was only the top to a Sprite bottle. Maddox peered at the electric meter in the back, then poked his toe into a bush. The yard was pristine. The gravel was carefully raked, like a Zen garden.

But when Maddox crunched around to the other side of the house, he stopped short. "Whoa." Tied to the railing of the lower deck, bobbing in the sky, was a shiny balloon with a rainbow peace sign printed across its front. Maddox's breath caught. That same peace sign was the logo on Gabriel's Bastille Day party flyer. "Guys!"

The others came running. Maddox untied the balloon from its post; the string went taut in his hand, the balloon tugging toward the sky. Was it a clue? There wasn't any writing on the balloon. No note tied to the string.

He let it lift into the air once more; the balloon recoiled when the string went taut. Seneca frowned. "Do that again."

Maddox grabbed the balloon between his hands, pulled it down, and let it bob to the sky once more. "It sounds like there's something rattling around inside," Seneca said.

Madison backed away. "An explosive."

Maddox gazed around. The street was so still. It was like no one lived in this town at all. Far away, he could hear a police siren. Overhead, an airplane groaned. When the wind shifted, he swore he caught sight of something moving behind the bushes, but when he looked away, it was gone.

He turned back to Seneca. "Should we open it?"

She nodded, her hands already at the gathered rubber at the bottom of the balloon. Within moments, she had pried it open. Helium began to leak out, and the balloon deflated quickly. She pressed the balloon between her palms. "There *is* something in here."

She worked to slash the peace sign in two. A folded piece of paper tumbled out, and Maddox gasped. On the front of the paper, generically typed with the same wonky typewriter as the one that had been used for his letter, was the name *Seneca*.

Seneca snatched it and unfolded it. Her eyes scanned, and she frowned. "Huh?" Maddox glanced over her shoulder, but the message made no sense to him, either.

Red, white, and awesome
With some caramel syrup and
a spot over the eye.
I met her, and it was love.
Thought she thought so, too.

CHAPTER 26

That afternoon, Seneca hefted her suitcase onto the bed of her new room at the Reeds Hotel. The sheets smelled fresh, and there wasn't a single cat or crotch-sniffing dog to be found – little details that should make her happy if her stomach wasn't shredded to ribbons and her mind wasn't swimming with questions. It was unclear whether people had hightailed it out of Lafayette because of Chelsea's disappearance or the news of Jeff's death, but all four of them were able to score their own hotel rooms – no more sharing. But the privacy was no longer welcome for Seneca. As soon as she shut her door, she started to tremble. The room was too empty. Too quiet. The gauzy curtains fluttered, and she jumped. She checked under the bed and in the closets just to make sure Brett wasn't there.

Then she sat down on the bed and unfolded the latest note from Brett in her hands. That weird little poem. What did it mean? It spoke about meeting Chelsea somewhere – so where had Brett and Chelsea first laid eyes on each other? At a party? In a parking lot? At the beach? The poem said *caramel syrup* – so maybe an ice cream place? They'd piled into Maddox's Jeep and cruised every ice cream joint up and down Lafayette, but they'd found nothing. Or maybe it was a Fourth of July reference with *red, white, and awesome*? They'd called J.T., Kona from the surf shop, Alistair, and even Amanda Iverson, Gabriel's boss from the rental company the press had hounded that morning. Mrs. Iverson didn't answer. Nor did Jeff's brother. When Kona spoke, he said, "Are we *sure* Gabriel's to blame in all this? I mean, he's so . . . *chill*."

Seneca had resisted explaining to Kona that Brett was many things, but *nice* definitely wasn't one of them.

She sat down at the room's little table, wondering if the message was encoded. Cryptograms? Rearranging the first and last letters of each word? Shifting the phrase several letters forward? An hour into her work, her phone bleated. It was the alarm she diligently set to check in with her father. She stared at it for a moment, trying to muster up the energy. Part of her wished she were home with her dad, curled up on the couch. Safe. Ignorant.

She dialed him, and her father answered on the second ring. He was in his office, she could tell – his voice echoed in the high-ceilinged room. "How are you?" he asked.

"Fine," Seneca lied. "The weather's great. Aerin and I took a paddle-boarding lesson."

"Ah, they didn't offer paddle-boarding when we vacationed there," her father said. Seneca's heart broke at the trust in his voice. Then he cleared his throat. "Listen, I've seen on the news that there's some trouble there – some kid jumped to his death?"

She tensed her shoulders. *Here we go*. "Yeah, I heard about that, too," she said carefully. "Off a balcony at some party? Is that what they're saying on the news?"

"I don't know." She heard a voice in the background, and her father paused to murmur something. "Just promise me you're being careful," he said.

"I am. I swear." She dug her nails into the comforter.

"You coming home soon?"

"Tomorrow," she whispered. "I'll definitely leave tomorrow afternoon." If Brett didn't kill her first.

Then her father hung up. Just like that. She could sense he was worried about her . . . but he was trying to give her some independence. Lying made her feel dirty and ashamed. *It'll be worth it*, she told herself. But would they ever find Brett? What if this was a dead end?

All of a sudden, she felt panicked. She stood, stepped into the hall, and walked to the room three doors down. It took Maddox a few moments to appear after she knocked. "Seneca?" His eyes widened at her expression. "Are you okay?"

"I can't figure it out, Maddox. We're going to lose."

"Don't say that," Maddox scolded. "You can't give up."

Seneca stared at him. "But I have no idea what Brett means, and we're running out of time."

"Hey," Maddox said softly. "We're going to get him, Seneca. I can feel it."

But Seneca wasn't so sure. She sat on his bed and tried to think, but all she could feel was the panic hammering at her. It was as though all her fears and worries and shame had been contained inside a shaken-up bottle and someone suddenly undid the cap. She was overflowing, out of control.

But no. She *couldn't* lose control. That was what Brett wanted. She sat up and took a deep breath. Maddox was watching her carefully. She couldn't imagine what she looked like. But suddenly, it didn't matter. Maddox was seeing her at her absolute worst, puffy-eyed, a total wreck, and it was . . . well, maybe not okay, but not totally horrible.

"You're right," she said. "You *have* to be right. We'll find him." She ducked her head. "Sorry about the freak-out."

"No problem," Maddox said gently. His throat caught. "I never mind you freaking out."

Seneca hid a smile, sadly remembering their talk at the party. It felt like a million years ago. Pushing the desire away, she unfolded Brett's note again and studied it as though seeing it for the first time. "Is this something Brett had said to us, once? Something buried in Chelsea's Instagram? What does he mean *a spot over the eye*? Did he *punch* Chelsea?"

"I don't think we can rule anything out," Maddox said. "Aerin and Madison are looking through her Instagram now, to make sure."

She carried the note over to Maddox's little table by the window and sat down. Maddox rolled off the bed and pulled back the drapes, revealing a brilliantly blue late-afternoon sky. "When was the last time you ate, Seneca? We should get dinner. There's a restaurant in the hotel."

Seneca shook her head. "Just bring me up something. I don't want to stop working."

What seemed like moments later, he was returning with a plastic bag of takeout. "Thanks," Seneca murmured, barely glancing at the cartons. She tapped her pencil to the note – she'd begun rearranging the letters, finding anagrams. The note contained the words *sneered, whitened, smote*. Meaning . . . what?

For a while, the only sounds in the room were Maddox's utensils clicking. He sat next to her and studied the note as he ate, but then he stood and announced he felt brain-dead and was going for a run. "Sometimes it clears my head," he said. "Helps me see things from a new angle."

The sun set out of the big windows. The door clicked; Maddox returned, sweaty and breathing hard. He disappeared into the bathroom, and soon Seneca heard the shower.

Anagrams were making no sense; Seneca crossed them out and decided to take a different tack . . . but what? Aerin, Madison, and Thomas stopped in, saying they'd made no headway and were going to bed. Seneca stared at the dark sky, her chest throbbing. They'd wasted a whole day. What weren't they seeing? What had they missed?

Maddox emerged from the shower and sat on the edge of the bed. "Stay here as long as you like."

Seneca glanced up at him, feeling grateful. Maddox seemed to understand she didn't want to go back to her room without her having to explain it. "Thanks," she said softly.

She bent over the letter. The TV hummed at low volume, but she barely registered the stream of programs that played. She thought of Brett's letter to Maddox. Brett's demeanor when they'd first met in Dexby. The conversation they'd had outside the Dexby Rec Center after Seneca caught Maddox and his track coach together. The look on Brett's face at the Easter Bunny party when he'd discovered that Aerin liked Thomas Grove, who'd saved them from Marissa Ingram. She paused on that memory – Brett had been so crushed. He'd left before Seneca had gotten the chance to ask if he was okay.

The next morning, when Seneca began to connect the dots and realize something was seriously up with Brett, she'd tried to reach out to him, but his number had been disconnected.

When she lifted her head again, the little clock on the bedside stand said it was 2:03 A.M. She glanced at the bed. Maddox was turned away from her, his chest rising softly, his toes sticking out from under the covers. She considered going back to her own room for a split second before deciding it wasn't an option.

She shifted onto his mattress. After some hesitation, she slid one foot under the covers and then another. She lay on the very edge of the bed, but that was so uncomfortable, and she was so tired. So she stretched out a little. Her hand hit his. Maddox might have been asleep, but his finger instinctively curled around hers anyway. Seneca froze, not knowing what to do. Their entwined fingers felt good. *Right*.

It was dark in the room, peaceful. She closed her eyes and tried to let sleep wash over her. Perhaps an answer would come to her in the morning. But just as she was sliding into oblivion, her eyes popped open, and she sat straight up. The letters in the clue, rearranged, revealed a word she hadn't thought of before. *Mother*.

Red, white, and awesome: a bull's-eye. *A spot over the eye:* the dog mascot. *Even caramel syrup:* They used that in Starbucks drinks sometimes. Maybe Brett wasn't talking about Chelsea when he said *I met her, and it was love. Thought she thought so, too.* He was talking about Seneca's mother.

He was sending them to Target.

208

CHAPTER 27

Early Friday morning, Aerin stood in the parking lot of the closest Target to the beach – the *only* Target, actually, for at least forty miles. The store had just opened twenty minutes ago – they'd meant to come first thing, but there was unexpected traffic on the bridge out of Lafayette – and there were a fair number of cars in the parking lot. Tourists, probably, stocking up on beach supplies. The sky was gray with low-hanging clouds, and though a huge storm had whipped through at daybreak, the humidity had rushed back in, and even Aerin's eyeballs felt sticky.

"You holding up okay?" Thomas's fingers closed around hers.

Aerin smiled at him gratefully. "Yeah. Thanks." It was weird how natural Thomas's presence felt. Like he'd been part of her life – and this investigation – since the start. All at once she couldn't remember how she functioned *without* him around.

Seneca got out of the Jeep and surveyed the parking lot. Her face was gray, and she kept pressing her hands against her cheeks as if making sure they were still there. Aerin watched her carefully. A Target in Annapolis was where Seneca's mom was last seen; Seneca had told her that she hadn't actually *been* to a Target since her mother was killed. Just driving by the stores gave her panic attacks.

Maddox pressed the LOCK button on the key fob. "So you think he means Starbucks, right? In his letter, that's where he said they spent time together."

Seneca shot him a look. "You make it sound like they were *friends*."

"I – I didn't mean it like that. I just . . ."

"It's not a crime that your mom talked to Brett," Aerin jumped in. "Brett charmed Helena, too."

Seneca stared at Aerin helplessly, and Aerin could guess at the thoughts churning in her brain. They were probably the same emotions she felt – fury, disbelief, devastation, all of it fresh and intense. The details in Brett's letter had ripped off a Helena-sized Band-Aid Aerin had tried so hard to keep adhered to her skin for years now. Underneath was a wound that was still bloody, raw, and very unhealed.

All at once, Aerin regretted losing touch with Seneca this summer. It felt selfish . . . but also self-destructive. If they'd been in touch, if they'd really talked, maybe handling this now – this pain so specific to both of them, this hell only the two of them understood – might be a little more bearable.

"Come here." Aerin pulled her into a hug. They stood like that for a long time, both of them silently suffering. "I'm sorry," Aerin whispered. "And if you don't want to do this, you don't have to. We can handle all of it. We can go in there."

Finally, Seneca broke away and wiped her eyes. "No," she said shakily. "Brett's trying to get to me. He thinks bringing me to a Target, making me re-create what he described in the letter is going to wear me down. But I won't let it. Come on. We don't have much time left."

She turned and marched toward the doors. Madison glanced at Aerin, and Aerin shrugged. Seneca wasn't any more over what happened than Aerin was. But they were alike in that way – they just needed a distraction, something else on which to concentrate instead.

Shopping carts jammed the front of the Target store. The air was cool and smelled like buttered popcorn. The Starbucks, set off to the right, was empty of patrons, and one of the sleepy-looking baristas was reading an *Us Weekly* next to the espresso machines. They didn't seem to care as Aerin and the others poked around the tables, the gift shelves, and big bags of coffee beans for a clue. Then Aerin noticed a lone drink sitting on the pickup counter. The name *Collette* was scrawled across it. Her heart stopped in her chest.

She pointed it out to Seneca. Seneca looked like she was going to explode. She darted over and picked up the cup. "Who is this for?" she asked the girls behind the counter.

The shorter of the two walked over and inspected the name. "Huh. Not sure."

"You don't remember who ordered it?"

The girl shook her head. "Sorry, no. We had a busy morning."

Seneca looked chagrined. Thomas nudged his chin at the register. "Go through your receipts. Figure it out. I'm a cop. This is official business."

"Thomas," Aerin felt uneasy. "What good is that going to do?" Brett wouldn't be stupid enough to use a credit card.

But to her surprise, the barista was compliant, glancing at the coffee order on the side of the cardboard cup and then looking at the register tape. "Okay, so there were only three Americanos," she said. "One at 7:33, one at 7:41, and one at 8:02. All of them paid with cash."

Aerin looked at the clock over the bar. It was eight thirty. Had Brett really been here so recently?

Thomas eyed the barista again. "Do you have security cameras?"

The barista looked suspicious. "Yeah . . ."

"Can we see them?"

The barista's eyes went blank. "I'll have to ask my manager. Unless, um, you have a warrant?"

Aerin groaned. That might take forever – and they didn't *have* forever. She snatched the Collette drink off the counter, looking at the cup from all angles. If this was a clue, what was it supposed to tell them?

"Uh, miss?" The taller barista peeled away from the counter. "You can't take that if it's someone else's . . ."

Aerin ignored her, walking straight out of the store with the cup in her hand. The others hurried behind. The drizzle had turned into steadier rain, and people were jogging in from the parking lot with jackets over their heads.

She pulled off the plastic sip top, and everyone peered into the cup. There was dark liquid inside . . . and a rolled-up piece of paper. "Whoa," she whispered as she pulled it out. Coffee dripped off the ends. Had Brett ordered this drink, stuffed this clue inside, and then left?

Seneca unrolled it with trembling hands. *Tonite at the Lafayette Boardwalk Aquarium, the Oddly Shaped Men*, read words across the top. Beneath that was a blurry, black-and-white photo of three guys with guitars. It listed today's date and the aquarium's address.

"So we go back to the aquarium?" Madison murmured.

Aerin shivered. The sudden rain had sucked the humidity from the atmosphere, and her skin felt chilled. "No way. That place was too creepy."

Seneca leaned against a stray shopping cart. "We can't just *not* go."

"Look." Madison pointed at the flyer. "More numbers are circled." Part of the address and part of the two phone numbers listed had faded pen marks around them.

"*That's* the answer." Aerin sat down on a red bench, pulled out Post-its and a pen from her bag, and wrote down the circled numbers – thirty-nine, eight, five, seventy-four, forty-seven. "Could they stand for letters?" She jiggled the pen.

"Sports jerseys?" Maddox suggested. "Joe DiMaggio was number five. Mickey Mantle's seven. And there's an NFL guy who's thirty-nine –"

Madison snorted. "You really think Brett would know that?"

Maddox looked surprised. "Doesn't *everyone* know that?"

"Wait." Seneca pursed her lips. "Maybe they're GPS coordinates."

"That's what I was thinking, too," Thomas said.

"So maybe longitude and latitude?" Maddox jumped in.

Thomas nodded. "The latitude coordinates around here start with thirty-nine, and latitude is seventy-four, which was what made me think of it. But you're missing a few numbers for it to give a precise location."

213

"What about the numbers circled on the menu?" Maddox asked. "It led to an address in Lafayette, but maybe it's part of a bigger picture." He wrote nineteen and ninety-three on Aerin's list.

"If that's the case, then we have to include this place, too," Madison said. "Brett might be using all the clues to spell out something."

"Target's address?" Madison pointed to the number on the building. Twenty-two.

Aerin grabbed her phone, opened Google, and found a site that mapped GPS coordinates. Once she plugged everything in, her eyes widened at a picture on Google Earth. The aerial image showed lush green wetlands just beyond Lafayette. Sitting off to the left was a dilapidated brown shack.

A rush of certainty flooded her. "This has to be it."

Seneca's throat bobbed as she swallowed. "It looks promising. But what about the aquarium? Is Brett trying to send us in two different directions?"

Aerin looked at the image again. This was where Brett had Chelsea. She could feel it in her bones. "I'm going here. I *have* to."

Thomas placed his hands on Aerin's wrist, and she felt the familiar jolt of electricity. "Then we'll have to divide and conquer," he declared. "Aerin, I'm going with you."

CHAPTER 28

Brett waited until nine a.m. on Friday before he made the call. "I'm such an idiot," he told the Starbucks girl who answered. "I ordered a drink for my wife but left it on the counter. Her name's Collette. Is it by any chance still there?"

"I'm sorry, but someone else picked it up," the girl said. "It would be cold by now anyway. If you come back by, we'll make you one on the house."

"That won't be necessary." Brett hung up without saying good-bye, just in case Seneca was having the call traced. He smiled. All the cogs were moving smoothly in the wheel. Now all he had to count on was his old friends doing exactly what he wanted, though he had a feeling that wouldn't be too difficult.

He burst into Chelsea's room. The girl shot up, her eyes wide, and she seemed to take in his close-cropped hair, his shaven face, his colored contacts, the makeup dusted across his cheeks and hands to give him a more olive complexion. For a moment, he could tell she thought he was someone new – a stranger. A rescuer. But then she noticed: It was the same old him, just changed a little. Tears filled her eyes.

"What gave me away?" Brett asked, annoyed. He'd worked hard on his transformation just now, shedding Gabriel in the same way a snake shed its skin. "My eyes? My build?" It would be easy to bulk back up, though. In only a few weeks, his body would be dramatically different. No one from here would be able to pick him out of a lineup.

"We're going to do a photo shoot," Brett said. "What do you think?"

Chelsea just stared. "Y-you look very handsome with short hair," she said in a frightened voice.

Brett eyed her coldly. He knew what she was doing, but it wasn't going to work on him. He lifted the camera and moved close to her face. "Smile, please."

Chelsea's eyes flickered to the phone again. Brett let out an impatient snort. "No, no. You can't see it. But don't worry. Your family will know how you are soon enough."

Chelsea's eyes widened. "Wh-what do you mean?"

Brett pressed the camera app. "I just need you to smile right now, okay?"

"But wh-why?"

"*Smile,*" he said through his teeth. "The world will want to see how pretty you were before."

Chelsea's eyes glazed over. Brett could practically see her little brain struggling with what that word could mean. *Before.* Her lip started to tremble. She didn't smile. Brett sighed and removed the knife from his pocket. It took only a second to push it to her throat. She made a small gurgling sound. "Smile like you mean it. Smile in the way you want to be remembered."

Chelsea looked terrified, but she straightened. As Brett pulled the knife away, she relaxed into an astonishingly convincing smile. Her eyes gleamed. Her teeth shone. Her skin seemed to glow. She was a pro, after all.

"Nice," he cooed, pressing the shutter. "Now, was that so hard?"

He pocketed the knife and phone and started for the door. Chelsea coughed, and he turned. "You're not going to . . ." She trailed off, but the end of the question loomed heavily in the air, like a swarm of bugs.

"Kill you now?" Brett liked how she flinched at the word. "No. There's something else I have to take care of first." Then, after a moment's thought, he tossed her the TV remote he'd carried in from Command Central. "Here. It'll take your mind off things."

Chelsea teared up again. "I don't want to watch TV. I want to *leave*."

Brett rolled his eyes. "Oh, please. You know you want to see yourself on the news."

Then he pivoted, walked through the door, and shut it. As he was making sure it was locked, he heard the fizzling snap of the television turning on.

Called it.

CHAPTER 29

As the clock struck nine thirty, Seneca, Madison, and Maddox stood at the aquarium on the boardwalk. Rain made sloppy puddles in the sand. The beach was almost empty save for two old men in rain hats panning the sand with metal detectors. Seneca peered at the worn, faded fish mural at the aquarium's entrance. The clown fish, its bright orange scales long ago eroded into a muted peach, looked like it was on the verge of a stroke. Someone had drawn a picture of a topless woman next to the shark.

There was an information desk, but no one was there. Seneca marched right past. Over her shoulder, Maddox had dug in his heels. He gazed around the desolate structure with disdain.

"Aerin was right," he muttered. "This place *is* creepy."

"The flyer pointed us here," Seneca argued. "It's worth it to check it out."

"It could be a trap."

"The shack could be a trap, too," Seneca said, exasperated. "Let's just do a lap, okay?" But she also felt a sense of foreboding. She didn't like that the group had split up. Their strength was in their numbers.

She marched into the aquarium. Fish swam languidly in illuminated tanks. A bright blue tang leered at her, baring tiny, razor-sharp teeth. The next room was even darker than before, boasting tanks of eels, rainbow fish, and a speckled sea blob with bulging eyes. Seneca gazed around, but she saw nothing. Not that she knew what she was looking for.

Someone shifted at the far end of the room, and Seneca's hackles rose. A man in a black shirt stood in front of a tank of electric eels. There was something rigid about his posture, as though he wasn't entirely comfortable in his skin. As she crept closer, she got a look at his profile and then read his gleaming name tag. Her body snapped to attention. *Wait*. Maybe there wasn't going to be a physical clue here. Maybe the clue was a *person*.

"Are you Barnes?" she said softly.

The man turned. She could feel his gaze upon her, even in the liquid darkness. "Who wants to know?"

"I – I have some questions about Chelsea Dawson."

Barnes breathed in sharply. "Are you a cop?"

"No. But I'm part of this group that . . ." Seneca trailed off. Explaining Case Not Closed was probably pointless to this guy. "I just want to know what happened from your perspective," she said after a beat. "You guys were friends, right?"

Barnes turned back to the fish tanks, not answering.

"And you know she's missing?" Seneca goaded. "Maybe you can help us find her?"

Barnes raised his chin, the light bouncing off his sharp features. "No thanks."

Seneca gestured to Maddox and Madison behind her. "These are my friends. They're helping, too. Listen, we need you. You knew Chelsea well. We saw your Instagram account. All those conversations you had with her . . ."

The dim, artificial lighting gave Barnes's skin a greenish-blue cast. He looked angry as he whipped around to face Seneca head-on. "Did you pay admission?"

Seneca stopped. "There's no admission. The aquarium is free."

"Well, you need to leave."

"Look, we're not the cops," Maddox pleaded. "We're not here to bust you or whatever. Chelsea obviously means something to you. We just want to know what that is."

Barnes's nostrils flared. "Stop talking about Chelsea, okay?"

Seneca felt a small, burning sensation in the pit of her stomach. Barnes was hiding something.

She sidled up to Barnes. He smelled unwashed and sweaty. "But if you keep acting like this, we *will* go to the cops."

Barnes's eyes flashed. "On what grounds?"

"You're acting suspicious. Maybe you *did* do it."

He puffed up his chest, almost like he was getting ready to sumo-crash into her. "You really think . . ." he sputtered. "You have no idea . . ." He turned his head. He seemed to be mentally wrestling with something, but then he wilted. "Look, I loved her. Deeply. I would never hurt her. But those comments you're talking about, on Instagram? That friendship you think we had?" He sighed. "I wrote those myself. My comments . . . and hers. I hacked Chelsea's account, I clicked on my photos, and I pretended I was her. I just . . ." He shook his head. "She doesn't really know me. We didn't really talk."

"So you . . . *weren't* friends?" Seneca asked in a small voice, feeling disappointed. Suddenly, she realized the possibility

220

that Brett had led them to the aquarium only as a distraction, running down the clock until the deadline was up. Had she made a grave mistake?

Barnes faced the eels again. His shoulders sagged. "Well, I saw her around a lot. And the day she came into the aquarium, last summer? Best day of my life. We talked. *Really* talked. I told her about all the fish. Afterward, she asked if I wanted to take a walk. Of course I said yes. She told me she was fed up with her boyfriend. He didn't understand her. He was jealous. At the end of the walk, when we were under this pier, she grabbed me and kissed me hard. It was . . ." There was wistfulness in his tone, but then his face fell. "I thought it would go somewhere, but I never heard from her again."

Seneca felt a cold, slimy sensation expand in her gut. There was something so emotionally painful about his words. Something, too, that reminded her of Brett, especially in that last poem he'd left for them. *I met her, and it was love. Thought she thought so, too.* He hadn't explicitly stated it, but Seneca guessed her mom had rejected Brett . . . and Helena had, too. Could they add Chelsea to that list? Perhaps that was Brett's MO: punishing women who wouldn't give him what he wanted.

"That must have been hard, huh?" she said softly. "You thought you had a connection. You thought you meant something to her. It was brutal when she ghosted you."

"I guess," he said gruffly.

"That's why you wrote the comments on Instagram. If she wasn't going to participate in the relationship in real life, at least you could follow through with the fantasy."

221

Barnes stiffened. "But I didn't *do* anything to her. I swear. If the cops look at my Instagram account, if they see what we wrote, and if they find out *she* wasn't writing it, well, I know how it looks." He shook is head. "I've been so on edge. This girl came in here the other day – got trapped in a back hallway where I was working. She looked just like Chelsea. I thought it was someone fucking with me, someone who'd found out that I'd lied."

"That was just my friend Aerin," Seneca assured him. "She wants to help Chelsea, too. We won't tell the cops anything. We think Chelsea blew off someone else, just like she rejected you. But unlike you, this guy snapped . . . and kidnapped her. We're worried he's going to kill her. So I need you to look at something for me. A clue he left. Chelsea *needs* you, Barnes. And if you help find her, we'll make sure she knows you saved her life."

Barnes stared at the ceiling for a moment, then shone his flashlight on the clues Seneca pulled from her pocket. His brow furrowed as he took in the menu, the Target address, and the flyer for the concert at the aquarium. "Oh. Yeah, okay. She's been to this sushi place. Took a picture there, actually. I still remember it."

"On Instagram?" Seneca demanded, letting out a breath she didn't realize she was holding.

Barnes reached for his phone in his back pocket. After a few quick swipes, he pulled up Chelsea's account and selected a photo of Chelsea lying across a table in a dimly lit restaurant. She wore a gold bikini top, hot pants, and white platform shoes. The look in her eyes oozed sexuality, and her lips were parted in a please-kiss-me-now pucker. The photo had over fifty thousand likes.

"This is taken at Sushi Monster?" Seneca asked. The photo wasn't location-tagged.

"Absolutely." He tapped the big fish tank behind Chelsea's head. "That's a peppermint angelfish in there. Sushi Monster is the only place around that has one. They're, like, ten grand a fish."

Madison ran her hand through her ponytail. "What about the other two locations in these clues?"

"No idea about Target, but she did come see this band play once." He pointed at the Oddly Shaped Men flyer they'd found at Starbucks. His eyes shifted toward the ground, and there was a tiny hitch in his voice. "I was there, too. The very next day was when she kissed me."

Seneca looked at her friends. "Could these clues be about people Chelsea hooked up with besides Jeff? When we were investigating Helena, we uncovered all her secrets – drugs, Ingram, running away. Our guy –" she paused, not wanting to say Brett's name out loud in front of Barnes – "seems to enjoy peeling back the layers of people, showing that they weren't as perfect as they seemed."

"So you're saying maybe Chelsea hooked up with someone at that house on Ninety-Third Street?" Madison suggested. "And then was there someone else at the Japanese place?"

"Maybe," Seneca said.

"So what?" Maddox argued. "Chelsea cheated on her boyfriend. Jeff already told us that. This feels like noise, not a real clue. How does it add up to where he's hiding her?"

"I'm not sure . . ." Seneca stared at the Instagram picture of Chelsea again. Something caught her eye: The photo had been taken fifty-two weeks ago exactly. She clicked through to get the precise date and found that it was yesterday, one year before.

She tapped on Chelsea's next image, also taken a year ago yesterday. Sure enough, it was inside a beach house – maybe the one they'd looked at on Ninety-Third. In the image after that, exactly one year ago today, Chelsea was in a makeup aisle – Target? In the next photo, taken only hours later on the same day, Chelsea made a kissy face on this very boardwalk. Seneca couldn't make out much more detail when she zoomed in, but she had a feeling that the blurry building in the distance was the aquarium they were standing in.

Connections began to form in her brain. "Last year's Instagram photos match up sequentially with Brett's clues. Could today's date be significant, somehow?"

"Yeah, but of what?" Maddox mused aloud. "July 16. It's not her birthday. It's not anything." He turned to Barnes, who was still standing there. "Do you know?"

He nodded. "It's her update day." There was a sheepish expression on his face. "She does an update video on the sixteenth of every month."

Seneca turned back to the phone. Sure enough, the next post was an update video – Chelsea was thanking all her followers and saying she had "big plans" for the page in the future. "Better photos," she teased. "Better makeup reviews. And lots more of *moi*." She made kissing lips at the camera.

Seneca looked at Barnes. "Do you know where she took this?"

Barnes squinted at the screen. "I've watched this one a lot. It's her friend's beach house. Her name's Ophelia something."

Seneca's heart started to pound. "Is this house nearby?"

"Sure. Out of town a ways, on a vineyard. But I don't think her family is here this summer – I haven't seen Ophelia around at all."

"Maybe that doesn't matter," Seneca said dazedly.

She thought of Chelsea's update videos. Barnes seemed to know every one by heart . . . and she bet Brett did, too. They were something he probably both loved and despised, fascinated by her beauty, disgusted by her narcissism.

Maddox cleared his throat. Seneca looked up, and he was staring at her, his lips parted, his eyes wide. Seneca could tell he was drawing the exact same conclusions, bridging the same gaps.

"We need to get to that house *now*," she said. "Call Aerin and Thomas. Tell them the shack might be a trap."

CHAPTER 30

Aerin and Thomas didn't say a word to each other on the bumpy drive out of town past a few lonely farms and through the entrance to the wetlands. She tried to distract herself by looking around the interior of his car, an old Ford Focus with window cranks and manual transmission. There were a bunch of library books and DVDs littering the backseat. She spied an Agatha Christie paperback that she'd read, too, and considered mentioning it, but then realized she was way too keyed up to make idle chitchat.

A big sign alerted them that they were now in protected space, so no hunting, littering, or trespassing was permitted. "There," she said, noticing something brown and pointed just over the trees. As they rounded the corner, a broken-looking house stood down a dirt road, in a clearing. The windows were boarded up, and the roof was black with rot. An old pickup truck, long rusted away, slumped in the gravel driveway. So did a big buzzard, chewing on the remains of a dead animal.

Thomas pulled onto the shoulder and hit the brakes. "Let's park here. This car will get stuck in the mud if we go any farther."

"Okay," Aerin whispered.

"Do you think we should call the cops before we go in?"

Aerin rolled her jaw. "What if Brett's in there and sees the police lights and kills her? Or what if just Chelsea's in there and Brett's watching from a remote location and he sees the cops and hits some sort of detonator and blows us all up? Or what if –"

"Got it," Thomas interrupted curtly, seeming nervous, too. "But I don't like us going in unprotected. I'm bringing this."

He popped the glove box and unveiled a small black handgun, perfectly palm-sized. Aerin recoiled. She'd never seen a gun up close before. "Has that been in there the whole time?"

"I got it after I quit the force. I feel more comfortable carrying one – it's totally legal, and I've taken courses on gun safety. I don't intend on using it, but I also don't want to potentially face a madman with my bare hands."

Aerin swallowed hard. The word *madman* echoed in her ears.

Thomas opened the car door. The buzzard lifted from the ground, flapping its enormous wings. The air was so still and quiet, Aerin could hear the thudding of her heart. She glanced at Thomas. His jaw was taut. His eyes focused straight ahead. The gun was in his hand. He was all business.

He started up the driveway. "Stay with me at all times, okay? I'll lead. You follow. Don't get out of my sight. Getting separated could be really dangerous."

Aerin scrambled after him. The air had a strange smell to it – like sulfur, wet asphalt, and burnt electronics. The wind picked up suddenly, brushing the blades of tall grass together. There were weeds all around the house, growing into the foundation. As they got closer, the shack creaked and moaned. It was even more dilapidated than she'd first thought – definitely uninhabitable-looking. No one had lived here in years.

Aerin stood on tiptoes and tried to peer into the single dirty window on the first floor that wasn't covered in cardboard. Was Brett in there? Chelsea? She stared hard, trying to make out shapes. She thought she caught something moving and widened her eyes, but it was too dark to tell.

Something fluttered in the grass, and she snapped up. How long had she been standing here? Thomas was gone. She could hear distant footsteps, almost out of earshot. Her throat felt dry. There was no way she was going to call out to him.

She tramped around the side yard. The grass was even higher, and there was a fence a few feet away that seemed to have been chewed apart by something huge and carnivorous. Part of the shack's siding had eroded straight through to the fiberglass. There were thick patches of weeds – and probably poison ivy – under Aerin's feet, but she trudged through them anyway. The wind swished eerily again, blowing her hair into her face.

Clang. She jumped and spun around. In the backyard, a rusted rooster weather vane mounted on a stump swung wildly with the wind, haphazardly knocking into a pile of junk behind it. Aerin's gaze scanned the heap: There was a rusty saw, some clamps, and an iron mallet that looked like it weighed more than she did. They reminded Aerin of torture weapons. An unsettling frisson fluttered up her spine.

Flies swarmed feverishly around something just out of view. Swallowing hard, she crept around the pile of rubble and looked down. The first thing she saw on the crumbling brick slab was a splotch of blood. She jumped back, bile rising to her throat. When she peered again, she swallowed a scream. Bones lay on the ground, the flesh picked clean away. Aerin raised a hand to her mouth. They looked *huge*. Maybe someone's legs. A forearm.

Something flashed behind her again. In the window? Aerin craned her neck, staring hard until her vision blurred. Her fear was doing a number on her balance, and she took a wobbling step back, nearly toppling over. This was a terrible idea. They couldn't be here. They had to leave, *now*.

And then she heard Thomas's scream.

CHAPTER 31

It wasn't hard for Maddox, Seneca, and Madison to track down Ophelia's family's house – when Maddox typed *Lafayette vineyard* into Google, it was the only property that came up. He drummed nervously on the steering wheel as they rolled on the secluded dirt road toward the property. Grape vines hemmed them in on either side, dry and twisted and fingerlike, and the clouds were thick and gray above them, threatening more rain.

"Shit," Seneca murmured, stabbing END on her phone. "Aerin still isn't answering. Where *is* she?"

"At least she's with Thomas," Madison said nervously. "She's got to be okay, right?"

There was a break in the road, and a small hand-lettered sign reading, *Wild Goat Vineyards*, with an arrow pointing in one direction. Maddox turned the wheel, and they started up a long driveway. In the distance, a monolith modern structure of steel, glass, and stone gleamed. "Holy shit," he breathed. The house had to be at least six thousand square feet.

Halfway up the drive, he slowed the Jeep to a stop. "Do you think we should park in the driveway? Brett will see us."

230

Seneca nodded. "At this point, he's expecting us. I think we should park as close to the entrance as possible so we have a getaway car if we need it."

Madison looked nervous. "If Brett's in there, how are we going to fight him? With our bare hands?"

"Let's call the cops," Maddox suggested. "Now. I'm not sure I can go in without knowing they're close."

Seneca seemed reluctant. "Brett won't like that . . . but then, maybe that doesn't matter. We go in first, but we have the cops close behind. Okay, do it."

"I'll say I'm reporting a break-in," Madison said, reaching for her phone. "That I see suspicious stuff happening at the vineyard's house." She pressed the buttons for 9-1-1.

Maddox maneuvered the vehicle up the path and into the empty driveway. There were no typical signs of vacationers – no towels hung on the porch, no beach gear propped against the door, not even rocking chairs on the patio. Everything seemed locked up, almost abandoned. If someone was here, they were hiding it well.

"Cops will be here soon," Madison said, slipping her phone back into her pocket.

Maddox stared up at the structure. The house was massive. Each level had a large deck, and Maddox noticed a pool off to the left. One of the striped umbrellas looked familiar from one of Chelsea's update videos. There were a few empty clay pots stacked against the back door; he strolled over to them and cautiously looked inside, finding only a dead spider and some clots of dirt. Suddenly, the hair on the back of his neck rose. He wheeled around and squinted into the thick vineyard, sensing something he couldn't put his finger on.

"What?" Seneca whispered, freezing, too.

Maddox blinked. "I don't know. It just feels like someone's . . . *watching.*"

Everyone stared at the field. Nothing moved. The dry branches cast long shadows on the ground. If someone was there, they'd turned to stone.

Maddox looked back to the house. "This place probably has a sweet security system. How did Brett override that?"

"You're forgetting Brett figured out how to break into the Dakota in New York City," Seneca muttered.

Maddox inspected the area under the porte cochere for anything that might indicate Brett's presence. A dropped gum wrapper. A sneaker print. One of Chelsea's long blonde hairs. His heart was racing, and any moment he expected an alarm to go off, or a car to roll up, or a bullet to shoot him dead. Then, as he turned, another strange sensation washed over his skin.

"Guys." When the others were by his side, he sniffed the air. "Do you smell that?"

Maddox shook her head. Seneca breathed in and frowned. But all sorts of synapses fired in Maddox's brain. "It's Brett's cologne."

"Would Brett wear the same cologne as he did in Dexby?" Seneca asked.

"It was distinct." Maddox was heady with the smell now, even though it was faint. "But I can smell it for sure."

Something in the vineyards rustled again. Everyone whipped around and stood straighter. A bird with a bent wing lifted above the branches. Maddox stared at its reflection against the window, then noticed something incongruous. The blinds were pulled down tight, but it seemed like there was a light on inside.

"We have to figure out how to get in," he said to the others. "A window? One of the patio doors? There's a little door on the widow's walk on the top floor . . ."

"What are we supposed to do, scale the house?" Madison went to the garage door again and twisted the knob. Then she stepped back and gasped. Maddox rushed over, afraid something had happened to her. Another blast of cloying cologne assaulted his nostrils.

"It's . . . *open*," Madison whispered, pointing. And indeed, the door was unlocked, pushed ajar a few inches. Maddox peered into the dark room. There was only one thing to do now. Go inside.

CHAPTER 32

"Thomas!" Aerin screamed, crashing through the weeds. Her foot caught on an exposed piece of pipe, and she flew into the dirt. When she stood, another screech pierced the air. There was a pounding sound, too, like metal against bone. Aerin thought of the pile of twisted objects in the backyard. The bones on the ground. What was Brett doing to Thomas?

She leapt to her feet and ran. As she circled to the front of the house, she caught sight of Thomas on the porch. He was standing, but his body was contorted, and there was blood on his arms. "Thomas!" she called again.

Thomas turned, his eyes full of warning. "No!"

Aerin darted forward anyway. She wasn't going to let Brett hurt him. He'd hurt too many people already. She was only a few feet away before she realized something was scuttling on the ground, a tail swinging, teeth gnashing. She stopped short, disoriented. This wasn't Brett . . . but an animal.

Thomas raised a rusty shovel over his head and smashed it down, crushing the creature's skull. The thing let out a wail and flattened to the ground, and a bald, pale tail whipped back and forth. Aerin screamed and covered her mouth. Two other rodents lay near a dilapidated porch swing. One had a gaping wound in its side. The other was missing half its head.

"Oh my God," Aerin gurgled.

Thomas stared at her from the porch. He was breathing hard, and his shirt was spotted with sweat. "Jesus." He sounded freaked. "Those were the biggest rats I'd ever seen."

Aerin took huge gulps of oxygen. "We have to get out of here. There are weapons in the backyard. And bones."

Thomas shot off the porch and grabbed her, first hugging her tight, then looking at her with fear. "Where?"

Swallowing hard, Aerin led him around the side of the house. Still clutching her hand hard, Thomas pulled his gun from its holster once more and held it at the ready. She pointed past the flies on the slab. "There," she said, averting her eyes.

Thomas crept over. He glanced down at the bones, then lowered his gun. "It's okay. These aren't human. I think it's a deer."

"Are you sure?"

Thomas nodded. He eyed the rusted pile of saws and mallets. "I don't know what to make of that stuff, but I'm not sure it qualifies as a weapon." He tightened his grip on the gun. "Are you up for checking inside the house?"

"Uh, *no*." Aerin wiped her eyes. The smell of death was making her stomach turn. "But I don't want to wait out here alone, either."

On the porch, the rats squeaked and moaned. Aerin willed herself not to look in their direction. Thomas touched the doorknob with his thumb, and the whole piece crumbled and fell to the porch with a thump. He gingerly tapped the door with his foot. A cloud of dust billowed, and half the structure crumbled inward, leaving a small space for them to climb through into the room.

Aerin was instantly greeted by a stale, earthy, rotting stench. She glanced at Thomas, and he nodded encouragingly. Holding her breath, she stepped over the boards and into the space. Thomas followed behind her, holding her hand.

The room was dark, wet, and stinky. Aerin cocked her head and listened for sounds, but she heard nothing. Thomas clicked on his flashlight and shone it across the floorboards. An ancient wood-burning stove was barely attached to the wall. The corners were littered with spiderwebs, dry leaves, and animal droppings. The bones of a carcass lay against another wall, but when Aerin turned fearfully to Thomas, he squeezed her hand. "They're a mouse's, or a squirrel's. Not a person's."

He stepped into the room, shining his light to the windows and the ceiling. The floor creaked precariously. "I don't see a basement," he said. "Or a trapdoor. Or . . . *anything*."

Aerin licked her lips, then nodded. It seemed like a dead end. But suddenly, she noticed a flash of something bright on the windowsill. She crept over, careful of the rotting floorboards. When she saw what it was, her heart stopped . . . then pounded in double time. It was a red paper crane.

"What the . . ." Thomas murmured.

Aerin held it in her trembling hands. It was *exactly* like the paper crane she'd found on Helena's dresser after she went missing . . . except more faded, the creases folded and refolded they'd turned almost white. She flipped it over, half expecting to see the initials H.I. on the bottom. Instead, there was something else, written in a cramped, tight hand: *Jackson*.

Thomas stared at her. "Do you know what this means?"

Aerin shook her head, swallowing hard. Instantly, she was transported to Helena's bedroom, smelling her floral perfume, surrounded by her vintage clothes, feeling her sheepskin throw rug under her feet. It seemed like a million heartbreaking years ago. And now, as she stood in the musty, moldy shack, she slowly undid this new crane's every fold, desperate to find another clue under a wing, or inside a beak – evidence that it *was* from Brett, and what it could mean. But in the end, all she was left with was a deeply creased square of origami paper, nothing more.

CHAPTER 33

Seneca used the flashlight on her phone to illuminate the basement. There was a pool table in the middle of the room, an air hockey table in one corner, and what looked like a pinball machine on the far wall. In another corner was a huge television and at least four different types of video game consoles. The beam of light swept across a bar stocked with every type of liquor imaginable and a tabletop slot machine.

"Here are the stairs," Madison whispered from the left. Seneca and Maddox tiptoed toward her. The three of them crept up to the first floor, carefully pushing the door open to reveal a gleaming modern kitchen. There wasn't a single item on the counters. The trash can didn't have a liner in it. A fruit bowl was empty. The only sound in the room was the gentle buzz of the appliances.

Seneca looked at the others. "Why aren't alarms blaring? Is this a trap?"

"Or maybe she isn't here," Madison said.

Maddox cocked his head to the left, then pointed down a long hall full of windows. "Wait. I hear something."

Seneca strained to listen. After a moment, she *did* hear

something: faint voices. An electronic hum. Her skin prickled. She met Maddox's gaze and nodded.

But Madison took a step toward the basement door. "Maybe we should leave."

Seneca gaped at her. "What are you *talking* about? We have to see what that is!"

"Hello?"

A voice drifted from down the hall. Seneca's heart froze in her chest. She wasn't sure the voice was real . . . but then someone called out again. "Hello?" It was a girl. "Wh-who's out there?"

Seneca rushed toward the sound. "Seneca!" Maddox called out behind her, but she kept going. At the end of the hall was a closed door; someone was pounding on it from the inside. "Help me! Help me, *please*! I'm locked in!"

Seneca's hands trembled on the knob, but it didn't turn. Hurriedly, she pulled a credit card from her wallet. She jammed the card below the bolt and swiped up quickly. The knob didn't budge. She swore under her breath.

"What's going on?" the voice cried.

Seneca tried the card in the door again, thrusting upward even more forcefully this time. The bolt released. The knob turned, and the door swung open. A girl huddled on the carpet, a girl whose face she'd memorized so intensely and thought about so continuously it was jarring she was actually a real person.

Chelsea.

The girl trembled as she stared at them. Her hair was clean and styled, there was color in her cheeks, and she was wearing a dress that looked like it had been ironed only moments ago. But her eyes were wide and full of tears. Her limbs were trembling. As Maddox took a step inside, she cowered back, shielding her chest. "Are you with *him*?"

"With who?" Seneca asked, even though she already knew.

"No," Maddox said at the same time. "Of course not."

Chelsea's eyes darted back and forth. "Then he's going to find you. He'll *hurt* you."

"Where is he?" Maddox peered around the room. There was a strange look on his face. "Is he here?"

Seneca peered around, too. It was only then she noticed Chelsea was being held in a luxurious master suite. A huge four-poster king bed sat in the middle of the room. The shades were drawn, but the television was on, tuned to Bravo. A pretty mirror, draped with a bra and several changes of clothes, stood in the corner. Past that was a massive marble bathroom, the counter messy with bottles and jars and powder puffs. The air smelled like perfume and fresh coffee.

She looked back at Chelsea. Her shiny hair bounced. Seneca also noticed she had makeup on: eyeliner, mascara, pink lipstick. There was a gold necklace at her throat and several bangle bracelets on her wrists. The terror on her face was positively incongruous. "H-he usually talks to me from another room," she said, wobbling as she stood. "It was only yesterday that he came out and I saw his face." She gazed into the hall in terror. "He's going to hurt us if he finds out. I know he will."

"It's okay," Seneca said as she rushed to her side. "We're getting you out right now. All right? Do you think you can walk?"

Chelsea nodded shakily. Seneca held out her hands and helped the girl through the door.

Behind her, Seneca heard the sirens. Out of the window, police cars kicked up dust in the driveway. Maddox opened one of the French doors and stood on the balcony. "We found someone inside!" he shouted at the officers. "It's Chelsea Dawson!"

Seneca and Madison held Chelsea up as they walked down the hall. Seneca's heart pounded the whole time, expecting Brett to appear. But as they opened the door and pushed Chelsea into the fresh air, nothing happened. Cops swarmed her immediately. She stepped back into the house, letting the emergency technicians look Chelsea over. They'd made it. Chelsea was safe. Now it was time to find Brett.

She spun around and got to work quickly, opening doors, peering into alcoves, bounding up staircases, knowing full well that Brett might attack her at every turn. But all she found was emptiness. The house smelled immaculately clean – the same sandalwood/cleaning products mix, she realized with a jolt, that Gabriel's condo had smelled like. Uneasy, she thundered down the stairs and swept over Chelsea's bedroom again. Peeked into the pool area. Ambushed a kitchen pantry. Nothing.

"Where are you?" she whispered, standing in the middle of the kitchen. It was clear he wasn't going to answer. This was another part of Brett's plan, and he'd executed it perfectly.

A police officer appeared out of nowhere and took her arm. "Miss, you have to leave," he urged. "We need forensics in here. This is a crime scene."

"But . . ." Seneca protested. Listlessly, she stepped aside and let the cops swarm in. She knew they wouldn't find anything. The house was empty. And as that realization slowly seeped in, Seneca felt empty, too.

CHAPTER 34

It was after eleven by the time Aerin and Thomas pulled up to the house on the vineyard, and the place was swarming with police cars, K-9 vehicles, paramedics, a fire truck, the bomb squad, and news vans from several local affiliates. Aerin gasped. Forty minutes ago, Seneca had sent her quite a few frantic texts, saying they were checking out the vineyard and that the shack might be a trap. Aerin hadn't noticed them because she'd left her phone on silent while checking out the shack. When she'd gotten back into the car she'd reached out to Seneca, but she hadn't been able to get through to her. What if something was wrong?

Thomas had barely thrown the car into park when Aerin spied Seneca, Maddox, and Madison standing under the carport. Her heart lifted with relief, and she bolted out of the car toward them. "What's going on?" she cried, gesturing at the police vehicles.

Seneca just stared at her emptily. Maddox stepped forward. "We found Chelsea." He sounded proud but also shaky. "She was in the house. Locked in a bedroom."

A mix of happiness and disbelief shot through Aerin. "You're *kidding*!"

"But not Brett," Seneca interrupted, her voice wooden. "He's gone."

Aerin stared at her, the words not quite making sense. Swirling lights from the bar atop a police car flashed against Seneca's face. "A-are you sure?" she asked.

Seneca lowered her head. "I looked everywhere. He's not in the house. I mean, I'm not surprised, really. Of course he's gone. I just thought . . . I just hoped . . ."

Aerin felt her heartbeat thudding powerfully at her temples. "Where's Chelsea now? Is she . . . alive?"

"She's fine," Maddox said. "The cops are questioning her inside."

"That's good!" Aerin cried, feeling a flare of optimism. She looked around at the others. "That means they'll get information about Brett and where he went, right?"

Madison smiled weakly. "A group of cops already started through the vineyards in hopes that Brett took off in that direction."

"This is all really good!" Aerin said, staring at Seneca, praying for her spirits to lift. But Seneca just shrugged. She seemed so disheartened.

Then Aerin remembered. She rooted around in her pockets until she found the origami, which she'd folded into a crane shape again. "This was at the shack."

Seneca opened her eyes and stared. Aerin turned it over for her. *Jackson*," Seneca read aloud, sounding baffled. "What does that mean?"

"I don't know. But maybe it's got his fingerprints on it. The cops could check."

Seneca sniffed. "I'm sure Brett wasn't stupid enough to leave a fingerprint." But she still inspected the weathered crane carefully, holding it gently under its wings as though it might shatter.

A group of police officers broke through the vines, empty-handed. One noticed Aerin and the others and trudged over. It was Grieg, the same freckle-faced man they'd spoken to after Jeff's death. "This is going to take a while," he said in a gentle enough voice. "We're going to need statements from Seneca, Maddox, and Madison at least, though maybe from Aerin and Thomas as well. How about we take you over to the station?"

"I'd rather wait here," Seneca said firmly. She was staring at something indeterminate out in the vines, her eyes glassy.

By the way Grieg shifted, it was clear he would rather they leave. The last thing Aerin wanted to do was make waves with the cops, so she trudged over to the police SUV. After a moment, Seneca followed. No one spoke as they buckled their seat belts. The only sound was the staccato raindrops as they pelted the roof.

Aerin stared at the house. Shadows shifted behind the windows – tons of cops were inside, canvassing the place for evidence. What would they find in there? What did Brett leave behind?

The SUV rolled out of the gravel drive. The air conditioner began to blast chilly air into the backseat, and the car soon smelled vaguely of mildew and wet upholstery. Aerin pressed her head to the door, feeling sick. Suddenly, her cell phone vibrated in her pocket. Maddox had group-texted them.

What are we going to SAY?

Madison wrote first: *We should come clean. Tell them everything.*

Agreed, Maddox pinged next. *It's the only way they'll be able to find Brett. We've done all we can.*

Seneca frowned at her phone's screen, and her fingers started to move. Three little dots appeared in the text window, then disappeared. That happened two more times, as Seneca struggled with what to write. Aerin could guess at what was going on in Seneca's mind. Her friend wanted Brett, and she wanted to do it on her own – without the cops.

Except now they'd been pushed into a corner. There was nowhere left for them to turn. They *needed* the police to help. This was bigger than all of them.

Seneca stared at the screen for a long time, as though in a trance. Finally, she lowered her eyes and sighed deeply, as if letting something go. The three dots appeared on Aerin's screen again, and then came Seneca's reply. *Okay. I guess we have no choice.*

Several hours and three bad cups of police-station coffee later, Aerin sat in the waiting room, cupping the paper crane in one hand and flipping through a year-old *Time* in another. The others were strewn about the small, cramped space, perusing their phones (Maddox and Madison), glowering at the closed interior door to the offices (Seneca), and, in Thomas's case, stroking Aerin's hair, which made Aerin oscillate between pleasantly sleepy and feeling guilty for feeling pleasantly sleepy. Despite a few clipped *they'll be right with you*s from the officer at the front desk, it seemed as though the cops had forgotten about them. Which was maddening. Didn't they realize they were wasting valuable time?

Finally, Grieg appeared in the doorway. "Let's go, guys."

Everyone shot up and followed him down the hall. Aerin mentally rehearsed how they were going to tell their story . . . and what it would mean. Would the cops be able to find Brett with the details they provided?

Grieg opened a door to a small room not unlike the one they sat in after Jeff Cohen was murdered. He shut the door behind him, slapped the same notebook he always seemed to carry around on the table, and said in a distracted, unenthusiastic voice, "Sorry to keep you waiting. It's been a busy day. So yeah, if you want to sum up what you know, we can probably get you out of here soon."

"Excuse me?" Seneca said sharply. She scoffed. "We have no interest in skimming over what happened. We want to tell you everything."

Grieg's eyebrow arched, and the look on his face was a mix of exhaustion and irritation. "*Okaaaay.*" He turned on a recorder. "Please state your names and ages."

They did so, and when Grieg asked his next question – *describe how you found Chelsea today* – Seneca blurted, "Because her kidnapper sent us to her."

Grieg's face clouded. He sat back and laced his hands across his waist. "Explain."

There was a long, awkward silence. Aerin glanced around. Seneca raised an eyebrow at her, and Aerin took a breath.

She walked Grieg through how she'd met Brett, the search for Helena's killer, and how they'd realized after the fact that

Brett had fed them every clue that indicted Marissa Ingram. Maddox jumped in next, telling about receiving Brett's letter. Seneca, Madison, and Thomas filled in the gaps of what the letter actually meant. Grieg's pen hovered over the notebook, but he refrained from writing anything down. After about five minutes, he held up a hand. "I'm sorry, *what* does this have to do with Chelsea Dawson?"

Seneca looked like she was going to explode. "That's what we're *getting* to."

She explained about Brett luring them to Lafayette, how he broke into the B&B, how he fed them clues, and how he pushed Jeff to his death because Jeff had figured out his identity. "Then he fed us more clues that led to finding Chelsea at the vineyard. He knew when we were going to show up, so he cleaned up beforehand and got the hell out. But look, he's killed others. If you don't go after him now, he's going to do it again."

Then she sat back with a grave look on her face. Oddly, though, Grieg seemed completely emotionless. At one point, his gaze had even slipped to his *phone*. It was baffling. Maybe cops all had to develop a strong sense of stoicism, but Aerin had expected *some* reaction – shock, certainly, and then gratitude. After all, they'd basically done Grieg's job for him, hadn't they?

There was commotion in the hallway, and Aerin peered out of the little square window. A K-9 dog sauntered by, its tongue wagging. A woman cop passed, her ear pressed to a cell phone. Finally, Grieg shut his notebook with a slap. He hadn't written down a single word. "That's all very interesting. But I don't think you're on the right track."

Aerin blinked rapidly, her mouth suddenly tacky and dry. "Excuse me?"

"You think someone *else* did it?" Seneca blurted. "You have another suspect?" She laughed incredulously. "Whoever you think it is, you're wrong."

Grieg licked his thin lips, busying himself with stuffing the notebook in his briefcase. "I'm afraid I can't release too many details at the moment."

Seneca edged forward in her seat. "Seriously? You're going to tell us nothing?"

"Seneca," Maddox said softly, taking her arm.

She wrenched it away. "We've been sitting here for hours," she said, her eyes hard on Grieg. "And *we* were the ones who found Chelsea – you owe us an explanation. Or else . . ." Her nostrils flared. "Or we're going to the press with our story. And we'll say you aren't listening, and that the town is in danger."

Grieg held up a warning hand. "There will be no going to the press. The last thing we need is to make this worse." He gritted his teeth. "Look, I commend you guys for bringing Mrs. Dawson home safe. But so far, our findings on the crime scene at the vineyard are . . . inconclusive. There's no sign of forced entry to the house. And no signs on Miss Dawson that she's been tortured or even mistreated – we had our best medics look at her. There's her mental state, of course, though that seems a little . . . melodramatic."

Seneca looked appalled. "Meaning?"

Grieg seemed to think something through, then said, his voice condescending, "Miss Dawson had on fresh clothes, she'd showered, and she was watching TV when you found her. That's not exactly common for abduction cases. Moreover, the stories Miss Dawson told about her captor don't exactly match up to what we've found."

"How so?" Maddox sputtered.

"Miss Dawson said her captor seemed to be talking through the wall, with a microphone system. And that he seemed to know what she was doing at all times – like he had cameras. But there were no signs of any of those devices in the room she was in or in any other rooms that we've searched. There were no wires that they might have been disconnected from, either. We're still looking, but we have experts on this. They would have found something by now."

Aerin shifted forward. "Maybe all his stuff was wireless. Seneca had a wireless surveillance camera in her room at the B and B."

Grieg gave Seneca a strange look as if to say, *What kind of girl carries around a portable wireless surveillance camera?* "I suppose that's a possibility," he said evenly. "But even if we do find evidence of a wireless camera, who's not to say Miss Dawson installed it herself? As another way to film herself?"

Seneca gawked at him. Aerin felt her stomach swoop. Was this really, truly happening?

"But when we got to her, her room was locked," Seneca said. "We had to unlock it for her with a credit card. How do you explain that?"

Grieg's brow wrinkled. "That, too, could have been staged. We found a key in the master bathroom. It was in a drawer, but it wasn't exactly hidden. Miss Dawson could have unlocked that door whenever she wanted, and we think she did. We don't have official data back yet, but there are a lot of fingerprints all over the kitchen. A few long blonde hairs, too. Preliminary searches also found those same prints on the doorknob that led to the garage, where we found a trash bag full of garbage – mostly food. We don't have a fingerprint match yet, and we don't have DNA evidence that *Chelsea* ate the food, but that's what we think happened."

Seneca shook her head. "No. That's impossible."

Grieg crossed his arms over his chest. "Miss Dawson also said she wasn't allowed access to her phone, though she saw it a few times. We found it just outside her room – that second phone, the one she used to speak to Gabriel. Her fingerprints are on that, too. When we accessed her photos, we found a lot of recent shots of Miss Dawson in the bedroom. She's smiling in every one of them. In fact, they seem . . . posed."

"Like for an Instagram shot, you're thinking?" Thomas murmured cynically.

Aerin stared at him. Slowly, her mind folded around the theory. Was Grieg saying what she *thought* they were saying? "But couldn't the kidnapper have arranged those photos so they *look* like selfies? Forced her to smile?" she asked. That sounded exactly like something Brett would do.

Grieg jangled loose change in his pocket. "Look. Miss Dawson has gotten thousands of new social media followers since this happened. She's on every news channel in the country. I should also add that we found a laptop in that bedroom, in a drawer. The first item on the Google search was her own name – it's almost like she *wanted* us to find it."

He rubbed his eyes. "We don't think there *was* a kidnapper. End of story."

"There was!" Aerin cried. "There had to be! Gabriel Wilton!"

"There's no real evidence Gabriel Wilton was involved," Grieg explained. "Yes, they were friends – good friends. And yes, Gabriel was the last person she spoke to before she was kidnapped, and it seemed she rejected him." He put *kidnapped* in air quotes. "And yes, he wasn't at his condo the day we went to question him, *and* someone tipped us off about him. But anonymous tips can be misleading. Sometimes people give false information to incriminate someone else – an enemy, perhaps. It's even possible *Chelsea* left that tip to throw suspicion off what she was really up to. Gabriel could be a victim here."

Aerin felt sick.

"In fact . . ." Grieg glanced into the hall as if mulling something over, then looked back at them. "In fact, I just got word that Gabriel Wilton's body has been found."

Aerin just blinked. Seneca clapped a hand over her mouth. "What? Where?" Madison cried.

"There was a car accident. A Toyota Prius smashed through a guardrail at a scenic overlook on one of the winding roads about a half hour away. The vehicle caught fire before anyone found it, but it's registered in Gabriel's name. There was one body inside – a male. And we were able to recover a license – Gabriel's."

Aerin's mouth was suddenly dry. "So he's . . . *dead*?"

Grieg nodded. His eyes were narrowed, but the corners of his mouth turned up slightly, almost as if to say, *See? You kids are so, so wrong.*

Seneca pounded a fist on the table. "Are you people that stupid? It's not Gabriel's body in that car. It's just someone who *looks* like him. Gabriel – *Brett* – is alive and well."

Grieg raised an eyebrow. "That's a pretty serious accusation to make, Miss Frazier."

"Let me identify the body, and I'll apologize," Seneca growled. Her face had gone completely red.

Grieg stood and curled his hands over the top of the chair. "Look, let's reconvene after we collect more facts. Which, I assure you, we will get." He scooped up his notebook and started toward the door.

"We're *giving* you the facts, and you're not listening!" Seneca's voice cracked. "If Chelsea faked all this, then who sent us that letter?"

Hand on the doorknob, Grieg turned. "The one about how your guy is a serial killer? Does the letter actually *say* that? Does it state, in bold facts, that he murdered those two women?"

"It . . ." Aerin started, but then her thoughts came to a screeching halt. *Jesus.* The reality seemed to drip over her, droplet by droplet. "It doesn't," she said finally, in a small voice. "Not really."

"Because he's very, very careful," Seneca jumped in. "But *we* knew what he meant. Okay, so even without the letter, why would someone send me clues? Why would someone attack me in the B and B?"

Grieg gave her a leveling glance. "I wish you'd reported that at the time, Miss Frazier."

Seneca looked blindsided, her lips parted slightly.

"We couldn't," Aerin eked out. "The kidnapper told us he would kill Chelsea if we got the police involved."

"I'm afraid there isn't much I can do about it now," Grieg said. There was a whisper of a smile on his face again, and Aerin could almost visualize what was going through his mind. Because they'd reported nothing, and because they could *prove* nothing, their story was as flimsy as Chelsea's. What did they have to show for Brett's wrath? Some take-out menus and flyers with numbers circled? A weird poem left on Seneca's windowsill and another shoved into a cup of coffee? A bent necklace that could have just as easily been damaged some other way? A few exchanges on an amateur crime-solving site?

It was possible, Aerin realized, that Grieg thought they'd been working with Chelsea, four kids desperate to make a name for themselves as expert crime solvers, eager for the attention. Her throat felt dry. She was filled with hot, liquid with rage, but she had no idea what to do with it.

Everyone filed out in a daze. Aerin gazed around at her friends, not knowing what to say. It was like they were trapped in a nightmare, where truth didn't matter.

Groaning, she stomped out the double doors and stood on the pavement. It was late afternoon, and though the humidity had lifted a little, the sky was still gray. It matched her mood. A single refrain thudded in her mind: Brett had tricked them – again. Brett had gotten away, *again*.

I'm sorry, Helena, she thought wearily, feeling acid rise in her throat.

"Hey."

254

Aerin turned. Thomas had stepped onto the pavement next to her and was squinting in the cloudy glare. "Hi," she said flatly, her eyes burning with tears.

He slung an arm around her and pulled her tight. "That cop is a disaster. We're going to find Brett. If he's still out there – if he's not dead – I'll do everything I can to find him."

Aerin shrugged. "I feel like it's a lost cause."

"It's *not*. When I get back up to Dexby, I'll reenroll with the police if I have to in order to get someone to look seriously into this case. This is a *huge deal*, Aerin. That letter Brett wrote? We're going to figure out a way to nail him. Maybe the answer is in that paper crane, you know? Maybe he's in Philadelphia."

"Or maybe he's just a Danny DeVito fan," Aerin grumbled. But she met his gaze anyway. His eyes seemed to anchor her into place, steadying her dizzy head. Slowly, she reached out and touched his hand. "Thank you," she said, and then hugged him tightly, feeling the disappointed tears run down her cheeks.

Only when his phone beeped did Thomas pull away. Aerin watched as he glanced at the screen, his expression slowly changing into something grim. "What is it?" Aerin said nervously. "Brett?"

Thomas shook his head. "It's from my grandma's doctor." He sounded dazed. "Sh-she's in the hospital. It sounds . . . serious." When he looked up, his eyes searched the room as if trying to lock onto something familiar. "I – I have to get back to Dexby. *Now.*"

"I'll go with you."

Thomas ran his hand over his hair. "Okay. Great." He glanced at her then, as if only now hearing what she'd said. "Wait. You'll really come?"

"Of course," Aerin said, clasping his hand. Thomas had been there for her, after all. It was the least she could do.

And it wasn't like there was anything left for her here.

CHAPTER 35

Maddox sat in the lobby of the Reeds Hotel gobbling down the first thing he'd eaten all day, a huge club sandwich overloaded with mayo plus a side of fries. The bathroom door at the back of the lobby opened, and his sister and Aerin appeared. He was about to ask them if they wanted to order when he noticed a guy in a local TV news affiliate polo stroll in and ask something at the front desk.

He sat up straighter. With his slick blond hair and gleaming smile, Maddox instantly recognized the guy as Matt Warburg, a reporter he'd watched commenting on the Chelsea Dawson Hoax, as it was now called, all day. The public thought Chelsea was a fraud. The end.

Aerin and Madison plopped down at the table. Madison picked up a menu but then put it down again, looking miserable. Soon after, Seneca appeared, too, listlessly grabbing a roll from the basket and slowly covering it with butter. Everyone was silent, staring either at their phones or into the middle distance. "I don't want to leave, but I told my dad I'd be back today," Seneca finally said. "I need to at least go back and check in, but then I can figure out a way to come back here. Or wherever."

"Wait, what?" Aerin looked shocked. "Why would you come back here? Brett's gone. We'll have to wait until he strikes next."

Seneca lay her butter knife on the plate. There was a sharp line between her brows. "No way. We have solid evidence he was here, even if the cops don't believe us. Brett *lived* here. Someone knew him well, and someone is going to give us a clue – we just have to ask more questions. And look, that message on Aerin's crane? Maybe it's another clue. We just have to figure out what it means."

"Are we *sure* Brett wasn't in that accident?" Madison whispered.

Seneca scoffed. "Please. Brett set up that accident to make it look like he'd died so the cops wouldn't search for him or ask any questions – *and* in hopes we'd drop the case."

"So who *was* in that car?" Aerin asked uneasily.

The sandwich churned in Maddox's stomach. He'd been thinking about that all day. Brett had taken another victim. It must have been his plan all along.

He felt a shift behind him and whirled around, on edge. A waiter passed with a tray. A woman in a navy dress slipped into an open elevator car.

Seneca took a bite of the roll and chewed. "I say we regroup, come up with a plan of attack, and find a lead on who and where Brett might be. There has got to be something. I can *feel* it." She sat back in the chair and crossed her arms over her chest. "Or is it just me? Am I the only one who wants to keep going?"

Everyone shifted uncomfortably. Madison stared at her nails. Maddox placed his napkin on his plate, feeling conflicted. Then Aerin said in a small voice, "I'm in."

"Enough that you'll come back and help?" Seneca's voice was hopeful.

Aerin nodded, her ponytail bouncing. "Yes."

"And you?" Seneca turned to Maddox. He felt his stomach flip over with a mix of fear and rage. "Okay," he said, hardly believing he was doing this. Searching for Brett now seemed so futile. The guy had orchestrated a complex kidnapping, turned around to make it look like a fraud, and then pulled off a Houdini-like escape. On the other hand, Maddox couldn't fathom going home. Lazing around the rest of the summer. Running. Packing up for Oregon. It all seemed so . . . illogical. Brett had hurt them. *All* of them. He couldn't walk away from that.

"I'll come, too," Madison said after a beat. "We should probably go home first for a few days, but then Maddox and I will come up with an excuse to get back here."

"Good." Seneca's mouth twitched, and her eyes were a little shiny – she looked so grateful, like she hadn't expected all of them to agree.

"I'll get back here as soon as I can," Aerin said. "I'll try to get Thomas to come, too. But I'm going to need a few days." Her face clouded, and she glanced at her watch. Then she grabbed the bag that waited next to her and stood.

"What's up?" Seneca asked.

"Thomas told me to meet him outside at two. We're driving to Rudyard – his grandmother's in the hospital. It seems serious." She turned to go, then hurried back to them and gave them all hugs. "See you soon. Everyone lock your doors at home tonight. And maybe install surveillance cameras, just in case."

Everyone laughed warily. After more hugs, Aerin tossed her long blonde hair over her shoulder and strode through the marble lobby. Maddox stared at her back, feeling a twinge. Long ago, he had loved Aerin's older sister, Helena, in that way only a dorky, misunderstood twelve-year-old could. It was astonishing how much Aerin suddenly looked like her now. From the back, the two of them could be twins. Then his gaze fell to the still image of Chelsea, frozen on the video screen. She looked so vibrant and happy. Who would she be after this? What horrors had she endured as Brett's prisoner? The worst thing about all of this was that no one would believe a word she said.

Madison tossed the menu to the table and stood, too. "Ugh, there's no way I can eat under all this stress. I guess I'll pack up so we can check out." Then she groaned. "Maddox, why did you tell me to bring two huge suitcases? It's going to take for*ever* for me to collect everything."

"I didn't . . ." Maddox started, but his sister had already spun on her heel and headed for the elevators. Maddox watched her go, smiling wryly. When they came back, Madison wouldn't pack so much. His stomach swooped again. He still kind of couldn't believe they were coming back . . . and so soon.

He started after her, figuring there was nothing else to do except grab his bags as well. But then he felt a hand on his arm. "Do you have a second to talk?"

Seneca looked nervous but hopeful. Maddox's heart lifted, and he turned toward her. "Of course."

CHAPTER 36

The hotel had a little patio off the lobby with couches, palm trees, a big fishpond, and a large bar. When Seneca and Maddox sank down into a chaise, she overheard a few patrons talking about Chelsea. "What kind of girl kidnaps herself?" a woman at the bar said as she sipped her red wine. The man next to her rolled his eyes. "A girl who needs to be the center of the universe."

If only they knew the truth.

Seneca slumped onto a couch, feeling a fresh wave of despair. Maddox sat next to her. She pulled it together for him; there was no use wearing her extreme disappointment on her sleeve. "I just wanted to say good-bye before I head out," she said. She checked her watch. It was a few minutes after two. "I promised my dad I'd be home by late afternoon. I'd rather things go really smoothly so that I can come *back* here."

Maddox nodded. "So he still doesn't know about . . . ?"

She shook her head. "And I don't intend to tell him. Not yet." She wouldn't until she had Brett behind bars. It didn't even feel like deception anymore. It was just the way things had to be.

She peeked at Maddox. He was hunching those muscled shoulders, and something about the lock of hair that curled over his left ear made her stomach swoop. "You know," he said gently, "we still don't actually know if Brett was telling the truth in that letter. He could have painted the relationship with your mom as way more friendly than it really was."

Seneca felt the now-familiar heart drop whenever she thought of her mom and Brett as friends . . . or whatever they were. "I guess," she said. "But I could also see it happening. Aerin's right – Brett seemed totally harmless. She flirted with him. I unloaded to him about my mom, and he was really sympathetic." She felt the prickle of tears. "Brett has this amazing ability to shift into whatever you need him to be. And I'm guessing that's what he did for my mom – and for Chelsea, too. I looked at some of the phone data that was released – apparently he and Chelsea texted each other nonstop on that second phone she had. Chelsea told him everything. School stuff. Family stuff. Brett wanted more, clearly, but she didn't."

"Do you think he's the guy Jeff thought she was cheating with?"

"Probably," Seneca said. She pulled her bottom lip into her mouth, reviewing the information Grieg had given them about Jeff. "Though it's ironic that Jeff even cared, given *his* history."

As soon as she said it, she felt cruel. So Jeff cheated on Chelsea. Maybe he had a reason to – people were complicated, or sometimes they made idiotic mistakes. They were mislead, or they acted impetuously and foolishly on hunches and impulses, the same as her mother might have done during that fateful kiss with Brett at Starbucks. Seneca couldn't shame Jeff for screwing up his relationship because she didn't know the whole story. It would have been nice if Jeff had been honest with her, but that was a moot point now.

When she shut her eyes, she pictured his pale body lying facedown in that vacant lot behind the hotel. Was it their fault that he was dead? Would she have to live her whole life feeling responsible for that?

A wine cork popped. The music on the stereo changed to something jazzy and full of saxophones. Maddox shifted beside her, and Seneca could tell they were both thinking about Brett and how he'd manipulated every aspect of this situation. "I still can't believe it," Maddox murmured. "Brett used Chelsea's life as leverage so we wouldn't go to the cops, and that ended up being why the cops didn't take us seriously."

"I know," Seneca said. "The other thing I don't understand is how there can't be any evidence at the house where Chelsea was staying. No cameras? No items out of place? Not a single fingerprint?"

"They're still collecting evidence. Maybe they'll find something."

Seneca grunted in doubt. Then she added, "The strangest thing about this is that Brett went to all that effort to kidnap Chelsea only to let her go."

Maddox cocked his head. "That seems like classic Brett. He shone a light on her biggest sin – that she's full of herself. No one will take her seriously now that they think she staged her own kidnapping. I heard a bunch of people dropped her on Instagram already. Her reputation is ruined."

"Yeah, but doesn't classic Brett actually *kill* his victims? I mean, he even murdered Jeff – and for what? Chelsea is the first person we know of that he turned loose. She has information about him now. Possibly even more vital information than we do. We should *definitely* talk to her."

Maddox's eyes lowered. "I heard her parents are putting her in a psychiatric facility."

"Well then, we visit her," Seneca said. "We ask her everything she remembers. We tell her *we* believe her, even if no one else will. But Brett should be thinking of that. He's taken a big risk, leaving her alive. Which makes me think Chelsea was never his end goal."

Maddox sat back on the cushion. "You think Chelsea was just a pawn, don't you? Brett had an issue with her, but his bigger issue is with *us*."

Seneca drummed her hands on her knees. "I do. Us finding her, us being here, somehow, is just another piece to the puzzle."

"And we played right into his hands."

Seneca massaged the back of her neck. It was a theory that had been kicking around in her brain all day, but it felt so chilling to say it out loud. "We did. We should have seen it coming. But all I was focused on was finding Chelsea . . . and having a standoff."

"You *wanted* a standoff."

She stared at him. "Of course I did. Didn't you?"

Maddox's green eyes narrowed, and then he took her hands. "I was scared shitless of that, but I would have been there for you. No matter what."

Seneca felt her mouth wobble. Their talk the other night at the party swirled in her head. As she shifted closer to him, her heart started to pound.

"Maddox?" she said in a small voice. "What *are* we?"

Maddox looked surprised. "You really don't know?"

She could feel her cheeks turn red. "Should I?"

Maddox stared at her for a moment, then took her shoulders and pulled her close. Seneca breathed in sharply, then felt all the tension in her body release as he pressed his lips to hers. She shut her eyes. The sounds of the bar fell away, and all she could feel were his warm hands wrapped around the tops of her arms and his soft mouth against her own. When he pulled away, he stared at her sweetly. She smiled back and ducked her head.

"Oh" was all she could think to say. "Well, okay. Good." She moved toward him again, not wanting to end kissing so quickly, but then her phone buzzed.

She glanced at the screen, annoyed for the interruption. It was an unfamiliar local number. She answered it and put the call on speaker. "Miss Frazier?" came a voice. "This is Amanda Iverson. From Golden Shores Realty?"

"Oh!" Seneca frowned. It was "Gabriel's" boss. "Hi?"

"I'm returning your call. I'm sorry I didn't get back to you sooner. I've had quite a hectic week. So are you interested in one of our properties?"

Seneca ran her tongue over her teeth, remembering how she hadn't given any details of who she was or what she wanted in her message to Mrs. Iverson. "Um, the reason why I initially called is irrelevant," she said, gathering her thoughts. "But I'm a friend of Gabriel Wilton's. I'm organizing a memorial for him, if you're interested."

Mrs. Iverson inhaled sharply. "Oh. I . . . I'm not sure."

"Why? Do you think the stories about him were true?"

"No!" Mrs. Iverson cried instantly.

"So you think they *weren't* true?"

"Of course not, but . . ." The woman sounded flustered. "I'd better go."

"Wait!" Seneca sat up straighter, desperate to keep her on the phone. "Look, I don't think he was a criminal, either. It's a shame how the press has demonized him." Every ounce of her being hated saying that.

Mrs. Iverson coughed. "Yes. Gabriel was a good person. I'm sad . . . well, I'm sad all of this has happened. He'll be deeply missed."

"I agree," Seneca said, her voice quaking with fake feeling. "Which is why I'd like his memorial service to focus on how good he was, not the false charges before his tragic death. So if you have anything you'd like to say about him –"

"When is the memorial service?" Mrs. Iverson interrupted.

"Yes, we're putting it together now," Seneca said quickly, praying someone *else* wasn't doing the same thing.

"I-is it in Lafayette? Or in Gabriel's hometown? Come to think of it, I don't *know* his hometown . . ."

Join the club, Seneca thought bitterly, exchanging a quick ironic glance with Maddox. "Yes, it's here. I've contacted friends. Coworkers. Family members. We're hoping to put together some kind words about what Gabriel was *really* like, and perhaps you'd like to contribute?"

266

"Family members?" Mrs. Iverson's voice had eased a notch higher. "So you've gotten in touch with his sister?"

Seneca's gaze met Maddox's again. Her heart was suddenly pounding. In touch with his *sister*? "Um, actually, we haven't been able to reach her yet. Do *you* know how we could?"

There was a long pause. "I . . ." Iverson breathed noisily. "I'm not sure . . ."

"Mrs. Iverson, please," Seneca said. "We'd really love to get in touch with her."

"All right," Mrs. Iverson said quietly. "I peeked at his emails this morning. It was for work reasons – he was handling some clients that I now need to take over. Gabriel was a model employee – he hardly contacted *anyone* unless it had to do with work. But I did find something in his deleted folder – he reached out to a woman named Viola with some sort of photo attachment. I didn't open it, but he called her *sis*. She has a different last name, though. Nevins. I already emailed her, but so far I've gotten no response."

Seneca dropped the phone on the cushion, staring at Maddox. He was clutching the side of his head. *Holy shit*, he mouthed. She picked the phone back up and conjured up her sweetest, calmest voice possible. "Can you tell me the email address?"

"Um . . ." Mrs. Iverson said reluctantly, but Seneca pressured her a little more, and she rattled it off. Then she said, "Now, where and when is the memorial?"

Seneca named a church she remembered passing in Lafayette and a time two days from now. Once Mrs. Iverson realized it was a lie, they'd be long gone. Then she quickly hit END and stared at Maddox. For a few beats, neither of them spoke.

"Do you really think this person is a relative?" she whispered. "Or is this another trick?"

"The email was in his deleted folder," Maddox said. "What if he meant to empty his trash but forgot? Could he really have a secret sister somewhere? And was it a mess-up, or intentional – yet another clue he left behind?"

"We'd finally learn his real name. We'd finally learn who he *is*." Seneca wanted so badly for this woman to be the answer the desire was almost tangible, a taste on her tongue. She pictured presenting the police with Brett's name. Telling her father. She pictured Brett standing trial, then shuffling off to jail forever. It wouldn't feel as good as having her mother back, but it would be justice all the same.

Her phone beeped, and she grabbed it, anticipating Amanda's email. But it was a text from a long, unorganized string of numbers instead – a line of zeroes and ones, a lot like the texts she got from Verizon Wireless when she'd gone over her data limit.

Don't bother looking for us. We're outta here.

She showed the text to Maddox. Her stomach was swishing again. "Do you think this is from . . ."

"I – I don't know." Maddox pointed to the word at the end of the sentence. *Us.* "What does he mean by that? Him and his sister? This Viola person?"

That didn't feel right. Unless Brett had bugged her phone, how could he know she'd learned about Viola at this exact moment? Seneca's thoughts returned to the sinking feeling

268

she'd had since Chelsea had been found – that her kidnapping was just a small part of a much bigger scheme. That everything he'd plotted had been deliberate, exact, and the worst was yet to come – something that would totally blindside them.

A chill went through her, cutting straight to her bones. Something had happened, she could feel it. She just didn't know yet what it was.

CHAPTER 37

Aerin stepped out of the hotel lobby and under the porte cochere. Thomas had told her that he was grabbing his belongings from a motel outside town where he'd been staying ever since he'd come to Lafayette to track her down, and then would swing back here at 2:00 p.m. It was a little after two now, but she didn't see his car in the drive yet. She jiggled her leg nervously. Thomas's grandmother meant so much to him. He hadn't had time to explain what had happened to her, but Aerin hoped she'd pull through.

The sun was out, and tourists were trickling out to the streets, beach bags in hand. Aerin leaned against the wall to the hotel, regretting that she hadn't been here to relax on the beach. Maybe she and Thomas could take a trip to Cape Cod once this was all over.

Then again, *would* it ever be over? She waited for the predictable clench in her stomach. It was there, of course, but so was a steady feeling of determination. This quest to get Brett was no longer just a lark, a *what the hell am I doing?* She was all in. She could almost imagine Helena standing behind her, seeing all of this, urging her on.

Her phone beeped, and she peered at it. *Mom*, read the caller ID. Aerin raised an eyebrow. It had been forever since she'd seen *that* number on her screen. Sometimes it seemed like her mom barely noticed she was away.

Miss you, honey, was all it said.

A tiny knot unloosened in Aerin's chest. Maybe her mom noticed their distance, too. How fucked up it was. How none of them were really recovered. She grasped the phone, trying to decide what to type. *There's so much I need to tell you. There's so much evil in the world. But I'm going to make it right. For all of us.*

But instead, she just settled on, *Me too. See you soon.*

A reply came in right away. *Definitely. Have a great time in LA!*

Aerin frowned. Since when was she going to LA? She didn't even *know* anyone there.

A growl broke her concentration. Thomas's white Ford had pulled up to the curb just beyond the overhang. Aerin hefted her bag on her shoulder and hurried toward it. She waved at Thomas through the windshield, but his head was down, his blue Yankees baseball cap obscuring his eyes. He seemed to be typing something on his phone. Her heart lurched. Something about his grandmother? Maybe things were even worse than they thought.

The trunk was open, so she dropped her suitcase in. Then she swung around to the front and climbed in. The air inside was cool and smelled like mint – much better, in fact, than the car had smelled earlier today, when they'd gone to the shack. Thomas must have had it quickly cleaned. She started to buckle her seat belt as the car reversed and pulled onto the street. "What are the doctors saying? Is she okay?"

"She's fine, Aerin. Just fine."

The world tunneled around Aerin. Instantly, her heart jumped to her throat. The voice wasn't Thomas's . . . but it sure was familiar. *Really* familiar. As he gunned the engine, cruising through a yellow light, the man in the driver's seat glanced over at her, and their gazes locked. Aerin took in his thick eyebrows, mischievous grin, and gleaming eyes. It felt like every cell in her body, every bone in her skeleton, might spontaneously combust. She knew. She just instantly, instantly *knew*.

It was Brett.

AFTER

Brett knew it was crazy to think Aerin would be happy to see him, but he was disappointed when she screamed. Where was the flirtatious friendliness she'd once felt toward him? Where was their old cozy bond?

He pointed at her sharply before she could do it again, his foot still firmly on the gas pedal. "*Quiet.*" And then, lightning fast, he grabbed her phone from her trembling fingers and shoved it under his thigh. "You won't be needing that where *we're* going."

Aerin pivoted toward her door, but he'd expected that, too. He pressed the childproof lock before she could wrench the thing open. "Seriously?" he teased, chuckling.

She gaped at him, pinioned against the backseat. Her bottom lip trembled. Her face was ashen. But, oh, how lovely she looked. That blonde hair. That perfect face. So beautiful. So *vulnerable.* All the pieces had fallen into place, and now he had her exactly where he wanted her.

Cruising through more yellow lights, Brett gave her a tight grin. "So . . . We meet again. It feels good, doesn't it?"

"Wh-what are you doing?" Aerin stammered.

"Driving, naturally."

She pointed out of the window. Buildings whizzed by; soon enough, they'd be on the highway. "I – I have to go. My boyfriend's grandmother is sick. I need to see him. He's picking me up."

"He's your *boyfriend* now?" Brett shook his head. "Jesus, Aerin. I thought you were smarter. Like I'm going to let you off at the next corner? Besides, I already told you. Your boy toy's precious Nana is fine."

There was a wrinkle on Aerin's brow, but then he saw the exact moment when it all made sense to her. *He* had sent that text to Thomas. Brett could hack into anything. He'd set *all* of this up – more than she could even imagine. The dominoes had finally lined up precisely. He'd gotten them all to Lafayette. He'd made them jump through hoops, find Chelsea, and destroy their credibility with the police. And now he could get the final part of his plan rolling.

Brett reached out and touched her cheek. "We're going to have such a good time together, Aerin. I promise."

Aerin trembled. A small, terrified noise escaped from her throat. When he touched her, she shut her eyes and winced.

Well. Might as well get to the next part of this. Making a turn onto the beach highway, Brett grabbed his leather bag on the backseat. When he found what he needed, he plunged toward her leg. Aerin saw it coming and thrashed, bumping against the leather, legs kicking high, but it didn't matter – no one was watching. Brett held her down and thrust the needle into the flesh. She gurgled. Her eyes fluttered back again. Her muscles gave out, and she slumped against the leather. Her eyes were still wide with disbelief, but she was suddenly too paralyzed to speak . . . or move . . . or run.

"Better," Brett said. And he gripped the wheel again, cranked up Bruce Springsteen, and rolled smoothly and gracefully away from the ocean. He had one arm propped out of the window and tried as hard as he could to drive casually, almost aimlessly, like he was just out for a nice little drive.

It was a lie, of course. He knew exactly where they were going. He had it all planned out, down to the end.

ACKNOWLEDGMENTS

It was so much fun to complete the second book in this series, and I couldn't have done it without the help of Josh Bank, Sara Shandler, Annie Stone, and Lanie Davis at Alloy and Julie Rosenberg and Emily Meehan at Disney. Also huge thanks to the Disney team for all their support for all things *Amateurs* – Mary Ann Zissimos, Andrew Sansone, Holly Nagel, Elka Villa, and Seale Ballenger, that means you! Super-cool Pop Sockets, spot-on swag, loving support. Thanks also to Crystal Patriarche and Kelly Bowen at SparkPoint Studio for their creative thinking and never-ending enthusiasm. And to all the authors I newly met or reconnected with in my months of touring – Sarah Mlynowski, Margaret Stohl, Katie McGee, Danielle Paige, Soman Chainani, Leigh Bardugo, Kami Garcia, Nicola Yoon, Kim McCreight (I loved our Padma sighting in Miami!), Caleb Roehrig, and so many more – you are all so lovely, and I'm so glad not to be doing this alone. Oh, and also, Caroline Kepnes, you are an absolute gem, and I probably wouldn't have stayed sane without you.

Also love and kisses to my family – Michael, who leaves golf tees in pants pockets and breaks our appliances; Henry, whose love of our cat has made our cat semi-domesticated, and Kristian, the only kid I know who enjoys singing the *My Little Pony* theme song as well as *Bad to the Bone*. You guys are the best of the best.

SARA SHEPARD

For as long as she can remember, Sara Shepard has been writing. However, when she was young she also wanted to be a soap opera star, a designer for LEGO, a filmmaker, a claymation artist, a geneticist, and a fashion magazine editor when she grew up. She and her sister have been creating joint artistic and written projects for years, except they're pretty sure they're the only ones who find them funny.

She got her MFA at Brooklyn College and now lives in Pittsburgh, PA with her husband and two children. Sara Shepard is the author of two New York Times bestselling series, Pretty Little Liars and The Lying Game, as well as the series The Perfectionists.

Visit her at www.saracshepard.com and follow her on Twitter and Snapchat at @sarabooks and on Instagram at saracshepard.

HOT KEY BOOKS

Thank you for choosing a Hot Key book.

If you want to know more about our authors and what we publish, you can find us online.

You can start at our website

www.hotkeybooks.com

And you can also find us on:

We hope to see you soon!